SMILE SO RED AND OTHER TALES OF MADNESS

SMILE SO RED AND OTHER TALES OF MADNESS

Mia Dalia

BRIGIDS GATE PRESS

BRIGIDS GATE PRESS
Overland Park, Kansas
www.brigidsgatepress.com
Printed in the United States of America

For Chelsea,

Every story

Always

Content

Smile So Red

It had been said that good things appear when you least expect them, but in Anton's experience, anything worth knowing or owning had always required a great deal of actively searching for it.

He spent several long uncomfortable years on dating websites before finding his wife, eight months obsessively checking realtor. com prior to buying his condo, and many more finding the best deals to furnish it. Nothing was effortless, nothing was easy.

His job search initially took just as methodical an approach, but after nearly two decades at the same company, he no longer thought about it, letting the employment stability it provided lull him into a false sense of security. Of course, he didn't know it was false until he'd been laid off. Budget cuts, they said. Unceremoniously as all that. Nothing to be done but smile, say thank you for the redundancy package, and walk away.

Now what? he thought, letting his heavy feet carry him away. Now what? No one started over in their forties, did they? Anton had never bought into the great myth of reinvention. For him, progress had always been a steady unidirectional thing. Getting laid off had unmoored him.

He put his boxed-up office things into the condo's basement storage unit and tried to think of a way to tell his wife what had happened. Nothing came to mind.

Anton had never been good at sharing, and bad news didn't seem like a good place to start. He did the next best thing which was to continue their daily routine with no interruption while trying to figure out his future.

It wasn't much of a plan, but it helped retain the status quo which had always been his favorite status of all. His wife's work schedule usually got her out of the house first anyway. All he needed to do was be elsewhere when she got back.

The rest of the day Anton spent job searching, which by late afternoon usually left him feeling sufficiently depressed and dejected to shut down the computer resentfully and walk away.

He'd pace, half watching the TV, half lost in his thoughts, dangerously close to wallowing.

It went against his stoic Eastern European upbringing but right along the lines of the emotionally overwrought zeitgeist he'd found himself a part of in his adopted country.

Anton had been brought up on the notion that life is a hard thing meant to be endured, and later, upon moving to the States, had struggled to wrap his head around the 180-degree opposite idea of a joyful existence, of happiness being important enough to get written into the constitution.

Unemployment had certainly constituted hardship. Something his parents, had they still been alive, would slap him hard on the shoulder about with that "what did you expect" shrug that had never quite passed for compassion. "Try again", they'd say. And he'd *been* trying. The news kept telling him about the booming employment market out there; one his search had found no evidence of. Where were these jobs? What were they? Certainly not middle management opportunities for the middle-aged.

Self-pity chafed at him. The Internet suggested fresh air. Anton began walking.

At first, it was merely recreational. Just around the neighborhood. Just to kill time until it was six, his normal return-from-work hour.

But then the city began to grate on him with its hustle and bustle, one he was seemingly no longer a part of. All he saw were people hurrying places, busy, important-seeming, all too drastically at odds with his directionless amble. The city, his lifelong ally, one whose rhythms were as familiar to him as his own heartbeat, no longer felt like home.

And so, Anton went into the woods. Trees instead of people, bird calls instead of car honks. A nice change of pace all around. In theory.

In reality, he'd never been one for hiking. It felt just like walking but on leaves and moss and grass instead of pavement. It took some getting used to.

The quiet was nice. The way it amplified his thoughts wasn't. He tried listening to an audiobook but couldn't concentrate. Music had never done much for him and didn't seem inclined to start now.

He opted for focusing on random things to distract himself, things one couldn't see in the city. The wildness of the wilderness. The distinctly uncity-like, uncurated quality of nature.

Best of all was how long some of the trails were. You could just follow the color markings on the trees and lose yourself for a couple of hours. He had to change his clothes before returning home to maintain the lie, but it was a minor detail.

The city offered nothing like this. Only a paved walking path sandwiched between a dirty river and a stretch of highway. Now Anton had to drive to walk, a funny concept. And he drove further and further each time, doing his research, finding more trails.

It was jarring to see all the wide-open spaces after the tight grid of the city. Once you left its bounds, there was seemingly nothing but trees. Forests of them.

Anton's latest discovery was the farthest drive away yet. A state park with an unpronounceable name undoubtedly stolen from the Lenape Indians who used to live in the area. Sad excuse for compensation if ever there was one. Nothing near an apology well deserved.

The best thing about the place was how empty it was. Time and again, Anton would walk for hours with nary a soul to be seen. An occasional mountain biker at a distance. Maybe a dog walker. None more than mirage-like silhouettes in the distance. He couldn't tell if this was because he came during traditional work hours or something else, something inherently to do with the park itself. Either way, it suited him.

He liked the lengths of the trails, the surprisingly robust river that weaved through the land, the stillness the air seemed to carry.

Anton walked and walked. Walked until his brain shut off. Until he no longer thought of his continuous lying to his wife, his inability to secure employment, his redundancy package running out, his age, his mortgage, his future. Until there was nothing but putting one foot in front of another and propelling himself forward.

He hadn't noticed anything unusual until well into his third visit. It was quiet here, but he had expected as much. Leaving the city had always created that ear-popping-at-altitude initial silence, and then you got used to it. But in this place, it was different. Something more. A profound absence of sound. No animals rustling around. No birds. Nothing.

The horror movies of his youth came to mind, silly frivolous things his parents had always made fun of. Things with ancient hauntings, possessed lands, Indian burial grounds.

The area was certainly rich in history. Or what passed for history in a country as new as the United States. The small town he'd driven through to get here proudly advertised 1800s dates on their outsized colonials. The war had come through here a long time ago, soaking the land in blood, leaving behind memories the town refused to forget even if it couldn't quite afford to upkeep. Façades in various states of disrepair glared at Anton balefully as he passed by. Brick and mortar tiredly hanging on to the past. Nothing like the proudly restored and gleaming historical mansions of the city, but somehow this seemed more honest.

After all, history *was* exhausting. It *did* weigh you down. Anton had been saddled with enough of his own; he could relate.

There was no way to tell whether some of the town's grimness spilled over into the nearby woods, but Anton began paying more attention to his surroundings. Not just to make sure he didn't slip and fall in his hiking-inappropriate footwear. The old running shoes had done perfectly well on most terrains on most occasions, but here the worn-out thread of their soles was proving to be a liability.

When he got tired, he strayed off the path toward the river. Got as close as the muddy banks allowed and just stood and stared. The water soothed him.

What he didn't understand were all the tires. The bottles—sure. Kids coming around to party, making a mess, sure, yes. But who'd bring tires all the way out here just to chuck them into the water? It made no sense. Seemed like too much effort for random vandalism.

Anton shook his head and decided to switch up the trails, picking a different color. There were three to choose from, and thus far he'd stuck to red. Why not try blue? Something new. He changed course at the next convenient intersection and followed the markings.

The first thing he noticed was the vines. Or *were* they vines? His city dweller ignorance was showing. They seemed to be the same color as the trees but twisted with all the sinuous grace of large snakes; coiling around each other, around the other trees, braiding themselves, slithering on the ground only to contort into strange ballet-like shapes. What were they?

Anton took some photos with his phone to look up later. His wife would be proud, he thought. She always said he was no good at paying attention.

He'd show these to her, prove her wrong. But then again, no, he couldn't. How would he explain traipsing through the woods when he was supposed to be hard at work?

With a deep sigh, he put the phone away and pushed on with heavy steps through the silent trees, as alone as the last man on Earth.

The sun had never come out despite the weather report's promises, he noticed. And yet he was sweating anyway, generating his own heat. These walks were probably getting him in shape for the first time in years. He'd always looked trim enough but knew it didn't quite equate with fitness. Not until now.

Anton paused spotting a nice outlook. Carefully, he slid his slippery sneakers along the mud to get as close to the edge as possible. There he stopped and drank some water. The first few times hiking he didn't think to bring any and ended up regretting it. Now he always carried a full bottle. An environmentally friendly plastic thing with the logo of a gym he'd once belonged to. A failed New Year's resolution. Another life.

A breeze dried the sweat on his face. Anton couldn't place the smell the air carried. Shrugged it off as nature's original. There was an unpleasant undertone to it. Reminded him of something.

Only later, after some distance and many more trees, it came to him. The smell—it was like the butcher shop his parents used to take him to back in the old country. If he closed his eyes, he could still see the fat man behind the counter, albeit vaguely. Only a shiny face and a bloody apron. Anton shook the memory away. Focused on the path.

The blue trail appeared to be significantly longer than its red counterpart. Anton could feel himself getting tired, the tensing of the calves, the protestation of the thigh muscles. He looked around for a bench to sit on; still too much of a city person to plop down onto the ground. Now and again the trail did offer a seating option. Some considerate soul had put makeshift benches together out of what looked like fallen logs cut to shape. A flat slab across two stumps. Plain and serviceable. There were none around now though. Maybe it was a red trail thing.

A sharp branch—a stick really—reached out as if to grab at his jacket. It was something to get used to out in nature. He'd already gotten a few snags on his favorite windbreaker, before wising up. Now he wore his old jacket while hiking, one pulled out from the very back of his closet.

Anton had bought it when he began courting his wife. Now the jacket was as old-fashioned as courting itself. Its owner moved on with the times but was never so enamored with the present as to disregard the past completely. And, presently, he was grateful for it.

The jacket was shiny with wear around the elbows, collar, and pockets. The trees could do their worst. And for a while they did,

narrowing to a two-foot-wide corridor. Bottleneck-and-pat-down maneuver, Anton anthropomorphized. As if he was entering somewhere important, somewhere sacred.

Alas, the only thing on the other side was more trees. And a maddening proliferation of the vine things. Wrapping themselves around the trunks as tight as lovers. Or pythons. Perhaps, pythons in love, Anton thought whimsically. Perhaps, this was a killing method—a passionate smothering.

It reminded him of a relationship he had in college. One that taught him what to avoid ever since. You couldn't hold on too tight, he learned. It squeezed the life out of a thing.

What he had with his wife was good. There was kindness, there was trust. The latter, he was likely violating these days, but at least it was well-intentioned. He had hoped to secure a job, then present it as a fait accompli. It was turning out to be more of a mission impossible, and he hated it. What good was he without work? What was his purpose? The meaning of him?

His parents had always worked so hard. Doubly so in their second life as immigrants due to the language barrier and the non-transferability of their degrees. He was the embodiment of their hopes and dreams; the one to have it all, to take all the right steps and reap all the awards. And he did until life made other plans.

Anton got lost in his thoughts. The maudlin labyrinth of them. The house snuck up on him. Or rather it stood perfectly still as houses tend to, waiting for him to notice it, and then said Boo.

Sure, in reality, it didn't say any such thing, but it could have for how striking its sudden appearance was.

Why was there a house in the middle of a hiking path in the woods, miles away from any sign of civilization?

And why did it look like *that*?

Anton got out his phone, because like most people of his generation, when struck with the inexplicable, he photographed it.

After a while, he put his phone down; he didn't think he was doing his subject justice.

There was something here. More than a sum of its parts. Something digital imagery couldn't quite grasp.

And he thought tires were the most incongruous thing in these woods. But no. This … this graffiti palace certainly took the proverbial cake.

Anton paused to take it all in. Tried to mentally peel back the years of abuse and neglect to imagine what it must have looked like once upon a time.

All his imagination brought back was a regular house. As unlikely as it seemed, that had to be it.

He could still see the floor plan: the outline of the living room with a long-disused fireplace, the adjacent kitchen with skeletons of cabinetry still intact. There was a drop that must have led to the basement. Another room off to the side. A bedroom?

It would have been a small house by modern standards, likely even smaller than his condo, but cozy, comfortable. With windows overlooking the woods and the river. Serene. Idyllic. Peculiarly isolated. How old could it have been?

The disuse and decrepitude had rendered it ancient beyond time, reminding Anton of pensioners in the old country, lining the cheap plastic chairs outside their ugly, blocky apartment complexes, gossiping and reminiscing the days away, their faces and hands impossibly wrinkled, their eyes windows to souls too tired to want more.

The building's windows had frames intact, but their glass was long gone. The doorways both front and back were doorless, Anton noticed as he walked around the place, carefully avoiding the thick layer of debris. Evidence of years of debauchery.

Who came here? It seemed too far out of the way to attract local kids. Then again, maybe that's what kids did around here.

Anton walked in. He couldn't resist it. Looked up. The roof was surprisingly sound. The floor moved beneath his feet unsteadily but didn't threaten to give way.

And if it did? he thought. What a stupid death that would be. What's the word? Ah, ignominious. Who'd even find him? No one knew he was out here. It would likely be some partying teens discovering his corpse. They'd be scarred for life.

He shrugged off the morbid thoughts and looked around some more. The place reminded him of people who tattoo every inch of their skin, turning themselves into living works of art. Equally, the house had almost no space left untouched. *Untagged.*

Graffiti reigned supreme here. Every surface, no matter how high or low. The walls, the floors, the ceiling even. Bright colors, brash styles.

From something as plain as names and hearts to wildly imaginative designs, the house made a statement. What it was trying to say, Anton couldn't quite tell, but it certainly drew the eye.

The other thing he noticed was that someone had swept up the floor. The carpet-like covering of leaves was tamed neatly in the living room, with all the mess pushed up against the walls, clearing the center.

Was that … was that a pentagram? Anton couldn't quite tell, but his heritage had rendered him superstitious enough to jump away as if from hot coals. There were things one simply did not mess with.

He walked into the next room. Unswept leaves crunched beneath his feet. The view from here was a drop straight down to the river. Or maybe more like a winding steep descent.

Anton took the path, unthinkingly.

It was slippery enough to warrant grabbing for stray tree branches, but he made it to the muddy bank. Peaceful, but there was that smell again.

A look at the ground made Anton shut his eyes and almost scream. Then morbid curiosity took over. Prying his eyelids apart slowly one by one like a kid at a scary movie, he waited for the full picture to sink in.

It was definitely a body. A body of what he couldn't say. Some medium-sized animal. A large cat? A beaver? His knowledge of local wildlife left a lot to be desired.

That wasn't the disturbing part. He'd seen plenty of roadkill on his drives outside the city.

The disturbing part was that the animal appeared to have been turned inside out. Or at least skinned to that effect.

And then there was the way it was laid out. Like a present. Like—Anton shuddered—a sacrifice.

Surrounded by gnarled branches that made a rustic sort of frame for it, there was an undeniable grotesque artistry behind the display.

Anton could see the animal's organs. Things he couldn't quite name. And a heart atop it all, flanked by a pair of unseeing eyes.

That's when Anton turned around and threw up. Afterward, with tears burning his eyes and acid burning his esophagus, he climbed back up.

Unlike most strange dreams, the house didn't dissipate in the absence of an observer. It waited for him just as he left it.

Anton chose to walk around instead of through to the other side, minding the glass on the ground. His sneakers, he noticed, had vomit splatters on them. Something he'd have to remember to clean up.

Once he got back onto the path, he felt torn. There was something about the house he couldn't just walk away from. The sheer macabre strangeness of it all.

He wondered if he could Google it and find out its history. Everything was Googleable these days, wasn't it?

There was no address and nothing like streets out here, but surely someone somewhere had to know about a graffitied house in the middle of the woods in a state park.

Some of the drawings were so good. Anton had never been much into art, no matter how many museums and galleries his wife had dragged him to. Stylishly framed and thoughtfully curated images hung on the walls there seemed dead and irrelevant.

This art was alive. Practically pulsing with life. So vibrant, so … vital. And there was so much of it. Anton felt like he could look and look and always find something new.

He also felt like if he gazed at it all long enough he might go mad.

As a compromise, he decided on one last long look before heading out. After all, he could always come back.

This time, his attention was drawn upward, above what must have once been a front entrance.

Abandon all hope, came to his mind unbidden. But that was so dark. And this graffiti was bright. The brightest red Anton had ever beheld. The red you saw when you closed your eyes against the sun. Brighter than blood.

The blinding splash of color was a smile. A smile that went on like hysteria. A Joker grin if Joker had been driven mad beyond all reason. A smile that felt like it saw you, followed you like those kitschy Kit-Cat clocks. A smile that looked like madness.

It was the sort of thing you could not unsee.

Anton felt it imprint itself onto his retina. When he closed his eyes, he could see its afterimage.

He tried it several times as he left the house, following the trail back onto the road.

The smile wouldn't go away.

He saw it as he made his way to the car. As he sat there cleaning up his shoes with a hand-sanitizing wipe. As he hydrated, got his GPS going, and drove home. As he experimentally tested closing his eyes at stoplights.

The smile followed him out. He had no choice but to bring it home.

"Why are you wearing that?" his wife asked by way of a greeting.

Shoot, he didn't realize he had forgotten to change into his work clothes.

"Office clean-up day," he lied clumsily. There was mud on his old jeans he hoped she wouldn't notice. The sweatshirt was clean enough, if—appropriately enough—sweaty.

"Well, if you're in a cleaning mood, you're welcome to tackle the bathroom," she tossed offhandedly, heading into the kitchen.

He gave her one of those that'll-be-the-day chuckles. You had to manage your loved one's expectations.

There was a sound of rummaging through the fridge. "Lasagna?"

"Sure," he said. "I'm just gonna go grab a shower."

"You've got—" He could just picture her squinting at the packaging instructions, neither of them cooked much, especially on weekdays. "—twenty-five minutes."

"OK."

In the bathroom, Anton discarded his clothes into the laundry basket and sprayed his shoes with a can of air freshener in absence of better options, figuring Fresh Linen beat stale vomit any day. On second thought, he took the shoes and put them in his closet, letting the offending odors percolate in isolation.

Then he took a shower as hot as he could stand it. When he closed his eyes against the water stream, all he could see was the smile.

Anton willed the shower spray to beat it from his eyelids. When that failed, he opened his eyes, turned around, and stared at the white tiles until the water turned tepid.

The lasagna tasted good, objectively. Subjectively, it felt like shoving three-day-old porridge into his mouth, flavorless and clay-like. He thought he could still smell that awful butcher shop stench, as if it somehow clung to his nose hairs and traveled with him through time and space. The meat layer of lasagna tasted sour, and he knew it was likely just him. Just his faulty taste buds.

They talked of work, trading real and made-up stories from their days.

Anton wanted, desperately, to tell his wife about the path, the house, the smile, but couldn't bring himself to expose the lie perpetuated so carefully and diligently. He'd find the way, he told himself, but not now, not like this.

Dirty plates in the sink, they microwaved some popcorn and took it to the couch. Netflix was calling their names. They took turns dozing to a haunted house mini-series Anton could think of no rational way to protest. After all, they did start it on his suggestion two days ago. Now every other scene reminded him of earlier. If he closed his eyes, there was that smile. He had to settle for looking away. Worrying the entire time about what sort of nightmares sleep would bring.

Alas, that night Anton slept as soundly as he ever did. If he dreamed at all, he remembered none of it in the morning.

For a fleeting moment upon waking, he felt genuinely happy. Then the weight of the day, life, lies dawned on him, and he groaned, catching himself enough to turn it into a loud stretch.

"Good morning to you too." His wife smiled. One of those obnoxious morning people, she looked positively perky even before the mandatory intake of caffeine.

Anton grumbled. It was way too early for polite conversation. She sauntered into the bathroom to perform an elaborate hair and makeup ritual. Operating on pure autopilot, he grabbed for his phone. No messages, no emails. Nothing. All those resumes he sent out. It was like throwing them into some great uncaring abyss. Anton sighed. And then, flashing back to yesterday's adventure, began flipping through his photos.

It wasn't a dream then. It really did happen. The house. The grotesque dead animal thing that he did not photograph but remembered vividly all the same. All that graffiti, too.

Not the smile, though, oddly enough. He seemed to have taken pictures of everything but. Oh well, it was enough.

Just had to get through breakfast as usual, and then he'd have hours for research.

Reluctantly, he rolled out of bed and proceeded with the morning charade of getting out office clothes for the day ahead. His sneakers, he noticed, had made everything smell like fake freshness.

Anton padded to the kitchen to set out some cereal and OJ. Making a gesture, he even sliced up a banana, half into each bowl. He hoped the food would have flavor today.

His wife came out of the bathroom and pecked him. *That* he could taste, warmth and face powder. The coffee maker finished sputtering into the glass carafe, making the kitchen smell like happiness.

"Busy day today?"

Anton shrugged, then changed the focus of the conversation, avoiding more lies. His wife had a meeting, a presentation, something. He nodded along at all the right conversational moments, years of training at work.

Afterward, he cleaned up the table. She reemerged from the bathroom, air-kissing him to avoid smudging. The lipstick she wore was bright red, and it made Anton's heart skip a terrified beat when she smiled.

After she left, he plopped down in front of the computer with his second cup of coffee to find out why.

As it turned out, there were still things in this day and age that Google knew nothing about. Neither did Bing. Anton checked, due diligence and all that.

If the house in the woods had ever belonged to anyone, there was no record of it. If it ever had a purpose, owners, or tenants, it was a mystery.

Anton read about the Lenape, the Revolutionary War, small-town histories, property records, local folklore. Nothing of relevance. He veered into newspaper archives, lingering on items as random as rare quintuplets born and a mayoral sex scandal.

He could spell all the Native American place names now without stumbling but remained no closer to finding out the one thing he was interested in. On top of it, he was getting hungry.

Anton fixed himself a pair of peanut butter and jelly sandwiches and went back to the computer. Perhaps, he thought, he might have better luck researching graffiti.

The peanut butter was chunky the way his wife liked it. He didn't much care for the texture, but he muddled through. The screen spat out image after image at him, anything from Banksy to cheap-looking tags. It recommended reading *Motherless Brooklyn* and watching *Exit Through the Gift Shop*. Showed smiles of all calibers from Mona Lisa to Cheshire Cat. Nothing even close to the one he believed was destined to haunt his nightmares.

In the end, he gave up, shutting down the computer with a resigned huff. He'd just have to go back. It was time to get moving anyway if he wanted to maintain the illusion of employment.

Anton put on jeans and a fleece jacket, stuck his feet into his now-aggressively-aromatic sneakers, grabbed a water bottle, made sure his phone had a full charge, and, carrying his day-at-the-office finest in a garment bag, left the house.

The drive felt pleasantly familiar, the radio cooperated riding the '90s nostalgia wave the entire way. Anton arrived at his destination, parked, and set off, his pace reflecting how he felt: a mixture of excitement and trepidation.

Despite everything, he clocked that he *wanted* to see the place again, *wanted* its weirdness, if only to distract him from the banal tedium of his life.

There was no one around. As per usual. Only quietude greeted him, refreshing after a drive full of loud grunge and alt-rock. Peaceful. Anton took a deep breath and released it.

Then he set off—wide strides, shoes slipping on wet leaves, arms swinging. In the city, he walked with small, hurried steps, fists balled in his pockets, but here it seemed the place demanded a different, more open gait. His explorer walk, he thought with amusement.

Soon enough, he arrived at his destination. The house greeted him with its shudder-inducing smile. Anton shook his head as if to say, "No, you're not getting to me this time," and proceeded to take more photos.

He couldn't tell for sure but thought some of the art was different this time around. Was there a new tag somewhere throwing off the balance? Had someone been here since he left the house yesterday?

Unable to tell with certainty, he looked around some more. He couldn't find any pipes inside, nothing like that. Were they copper and therefore stolen at some point in the past, or were they simply never there to begin with? How would the house have gotten water or power? Even if the fireplace provided enough heat in its heyday, it still would have required other things to make it livable.

And then it struck him: what if this was never a real house at all but a prop? Something built for a movie or some such purpose and later unceremoniously discarded. That would explain its façade-like quality and the absence of property records.

Of course, *of course*, that had to be it. A place built on a scenic lookout to stand in for some fictional location. That made perfect sense. Mystery solved.

Creepy graffiti remained, but that had to be local kids. Idle hands and so on.

Anton laughed out loud with relief of having figured it out. If only everything in life had been that simple. It was almost disappointing. Like figuring out the plot twist in the middle of the movie.

And then he remembered the other thing. The one he'd been desperately trying to forget. And slowly, so slowly, he made his way down to the water.

The animal corpse was gone. Like it was never there at all. Which made sense, he supposed. Circle of life, food's food. Some creature out here had itself a tasty meal not worrying for a moment how sinister it might have looked to an untrained and imaginative eye.

Anton climbed back up. He even walked through the house this time to get back to the path. The floorboards groaned their half-hearted protestations. He looked up at a bright green tag in the corner of the room and felt his foot go from under him. A slapstick comedy special of pinwheeling arms ensued. He remained upright but only by catching himself on a wooden beam, one of the longer ones going all the way into the basement. Or the open space where he presumed the basement might have been.

Anton felt a splinter going into his palm, the tiniest of assaults but a distinctly unpleasant one. Could have been worse, he told himself, could have ended up taking a dive and breaking his leg or his neck.

He straightened out, wiping his slipped foot on the floor to regain traction, and studied the damage to his hand.

The shard of wood was sticking straight out of his palm in a nauseating fashion. A drop of blood around the wound looked oddly artistic.

Anton grabbed the splinter's tip with the thumb and index finger of the opposite hand and pulled. It emerged easily enough, a full knee-weakening inch of it. A few more drops of blood.

He patted his pockets down, looking for hand sanitizer to clean the wound and settling for an old napkin.

The fall to the basement would have been a sharp drop straight down. There was something there Anton couldn't quite make out, glistening on the floor. He got out his phone, turned on the flashlight app, and shined it down.

What he saw was … No, no, it couldn't have been. Gross. Was it really the animal carcass from the other day? Did someone or something drag it down there?

He looked around his feet and saw the thing that made him slip. It appeared to be a bit of an entrail. Anton gagged. Gagged again. Dry heaved but held steady. No more vomiting for him.

So there were some bloody innards on the floor. So they were placed in the middle of the faded pentagram design and now smudged and dragged out by Anton's errant foot. So what?

He read about that phenomenon once. Pareidolia. Seeing patterns where there were none. Letting your imagination run away with you.

If idle hands created graffiti, idle minds could go further still, crafting entire scenarios out of coincidences and suppositions.

It meant nothing. Most things meant nothing. Patterns were only sought out to convince oneself of the universe's grand benevolent designs. To ward off the bleakness of potential indifference.

He knew that. Any intelligent person knew that.

Anton shook his head. It *was* creepy, though. He left the house, putting pressure on the napkin around his palm, watching a small red circle blossom there, like some flag of Japan simulacrum.

He tried not to look up once he was outside, but it was impossible. He couldn't resist the siren song of it, the hideous call of it.

If anything, the red smile looked *more* repulsive. There was a satisfaction about it this time, like it had just finished licking its lips after a particularly tasty treat.

"What's so funny?" Anton whispered, looking at it.

"Why so serious?" he imagined it reply, Joker-style.

A grin like that would turn Arkham Asylum's walls inside out.

Anton thought he heard a rustling in the trees; a sound common enough on any other walk and unusual here because of how quiet the trail normally was. He spun around like a top, sighting what he thought was a figure at a distance. A biker? A dog walker? A fellow hiker?

But no, it stood still, tall and thin. A distinctly corvid-like outline. Sharp, dark.

Something about the silhouette made Anton remain shock still, holding his breath. Fear had no place outside of the city, surely. People out here were uniformly, overwhelmingly friendly, always quick with a hello and a smile.

And yet, Anton knew with bloodcurdling certainty that he did not want the far-away man—and he was suddenly certain it *was* a man and not a nice one—to ever greet him or get close enough to.

Then the wind blew, stirring the trees, and the figure vanished. Like it was never there to begin with. And was it? Or was he seeing things now? It *was* getting darker earlier these days. The sun retreating sooner as if eagerly washing its hands of earthly concerns, knocking off a few minutes here and there from its workday.

Anton peered into the distance. He saw nothing but trees. No man among them. Who'd he think it was anyway? Some practitioner of dark arts? A Lenape ghost? Sheesh. He shook his head. The place was obviously getting to him.

He'd just have to find another place to hike. A new trail. Better yet, a job to end all this aimless wandering around.

For a moment, he let himself imagine that the man was indeed some local warlock. That he bloodied the pentagram and made a dark wish or two.

What did he ask for? Anton knew what he would have.

If only it were that simple. He huffed. Then, on a whim, made a wish. Because what was the harm? It would work like everything else has worked so far which is to say not at all.

Maybe the corvid warlock would do better with his ambition.

Anton sighed and headed back. Home was still a walk and a drive away, and he had to remember to change his clothes this time.

He feigned normalcy as best he could. They shared another pleasant evening of white lies, small talk, carb-based ready-made meals, and Netflix. A few hours later, his wife was sound asleep in the bed next to him, and Anton tried desperately to follow suit. When he finally dozed off, the smile came to him, razor-sharp and fire-red. In his dream, the lips were moving, mouthing words he could not understand.

'What? What are you saying?' he pleaded with it, but no sound emerged. He only had to guess at its meaning, only had to …

Anton woke up to his wife's phone alarm shrieking good morning at him. His heart pounded like the bass in an EDM nightclub. The clammy bedsheet clung uncomfortably to his sweaty body.

"You had a nightmare, I think," his wife said. "Kept tossing and turning."

"Yeah, I think I might have," he replied, rubbing his hands over his face. The familiar creases and stubble offered a reassuring sensation beneath his shaking fingers.

"Poor baby." She leaned over to kiss his head. "Wanna talk about it?"

"Nah." He never wanted to hear anyone's dreams and couldn't imagine someone genuinely interested in his. It was just a way one's psyche processed the detritus of their daily life. Like shitting, really. Why would you want to show someone your turds?

The dream left him jumpy. The details of it stubbornly refused to fade away in the daylight weakly streaming through the windows.

The mechanical ka-ching sound of waffles popping out of the toaster gave him a start. The slam of a car door outside had the same effect. He couldn't wait for his wife to leave so that he could relax. Faking normalcy was exhausting enough *with* a good night's sleep. He'd just have to bide his time until it returned organically. Meanwhile, there was TV and the internet.

Once alone, Anton checked his email reluctantly.

There was always the same process to it. He'd pause, mentally preparing himself for nothing: no satisfactory replies of interest, just rejections and spam. And then he'd click on it and be proved right.

This time though there was an email that didn't say, "No, thanks," and didn't offer free shipping on pet products or male performance enhancers. Anton clicked on it reluctantly. It was an invitation to a job interview. Nicely worded, polite, official. A real or at least a real-sounding job at a real company within an easy commuting distance. Anton had almost spewed his coffee at the screen in a comic-gold surprise of it all. But he didn't. That sort of thing only happened in the movies.

He read and reread the email, and at last, finding no fault with it, wrote a professional reply straight out of the best job-hunting websites.

They usually gave more notice, but it wasn't worth contemplating.

Anton showered and used some of his wife's more neutral-smelling hair products. He was shaggy, but there simply wasn't enough time to fix that.

It was nice to put on his work suit and a good tie and not have it be a part of a charade. He drove the speed limit listening to the oldies station. Nothing too exciting or too moody, he had to maintain an even keel.

Afterward, he sang along to the '90s songs as loud as he could, drumming on the steering wheel and veering in and out of traffic with the assurance of a Formula One driver.

The interview went well. He could feel it in his bones. They said the company was looking to make a hiring decision within days.

He tried not to get excited about it, mitigating any potential future disappointment. Odds were, it wouldn't work out. Something would come up. They'd find another candidate ever so slightly more their speed. Et cetera.

But he had to allow himself this small celebration if only for the duration of the drive back. A recognition of this one win in a line of steady losses. Like the sun peeking through a curtain of clouds drawn across relentlessly grey skies. He'd revel in it for a bit more.

Then he was home. And there was still all that pretense to go through. He decided to stay in the suit for convenience's sake. Just drive around somewhere, kill some time until six p.m. He wouldn't miss any of this, not one bit. If only this job would …

Anton sighed and left the house. He didn't realize his driving destination until the woods came into view. It was almost as if he'd arrived on autopilot. Unthinkingly.

He wouldn't hike in his good suit, though. He'd just sit there, he figured. Do nothing. But sitting got tiresome, and Anton began walking. Only on the paved path connecting the small, interspersed parking lots. Nothing to avoid there but the puddles. The uneven pavement was diligent in holding on to remnants of the days-old rain.

Anton walked and thought about the house. The sacrifice, the figure, the smile. His wish. It was all a coincidence, of course. What else could it be? He was bound to get an interview out of all those applications he submitted. It was merely a matter of time, a numbers game.

There were some cars in the parking lots, he noticed. Where were their owners? Hiding from each other among the trees? He hadn't seen a single person getting in or out of their vehicles the entire time he walked.

Weird, weird place.

He'd never come here again, he realized. Not if he got a job. It would feel too far then. He would be too tired. This was a "for now only" destination.

The trails were snaking up from the parking path upward. He craned his head looking for anything, anyone. Only the trees looked back.

Not until his walk back did he see the now-familiar corvid-man figure lurking above. Or no, not lurking, but rather looking distinctly like it belonged there. Like Anton was the one intruding.

Did they lock eyes? Could you lock eyes with a shadow? From certain angles, the man seemed like a sharp rip in the fabric of reality with nothing but darkness behind him. From certain angles, there was nothing up there but the trees.

A rhyme about the man who wasn't there came to Anton, unbidden and unsettling. He had to force himself to look away, to focus on his dress shoes, incongruous amid the shabbily paved road. One foot after another. Until his car came into view. Until he was safe within its metal and glass shell. Until it was whisking him away back to the city, back to where things made sense.

I won't go back again, Anton told himself, not ever. The thin man could have his woods all to himself.

But then, days passed. Days of obsessively checking his messages and coming away disappointed each time. Days of discouraging silence and depressing nothingness. And Anton found himself back in the woods once more.

This time it felt different. As if the woods expected him. As if the wooden vines had rearranged their contorted bodies to welcome him. As if they could read his churning mind, see his twisting gut, and *know* him the way no one ever had before.

This time he had a mission. Impossible, unlikely, one he had barely put into words for himself. Just a feeling, really. An itch at the back of his mind. The maddening what if.

He'd brought a mouse. A tiny helpless thing he found stuck on a glue trap behind the fridge. One of the unavoidable nuisances of city living—small vermin that seemed to travel between the neighbors and was virtually impossible to get rid of. An unwinnable war with only these small victories. His wife had always been squeamish about it, so he was the one forever setting up traps and getting rid of the victims.

The night before his wife heard squealing, and after some searching, he found the poor thing, hopelessly entrapped yet valiantly struggling still. And he had this wild thought …

Because it would cost him nothing. Because he was becoming hopeless, and there were too many quiet hours in the day whispering to him of failure. Because he stopped understanding the inner workings of the world and increasingly felt like he had entered some twilight zone where anything was possible. Because no one would know or ask, and it would die with him like so many wishes, hopes, and dreams. Because …

Anton took the glue-stuck mouse out of the hummus container he brought it in. He had made a few cuts in the plastic lid for air, so the poor thing wouldn't suffocate. What fate had in store for it was equally gruesome but quicker. Small mercy, that.

He just wouldn't think about it. Thinking about it made it so much worse. He walked as fast as he ever had, his pulse deafening in his ears. There was nothing else, only the path, only the air, only the sound of blood rushing through his veins. And soon, only the house.

All he had to do was … Anton laid the small body—glue trap and all—on the floor of the long-abandoned living room at the center of the pentagram. Then he made a silent wish as fervently as he knew how, unsure of whose ears he meant his pleas to fall on, and stomped down.

He wouldn't look. He refused to look.

The trap glued itself to his sneaker sole, insult to injury. Anton thought he could feel the tiny body squirm through his shoe, but of course, that was impossible. He tried dragging his foot across the floorboards to discard the trap, but it was stuck fast. In the end, he found a stick on the floor, pushed it against the corner of the trap and pried it away. All while trying to not look, not to gag. A stupid idea that intended to make him pay for it. Something he would just have to put out of his mind, because you couldn't carry certain things with you—they ate straight through the soul, corroding like acid.

His foot left a bloody print on the dirty wood floor as he walked away.

If there was a dark figure lurking in the woods, Anton couldn't see it through the tears in his eyes. He hunched over, stuck his hands in his pockets, and hurried away. The smile graffiti burned his back like the summer sun at noon.

He didn't remember the drive home, the change of clothes, the meaningless exchanges over a microwaved meal. After so many years of marriage, he could do all that on autopilot.

The phone was placed beside the computer. Both sat on the desk expectantly, but Anton didn't have the heart to check his messages. Not just then.

It took hours to fall asleep that night, and when Anton finally did, the nightmares made him regret it. Stumbling out of bed, he made his way to the bathroom. The condo was never dark at night—too many streetlights, neon signs, passing cars.

Bet the house in the woods gets dark at night. Really dark. Anton shuddered. Flipped the light switch to stare into eyes best described as haunted. Was he the only one to see it? Did his wife glimpse his despair during the brief shared time together that bookended their days? Did she choose not to say anything? What was there to say anyway? The Hell people carried within them was a private matter.

Anton shut off the light and went to sit on the couch, staring at nothing, willing the dawn to come.

He got the phone call the next morning. The company had hit a snafu in the hiring process, they were sorry about the delay, but all-in-all, he was the strongest candidate. How soon could he start?

The relief of it all was enough to make one weep. Anton stayed dry-eyed, though. Thinking thoughts he wished he didn't—dark, bleak notions about the inner workings of the world. Surely, it was all a mere coincidence. It had to be, didn't it? The alternatives were unfathomable.

The starting date was agreed upon as first thing next week. Easy enough. All he'd have to do was come up with something to tell his wife. A plausible lie. He'd been headhunted, made an offer he couldn't refuse. Something like that.

They'd discuss it over the weekend. For now, there was still time to kill.

Back in the wild days of his youth, Anton had gotten drunk enough to lose time. Only once or twice but it terrified him enough to slow down his partying ways. The blackouts didn't agree with him; it was too out-of-control, too much like a freefall, too contrary to his nature. He liked being able to account for his time and actions.

Standing in front of the house in the woods once again without any idea of how he got there felt too much like a blackout. Alarmingly so.

Anton took a deep breath, staring, just staring at the place. There was a certain dark poetry in the way the trees framed it. The fall had stripped the branches of their leaves, making them look like gnarled fingers, pointing in awe or accusation at the incongruous building in their mix.

Look, they seemed to say. Look and despair.

The trees dwarfed the single-level house, and yet it managed to dominate the view. Its aura emanated unsettlingly, eerily—a sinister whisper in the middle of the night, a bone-stilling brush-up by a ghost.

Anton came closer. Then entered through the doorless doorway. When in Rome …

It was impossible not to look down. The floor appeared to have been swept again by a broom unseen. No mouse, no glue trap. Only a smudge of blood across the satanic design on the floorboards.

He'd been brought up on a version of *better safe than sorry,* and it stuck. Only later, during his college years, he had reframed it as a sort of Pascal's Wager concept, following a surprisingly good philosophy class.

In spirit of both, he now said "thank you," desperately trying to not think about where his gratitude might be going. There was no answer. None was expected.

Anton let out a laugh, more of a chortle, something to relieve the internal pressure building up. There hasn't been anything funny in a long time. He'd been in his head for far too long. His wife, too busy with her work, had taken to falling asleep on the couch shortly after supper. And he couldn't very well talk to himself. It was bad enough he was thanking unnamed entities in an abandoned house.

The new job ought to take care of all that. He'd make new friends the way he did at his old company. Sure, they fell away like autumn leaves the moment he was laid off, but still, he'd have someone to talk to, some social outlets. More importantly, money to buy his mind some peace and replenish his bank account. And with it, his self-worth.

All he had to do was wait a few days.

"I won't be back," Anton told the house. He didn't know why he said it. He didn't like that he said it. Time to leave, he thought.

There was a thud. Sounded like a bird hitting a window, but of course there were no windows to hit here, only empty places where they once were.

Anton looked around, his heart thumping. A small ball was rolling on the floor toward him, unevenness of the surface aiding its progress. About the size of a tennis ball, but instead of the customary rubber topped with neon felt, this thing appeared to have been made of twisted twigs covered with cobwebs.

Some creepy Blair Witch crap, Anton thought, and shuddered. Eerie as the ball's sudden appearance was, the most unsettling thing about it was that someone had to have thrown it in.

Kids? It had to be kids. Likely the same ones that tagged up the house in the first place.

Anton rushed outside, ready to do his best fist-shaking why-I-oughta act, but there was no one there. Kids would have stuck around, pointing and laughing. Taking photos.

He thought he heard someone say something—maybe "Hey," maybe even his name—but it could have just been the wind. It *had* to have just been the wind.

His head tilted upward as if on its own accord. The red of the graffiti above the entrance appeared to be bleeding. Someone must have applied a fresh coat recently. Or …

No, Anton refused to let his mind even go there, though the hideous smile seemingly encouraged him, twisting itself into a knowing smirk.

"Go on," it appeared to be saying. "I dare you. Let your mind take a walk on the dark side."

Anton looked away. There was an extra shadow amid the trees. Sharp and thin and man-shaped.

Nothing, Anton repeated to himself, nothing there. Nothing anywhere. Only his imagination playing tricks on him.

By hook or by crook, he got a new job. If there was something here in the woods that helped him, so be it. Perhaps, all of this was a good thing, albeit presented in a nightmarish gift wrap.

Why question it? What good would come of it? That saying about gift horses existed for a reason.

If there was a mystery here, perhaps it wasn't meant to be solved. Not by him, anyway. It was important to know when to leave things well enough alone.

Anton walked away slowly, heavy feet to match his heavy heart, hoping no one had followed.

The conversation with his wife went better than expected. She was too tired from her work week and too glad that he'd be making more money to ask a lot of questions. It allowed Anton to keep his lies down to a minimum. Soon, he'd be putting the rest of it away for good. All would be just as it should. Back on track. He hated lying, the convoluted effort of it all. Life was complicated enough.

He didn't go back to the woods. Not deliberately, not on autopilot. He tried his hardest to not even think about it.

They ate takeout and watched TV. They walked around the neighborhood. The pavement was steady beneath his feet, and people were nothing like trees. All the houses they saw were intact and graffiti-free. Everything made sense.

The new job was conveniently similar to the last one. Meaningless shuffling of papers, tedium of meetings. Nothing to love but not much to hate either. Ropes were quickly learned, new names memorized. Anton hoped to stay put. Endure a slow and steady papercut-death-trudge toward retirement. Only a couple more decades and then freedom. It seemed reasonable enough.

He could feel himself falling out of shape. Staying out of the woods and getting regular drinks with his new office mates saw to that. He'd pat the soft tire slowly accumulating around his waist, clock the huffing and puffing of climbing the stairs, and frown, but there was never enough regret—or enough energy—to motivate him to pick hiking back up.

It didn't matter. It was only his body conforming to its—to his—regained place in the grand scheme of things. All was as it should be.

Life went back to what he knew and recognized as familiar and serviceable. To Anton, it was as good as a ringing endorsement. He'd never had particularly high hopes for it; after being brought up on a steady diet of perseverance and managed expectations. Happiness was a sucker's game as far as he was concerned, an impossible pursuit, a way to invite frustration in. He'd take contentment instead any day. A steady procession of comfortable routines. An easy, agreeable, congenial life. What more could one ask for? Wasn't *that* the good thing everyone was searching for?

And it was perhaps because he wasn't programmed for happiness that he failed to recognize the absence of it in the only person who really mattered. By the time his wife finally mentioned something, it was much too late.

She said all the right things. That she loved him. That she didn't mean to cause any harm. She simply—she had the decency to hesitate here—didn't feel alive in their marriage. Not enough. Not in that living-out-loud-everyday-is-an-adventure way.

"It's like our entire life has been laid out for us. Like I can see the future, and every day of it is the same. And ..." she said with a sigh, "I'm too young to feel this old."

Anton noticed his wife didn't say *we're* too young and couldn't fault her, for he had always been the old soul of the two of them.

She had an entire plan, he was surprised to find. A new job, a new city. Presumably, a new love interest, though she'd been mercifully circumspect on details. She'd already started this reinvention by chopping off her long hair into a striking pixie cut and introducing bolder color choices into her wardrobe. All these changes he complimented her on whenever noticed but failed to recognize as clues.

And now, there was simply nothing to say. Her mind had been made up. It was like getting laid off all over again only on a much grander scale. He couldn't protest this either; it wasn't meant to be fair. It was just one of those things.

Anton didn't scream, didn't cry, didn't hurl accusations. A sudden bone-tiredness descended on him like gravity. He simply nodded his assent, grabbed a bottle of vodka—an old Christmas gift neither of them had managed to get through in years, went to the office-slash-guestroom, and shut the door.

The space, square and plainly furnished, was seldom used and felt like it. Like a spare. Small, it had nothing more than a desk holding the computer, the printer, and all sorts of office accoutrements, a rolling desk chair, and a cheap but surprisingly comfortable futon that had been with them since the early years of marriage.

Anton didn't bother dragging out the sheets and pillows from under the futon to make the bed. Instead, he sat down and took a sip straight out of the bottle. The clear liquid burned its way down. He wondered how many shots it would take for a proper all-obliterating inferno.

That night Anton drank until he stopped tasting the vodka, yet his mind refused to shut off. It still churned over the same sad, self-pitying thoughts by the time he finally dozed off. His dreams weren't much better either. He woke up with a start. Falling asleep sitting up had left a vicious crick in his neck, and he rubbed it uncomfortably with one hand thinking how he no longer had someone to ask for a massage. He no longer had someone to ask for anything.

Their separation wouldn't be immediate. The continual sharing of the condo would continue for logistical and economic reasons only. Just until the end of the month. Anton didn't even want to imagine all the awkward moments the upcoming weeks were sure to bring, all the conversations stopped short by their realized irrelevance. Like reaching for a limb that was no longer there. An amputated heart, an amputated life.

He stood up on unsteady legs, feeling every vodka shot he downed a few hours ago. It was dark outside, but the streetlights provided enough light to see by. The sole window of the spare room offered a dour vista of the backlot: parking spots, a communal mailbox wall, and large metal trash bins at the far end. Nowhere anyone needed to be in the middle of the night, and yet ... someone was there. Anton willed his vision to focus. Was it a play of shadows, or did a man-shaped, sharp-featured figure separate itself from the mailbox wall and walk to the center of the paved lot?

In the ambient light, Anton could make out a long dark coat that gave the impression of folded wings. Long dark hair that hung curtain-like bordering a razor-thin face. The stranger seemed to be looking down, but then slowly—at the pace of a blood stain spreading or a nightmare creeping in—he lifted his head. Eyes like burning coals, a beak-like nose, a pointy chin. And a smile that went on and on …

Anton knew he shouldn't have been able to make out all those details in the poorly lit lot, but he saw the man clear as day.

Suddenly, there wasn't enough air in the room, and breath wouldn't come. Anton could swear the man was there for him, looking right at him, right *through* him.

And that smile. Thin lips stretching impossibly far as if to envelop the entire head. The entire world.

Anton did what anyone faced with something too terrifying to process might—he closed his eyes. Shut them tight enough to produce an afterimage. And then, following another instinct as old as time, he opened them again. A danger seen is a danger avoided, or something like that.

But there was nothing, no danger anymore. The man was gone. If he'd ever been there at all. There was just a parking lot lined with budget friendly sedans, surrounded by some maintenance-groomed shrubbery, and the dark windows of his sleeping neighbors.

Drunk and seeing things was Anton's first thought. He clung to it like a buoy. But the undercurrent still threatened to pull him under.

He sat back down on the futon feeling terribly— uncomfortably—sober. And frightened. He could be honest with himself now: he *was* frightened. Of his wavering sanity, of his life about to change, of the uncertain future.

There was an undeniable comfort to wallowing. It saw Anton through to the dawn that night and for many to come.

The corvidian man came back, time and again. Just standing there and smiling his terrible smile. Sometimes he spoke to Anton, mouthing words that sounded like commands. Things Anton didn't and couldn't understand.

During the day, he played at normalcy. Drank extra coffee to stay alert. Joked with coworkers. Made small talk. If anyone saw the deepening dark circles of sleeplessness and the ever-increasing desperation in his eyes, no mention of it was made. All interactions stayed at a comfortable surface level. During the long busy days, ones that ended with drinks at local pubs and saw him home well after dark, he could almost believe in a certain degree of sanity and balance restored. Then he'd get home to a silent condo with his wife behind the closed door of their once shared bedroom planning her future without him, crash on a futon dreading his nightly visitor, and reality would come crashing in, pouring over him like a bucket of ice water, reminding him that any normalcy achieved during the day was of a purely performative variety. This—this waking nightmare—was his life.

One evening he heard his wife laugh through the door. She was on the phone, her voice too quiet to make out, but the sound of laughter carried: so bright, so airy, so *delighted*. When was the last time he had made her laugh like that, like the person on the other end of the line did?

It was so good for so long between them. Where did the good go? Would he ever have it again, or would life now offer nothing but a steady decline in quality? Didn't he work for this? Didn't he try? Wasn't it enough? Wasn't *he* enough?

The small ugly voice inside of him whispered no, and Anton poured himself some vodka to silence it. The old bottle was done and gone, this was its latest replacement, grabbed from a bodega on the corner.

That night he finally made out what the dark man was mouthing to him. "Return," he was saying. "Return. You know what to do."

I do know, Anton realized, of course, I do. I've only been trying not to.

The man smiled. It was enough to keep Anton up the rest of the night.

He waited until the weekend, thinking of almost nothing else. There was no one he could talk to about it, no one who would understand. It was a very particular sort of loneliness; one that had nothing to do with being alone and was all the more suffocating for it.

And then of course there were practical considerations. He couldn't just bring another mouse. Ever since the last time, he'd taken to buying snap traps, trusting the cheap mechanism to do the killing for him. He saw a dead bird on the street on the way home but knew that wouldn't do either. Eyed a neighbor's chihuahua for a while, but yappy as it was, he couldn't bring himself to do it. In the end, he bought a squirrel cage from a local exterminator business, set it up out back, and waited. There were always squirrels around, the same as mice. Nuisance. Forever climbing up the walls, tearing at window screens, digging at the roof corners trying to sneak into the attics. It was practically a public service he was doing, he told himself. There were no accusatory glances being cast in his direction by the tiny black eyes of the caught and caged creature, he assured himself while making the still-bone-familiar drive that weekend.

The squirrel chittered and scurried around the entire walk, making carrying the trap all the more unwieldy, but Anton made it.

The house greeted him like a prison might a recidivist criminal. With a satisfied silent, "Ah, I knew you'd be back."

Anton sighed heavily. The red of the smile graffiti scorched his retinas as a welcome.

The trap wasn't built to murder. It was strictly a catch-and-release system. Anton had never thought he was built for murder either, but extreme times invited extreme measures. Nevertheless, it took time and effort—both of which he hoped to forget or drink away in the near future—to make the squirrel dead.

There were sticks involved and the longest kitchen knife he owned and now would never use again. He was afraid of getting bitten, but the work gloves—bought once optimistically as a new homeowner and never used since—had kept his hands clumsy but safe.

In the end, the poor thing was dead. Bleeding out at the bottom of the cage. Anton poked it with a stick just to be sure, then opened the trap's door, and released the body onto the floor. The pentagram design began turning red.

And Anton made his wish as fervently as he knew how.

He thought he heard laughter coming from somewhere in the woods, but surely it was only his imagination. After all, who'd ever laugh if they had a smile like that?

A smile Anton was sure had marked him like a brand as he walked away from the house, the weight of the world collapsing his shoulders inward. He could feel the dark man walk beside him, could hear the rustling of his long black coat, but didn't dare look.

To him, it was only the wind. Another convenient lie. As if the wind could ever be that sinister, that self-satisfied.

It was one of those freak things. The car came out of nowhere, everyone said, going way too fast, blowing straight through the red light. It caught his wife just as she was crossing the street, heading back to work from lunch. She'd never walk again, that much was clear from the start. The rest of the damage was harder to estimate and would take a while to make itself known.

By the time his wife came home, pinned and sewn back together like some modern-day Frankenstein monster, Anton had all but destroyed himself with remorse. It was his wording, he was sure of it. All he had asked for was that she would stay, that she would never leave. He should have gone into specifics. But who would ever think of such a thing?

He was sorry now, so sorry, so terribly, suffocatingly sorry. But it was much too late. And no forgiveness would be forthcoming.

He'd dedicate his life to her, he decided. He'd take care of her, help her heal and recover, listen to every word, every concern. He'd make her laugh again. It didn't matter how much time it would take. Till death did them apart ... as they had originally intended.

Except that, of course, good intentions can only carry one so far. Life had a way of crashing straight through the best-laid plans.

You couldn't help someone who didn't want to be helped, who'd given up. The speeding car didn't just take away his wife's mobility, it stole her spark. Her soul, her hopes and dreams, whatever it was that animated her and made her *her*.

What remained was a spiritless vestige, a ghost, a shell, crushed and indifferent. Getting cut down on the brink of a much-awaited and perfectly-planned second act had broken his wife beyond bones, tore her beyond ligaments. There was nothing he could do or say. Not enough love in the world.

She tried to kill herself, He stopped her. She began resenting him. The resentment felt doubly sharp as it echoed his guilt.

Eventually, they settled into something like a routine, though increasingly recognizable as more of a rut. A joyless drag of days, a trudge toward nothing by two people who have all but exhausted each other's good graces.

Their lives were inertia giving way to entropy, with nothing to look forward to and no way out. Hopelessness permeated their condo like a sour smell of spoiled food. Even their détentes were bleak, mired in bitterness and unspoken sorrows.

And through it all, Anton couldn't stop thinking that there was a way to fix it. Fix all of it. But he was afraid now. So very afraid. Now that he knew what terrible weight words could carry, how would he dare to ask for anything more?

He drank. He sulked. He apologized and tried again. He brought his wife cake for her birthday when what she asked for was euthanasia.

She dressed up for their party of two, her shaky hand drawing red lipstick across her mouth. She spat a vicious smile at him. Later that night, Anton threw up the cake. The technicolor-hued vomit reminded him of the mad graffiti of the house in the woods. He washed down the thought with a shot of vodka.

His work held on to him out of sympathy, but their compassion could only stretch so far. Eventually, he was let go. Crippled wife or not, he had become simply too incompetent to employ.

The money he was given wouldn't last. It was much too expensive to take care of someone in his wife's condition. He did the math, redid it. Double-checked the numbers. The story they told was grim. But at least they didn't lie or mince words. Anton could appreciate that.

He told his wife. It seemed like the right thing to do. And then, empowered by the newfound freedom of confession and liberal helpings of alcohol, he continued talking. Studying the patterns in the carpet and drinking, his foot tapping out a self-soothing rhythm as he spoke, Anton told her everything. And in the end, horrified at himself, he clamped his mouth shut and looked up.

What he saw in his wife's eyes was pure hatred. He knew he deserved every ounce of it, but still, it cut like a knife. He flinched and looked away.

Always looking away. From the dark stranger who never even visited anymore to the truth itself, it seemed Anton could never face reality head-on. Forever trying to find a trick, a gimmick, a cheat.

His wife didn't speak to him for days. When she finally did break the silence, he'd been grateful enough to get teary-eyed, but what she wanted was just one thing. Terrifyingly simple.

"Take me there," she said.

And so he did. How could he say no to her after everything?

Anton still remembered the drive but hiking to the house on a path never meant for a wheelchair took ages. The weight felt right, *just and fair*—the Sisyphean boulder of a punishment richly deserved. In the end, exhausted, feeling like his arms were going to rip out of their sockets and his legs give out from under him, he made it. They made it.

He dragged the wheelchair backwards over the stone steps leading into the house, wondering what his wife was seeing in the woods. If it was a thin man with a dark expression and a hungry smile.

Once inside, he leaned against the wall, panting. Out of shape, with no exercise, poor diet, and steady drinking, he was surprised he had made it at all. But then again, it seemed he always managed to rally for the occasion.

His wife wheeled herself around, taking the place in. It was the most animated he'd seen her in ages. She rolled back to study the pentagram. The floor, he noticed, was still—or again—swept. The old blood stains plainly visible on the floorboards amid the morbid design.

Anton wanted to say something stupid, like, "This is where the magic happens." To somehow laugh it all off, make it less real. But it was much too late for anything like that.

As he entered, he saw the smile above the entrance curling its corners like snake tails and knew with a crushing certainty that *this*— the madness inside this house with its garish impossible walls and sightless windows—was the only real thing in the world.

He felt apologies bubbling up to the surface, but it was much too late for that either. There wasn't a sorry in the world expansive enough to cover the damage.

Pushing off the wall, Anton took a tentative step toward his wife. Then another. There were no words, but then, they were past that.

He didn't feel the knife going in. Or rather he felt something pushing against his body and dismissed it initially as walking into some part of his wife's wheelchair which was forever trying to injure him. There was no accompanying sensation of the parting of the flesh or even bleeding. Only when he looked down did he see the hilt of it sticking out of his stomach, a red stream leaving his body.

It didn't seem quite real; the numbness made it feel dreamlike. He met his wife's eyes, afraid to see the same burning hatred there, and was glad to find the expression mitigated by something milder this time, something almost like an apology.

"I had to try," she whispered. "You understand." And then, she drew back the knife with her good hand and plunged it into him again. And again.

Anton collapsed onto the floor, pawing at his stomach, slipping in all the blood. Sisyphus fallen at last, crushed by his boulder. It felt strangely peaceful, this letting go. He knew he deserved every moment of it. It was an ending apt enough for a fable. A built-in moral and all.

He tried to tell his wife that, but when he opened his mouth, blood poured out instead of words. So, he tried to smile to let her know that it was okay, that he got it, that he was sorry it had to come to this but hoped it brought her some small satisfaction or peace. His smile, strained and red, must have been horrific, he realized.

And then he thought about the house and the pentagram on the floor he was bleeding all over, and the very last thing that went through his mind before the darkness took him, the one he desperately tried to make his wife understand was, "I hope it works."

She stared at the body on the floor in horror. She'd never seen a dead body before. Only on TV. Never even went to any funerals. And now it was right in front of her and so very real. What was he trying to say to her? His lips moved at the end, but no words came out. She hoped it was something like forgiveness. Life had been so short on acts of kindness lately.

She wheeled herself around. All along she'd been making a wish, as fervently as a kid with a birthday cake but more desperately, and now she'd just have to wait and see.

It seemed impossible, but then nothing has been making any sense for a long time. And she had made her peace with the alternatives.

As far as she could figure, she'd either get her wish granted and walk out of here or stay moored in the middle of nowhere with no way to leave and eventually die. She could live with either outcome, but something in the eye of the man she saw in the woods outside made her think everything would be okay.

The man reminded her of a tall black bird, the way he looked, the way he tilted his head to the side, studying her. Before he vanished into the trees, he smiled sharply, breaking the illusion. But she was hoping to see him again. Even that smile. It wasn't so scary once you got used to it. Probably.

Would he come to her now? Would he wait with her? The sun was going down, the wind was picking up. The trees around the house swayed as if performing some ritualistic dance. She thought she heard footsteps behind her and felt her toes give a sympathetic twinge. Then another, a stronger one.

Slowly, very slowly, she grabbed the sidebars of her wheelchair and pushed up, simultaneously sliding her feet off the footrests toward the floor. The gravity rushed in like a tidal wave, threatening to pull her under, but with a feathery touch, a steady hand appeared to catch her elbow. The smiling man had steadied her. Together, side by side, they took a step toward the woods.

SPINDEL

When we are children, our imperfect worlds make perfect sense to us. It is only later, through the wear and tear of years and experience, that reality unravels presenting a much different, infinitely flawed tapestry of life.

My name is Johnny Walker. I was twelve the summer my life changed forever.

My dad always said he named me "after his best friend." He generally preferred whiskey to fatherhood and had a peculiar sense of humor, but I learned to live with it all: the man, the humor, the name. Not like I had much of a choice.

I was tall enough for my age, but skinny, like a reed, with outsized feet and hands and a large nose and mug-handle ears I was hoping to grow into before long. After all, my older brother, Beau, was handsome and popular, and everyone said we kind of looked alike. Well, our mom did, anyway.

We lived in the same small two-story house, in the same small town my entire life. Just the four of us. When he was sober, my dad worked construction. At other times, he could be found sunk into the old living room recliner that could no longer be straightened out into a chair, watching sports or reading crime stories. My mom worked the reception desk for the local police department, and my brother was the star of the high school football team. It was a nice and simple life. I had a best friend and a paper route. I did okay in school. My brother had always been my best and only babysitter; most of what I knew about anything important came from him, be it what music to listen to or what movies to watch. I don't know if I liked his choices back then, but I knew I ought to. Beau was the preeminent authority and tastemaker of my formative years. I certainly don't like the same things now. Beau was funny, too. He could do all sorts of voices, imitating the people on TV or in real life, always making me laugh.

Looking back on it makes it seem idyllic, like a perfect slice of Americana, but far be it from me to wax nostalgic. I know better.

With the certitude only a twelve-year-old can have, I believed that every small town had its own boogeyman. It was probably all those horror movies I watched with Beau, peeking at the bloody mayhem on the TV screen through splayed fingers as my brother chuckled.

"Oh, don't be scared, little dude," he'd tell me. "All the monsters are in the movies. Well." He'd pause dramatically. "*Almost* all of them."

The boogeyman of my childhood had a name. Mr. Spindel. Karl Spindel on his newspaper address. He lived at the end of Maple

Avenue in a boxy, meticulously kept grey house. There was nothing ever on his front lawn to indicate anything about him—no children's toys, no blooms, no trees, no decorations, or broken-down cars. Only perfectly, evenly cut grass.

The man himself looked to me like a cartoon villain. Mr. Spindel was tall, with a smooth hairless skull, small, deep-set eyes, and a wide mouth. He had long spindly limbs and a small round torso. He wore suits to work. Plain dark suits. I knew he was a bank manager, but having never had any reason to go in, I never saw him at work.

In my imagination, Mr. Spindel led a dark and sinister double life. I believed the man had only pretended normality during the light of day and committed terrible atrocities under the cover of darkness. Had I been braver in those days, I'd probably attempt to follow him around and prove my suspicions true, but courage had never been my strong suit.

So, I speculated. Imagined. Sometimes I even dreamed about the man. Karl Spindel in his ugly brown suit, scowling at me like he could see right through me. I'd wake up tangled in my sweaty, twisted bedsheets, grateful for the daylight streaming through my windows.

This morbid fascination had been going on for years, ever since I'd started the paper route, but the summer I was twelve, the slow-simmering suspicion boiled over into something else entirely.

That was the summer the girls went missing.

First, it was Sandy Morgan, who never came home from her shift at Dairy Queen. Then, it was Alice Chang, who left her piano tutor and apparently disappeared somewhere on a three-block walk to her house. And then, Amanda Teller. My brother's on-and-off girlfriend. That was the one that had really brought it home.

Beau and Amanda were off at the time of her disappearance, but of course, he still came under suspicion. Police officers showed up and asked questions. They were the people we both knew from Mom's office holiday parties, but we'd never seen them like this, in their professional roles, all serious and solemn.

Beau had an alibi—he was working the closing shift at the local video store. Pushing the latest horror flicks on the unsuspecting locals, I'm sure. So he was off the hook. But still understandably distraught.

Amanda was his first real girlfriend. Their flame waned and relit itself over the past two years, but the fire was still there. I could tell he was upset by the way he was acting, by the mournful sound his music selection had acquired. I didn't even know they *made* sad metal songs.

Me … I was convinced the disappearances were the work of Karl Spindel. But because I had nothing by way of proof outside of personal antipathy, no one would listen to me, not even my brother.

Everyone was stressed as the summer went on. My mom was working overtime, fielding phone calls pouring in through the specially set up helpline, trying to separate the useful from the useless—or the wheat from the chaff, as she liked to say—and coming up empty-handed. My dad suddenly got extra work, helping install security cameras and additional locks.

Everyone was worried, everyone was scared. Nothing like that had ever happened in our small town. Nothing like that ought to ever happen in places like ours—nice, good places. And to such nice, good girls, too. Not at all the sort of girls who stayed out late, partied, flirted with danger. "This was all wrong," people said, frowning and shaking their heads. "It didn't make sense."

But then, they didn't know about the boogeyman.

From the small window on the opposite wall, she could see a spider web. A large messy affair beginning at the top right corner and spanning downward. She hadn't seen the spider weave it, but she had seen him visit it. A disgustingly thick body ambulating on sharply angled legs as thin as pencil lines. He didn't come by very often, and she imagined he must have other webs to visit. The thought made her shudder.

Still, she watched the web, even when it did nothing more than sway in the wind because there was nothing else to do or see. It was either doing that or thinking about what lay covered by the dark stained tarp in the far corner, emitting an eye-wateringly nasty smell. The worst thing was that she was getting used to the smell. Just as she was getting used to this creepy small room and its soundproof walls and the old sleeping bag and the rust-stained bucket she'd been given for her convenience and the plain, barely palatable meals slid under the door twice daily.

What she couldn't get used to were the chains. There was no way to get used to the chains.

She had long ago lost track of time. It was almost as if there were two lives she'd been given—a happy, sunny one where she was a popular high school cheerleader with a cute, athletic sometimes-boyfriend, and this—endless darkness.

Or maybe not endless. There was some light streaming in through the window, albeit low. She speculated there had to be a tree right outside or something, obscuring the sun. From where she was chained, there was no way to reach the window. She tried screaming for help the first few days, but it proved futile.

The man came by and knocked on the glass for her, his gloved knuckles sounded like they were meeting with something infinitely more solid than a mere windowpane.

"It is soundproof," he said. His voice was low and muffled by the mask he wore. Obviously, he didn't want her to see him or know what he sounded like.

This gave her a glimmer of hope. If he didn't want to be recognized, then perhaps he was still considering eventually letting her go.

The man came by infrequently and spoke even less so. It was almost as if her mere presence there was enough for him. The worst things he could do to her, the morbidly imagined scenarios that kept her awake at night, he did not do. Not yet, anyway.

The night she was taken, she had been walking home from Stacy's house. Five blocks. A walk she'd done a thousand times.

Of course, she'd heard about the others—poor Sandy and Alice, the school had a special assembly for them—but somehow it didn't seem quite real, didn't quite tip her world into the red-lights-flashing danger zone. Youth, after all, is the best protective carapace; the way it makes one so sure of their invincibility.

Stacy was considering asking her dad to drive them, but by the time they came downstairs, the man was snoring on the couch in front of the TV. He sounded like a motor engine in need of oil.

She would have asked Beau, but they were on the outs just then. Another stupid fight about nothing.

So, she said she'd walk. Told herself it would be fine. And it was, for about two out of five blocks.

The man had come out of nowhere, it seemed. It was like one moment he wasn't there and the next he was. The suddenness of it had knocked the fight right out of her. He grabbed her, put something nauseatingly sweet-smelling over her nose and mouth, and the next thing she knew was this room. And the man looming over her. Still dressed in black from head to toe.

"Behave," he told her. "If not …" He walked over to the farthest corner and lifted the tarp. She never made it to the bucket; the vomit splashed the floor, ricocheting onto her. It didn't matter.

She'd never seen a dead body before outside of TV, let alone two. Let alone people she knew. Death rictus twisting their pretty features.

She didn't know Sandy well, but Alice was on her cheerleading squad. Her golden necklace—an ornate half-heart she shared with her sister—glistened brightly amid the purplish viscera. It was too much. She threw up again. When she was done, she felt horribly, terribly empty.

The man said nothing, simply left, and came back with an old towel, motioning for her to clean up. She did the best she could, throwing it in the bucket once finished. The man watched silently.

He brought the bucket back later. Also, a tall glass of water, a plain cheese sandwich on white bread, and an apple. *He doesn't want me to die*, a curious thought occurred to her. *Not yet, at any rate.*

She didn't think she'd be able to eat and ended up surprising herself by scarfing it all down. Then, eventually, she passed into an uneasy restless sleep. That was day one. She didn't know how many there'd been since. She should have kept track, but it seemed so oddly immaterial.

Time had ceased to matter. Perhaps she had, too.

It was difficult to imagine her mother—who when drunk, shouted at her regrets for not having an abortion—putting too much effort into finding her. The police she didn't expect much from either. After all, they had never found the other two girls.

She'd like to imagine Beau searching for her heroically, but that was just for movies and fairy tales. In real life, princesses stayed locked up in the dungeons, and the princes never came.

She shivered and pulled the sleeping bag tighter around her.

I decided that I at least ought to talk to Mr. Spindel. It was terrifying enough of an ordeal, but to me, an essential part of my investigation. If I was to have an investigation.

As a rule, the things a twelve-year-old and an adult had to talk about were few and far between. Unless that adult was Zeek who worked at the comic book store. I needed a plan. Failing to come up with a solid one, I improvised.

Walking into the bank felt weirdly grown-up. I was glad I put on my church best: a blue button-down and a pair of khakis. Our family almost never went anymore. The outfit had been mostly gathering dust at the far end of my closet. Sprung free from its baseball hat imprisonment, my hair resisted a comb, so I opted for watering it down instead.

The bank smelled like paper and air-conditioning. There was a security guard posted at the door, but he seemed too fat and jolly to offer much protection. In fact, I wondered if it wasn't the same man who played Santa Claus every Christmas for the town's festivities. The beard wasn't there, but maybe he shaved for the warmer months.

The teller windows were straight ahead, and to the right and further back there was the manager's desk. I made a beeline straight for that.

I had originally considered confronting Mr. Spindel at his house over some made-up unpaid newspaper balance, but cowardice had led me to seek the safety of a public place.

He seemed busy and serious. There were thick glasses on his face, and his creepily thin fingers were shuffling through the papers on his desk.

He looked up at me as I approached. "Yes, young man?"

"Um … yes, hi … hello. I was …" I took a deep breath and fired out my preprepared lie. "I was hoping to open a bank account."

"Oh," he said, taking off his glasses. His eyes immediately shrunk without the thick protective lenses magnifying them. His eyebrows, I noticed, were repulsively bushy.

The blindingly bright overhead lights reflected off of the shining dome of his head.

"And why do you wish to open a bank account?" he inquired politely.

There was an accent in his speech, too light to place. Not that I was an expert.

"For my money," I said.

He gestured for me to sit down. The chair was upholstered and cushy. My dad had always said banks fleeced people out of their hard-earned cash. I figured they must want them to be comfortable for the process.

"How do you make your money, young man?"

"I have a paper route."

"Ah." Mr. Spindel tapped a long, tapered finger to his temple. "Now I know why you look so familiar. You deliver my paper, yes?"

I nodded.

"You do a very good job," he said with something like a smile. His mouth was too long for a smile, and it didn't look right.

"Thanks," I answered politely. 'So, I wanted a place to put my money."

"How old are you?" he asked me.

"Twelve."

"Ah. Yes. I thought as much. Unfortunately, that's a bit too young to open your own bank account. Perhaps, one or both of your parents can come by with you and sign some papers?"

This was the opening I was waiting for. "But see, I don't want them to know. I want it to be a secret. Don't you think people should be able to have secrets?"

He gave me a curious look for a moment, then his mask of politeness slipped back on.

"Of course," he said, his accent adding a light whispery quality to his syllables. "Of course. But I am afraid, one must still follow the letter of the law. Rules and regulations and all that. And our bank's rules and regulations stipulate that you need an adult if you wish to open an account."

I must have faked the dejected look well enough for him to attempt to comfort me.

"I think it is very good for a young man such as yourself to be so smart about money. I would be happy to help you if you bring an adult with you."

He glanced down at the papers in front of him as if to indicate our conversation had come to an end without saying so.

His fingers lifted gently, then touched down one by one, making a light tapping noise on the polished surface of his desk. He tried to smile that terrible smile at me again.

"Okay, thanks," I mumbled, getting up.

"Would you like a lollipop or are you too old for such things?" he asked me, reaching for the small square container full of brightly colored sweets.

That's when I did something I had never done before, something unimaginable—I refused candy.

I walked out slowly, steadily, like a person with nothing to hide, only sprinting for home once I was outside and down the block from the bank. I couldn't wait to get out of the uncomfortable clothes and slip back into my summer uniform of denim cutoff shorts and my brother's old hand-me-down T-shirts.

All the while, I was thinking, my mind whirring and whirring. What had I learned? Nothing about Mr. Spindel's demeanor screamed serial killer. Not outright, anyway.

I'd need some actual evidence, something more than gut feelings. As I rummaged through the kitchen cabinets for snacks, I resolved to find my courage and follow Mr. Spindel around. After all, everyone was always on their best behavior at work. Dad didn't even drink at his. It's what happened after hours, when no one was watching, that revealed one's true self. And I was determined to reveal Karl Spindel for a monster.

The spider web caught a fly. A large fat fly, the kind she would have swatted to death if she found it in her room. Now it was her only company. All too bitterly relatable.

The fly struggled at first but then gave up. Resigned to its tragic fate, it hung suspended by the web, blowing in the wind. The strange thing was that the spider never came. Not during the day anyway. She watched and watched, having nothing better to do. Imagining some arachnid drama that prevented the creepy thing from collecting its due.

Maybe he came by at night. Maybe he was a she. Biology was never something she paid too much attention to in class, and so she knew nothing about spiders.

The fly began to look more and more desiccated each day. After a while, its body separated into two halves. One day one of the halves was gone. Then, soon after, the other followed suit.

That'll be me one day, she thought. *Gone.*

Tears wouldn't come. She was too dehydrated to cry anyway. The man never seemed to give her enough water, and she was afraid to ask.

She had so many questions for him, but then he'd come and stand there towering above her, considering her like she was something lesser than, a puzzle for him to solve, or perhaps, a fly in the web, and the questions died on her tongue.

One day, he came to take her bucket, a disgusting thing even with the lid firmly on, and paused for a while, leaning on the wall opposite the one she was chained to.

"What are you?" he asked her after a while in that strange voice of his.

She tried answering, but her tongue wouldn't cooperate. She took a sip of water and tried again, daring to look up at him.

"I am Amanda Teller. My parents are Bill and Karen Teller. I am sixteen. I'm a cheerleader. I have friends and family who love me and worry about me." She stopped, afraid to continue, afraid of having already said too much. It didn't matter if it wasn't all true. It was close enough, anyway.

There was a pause, only a beat that felt like an eternity.

Then he said something so quietly she could barely make it out. It sounded like, "Then what am I for keeping you here?"

"A monster," she wanted to scream at him. But what good would that do?

She lowered her eyes in what she hoped was a look of deference. After a while, he left.

She watched the window for days to come, but the spider never returned. Was he ever there? What was his web's purpose if not to feed its creator? Did nature have such cruel designs?

Eventually, the rain came and washed the web away.

I began following Mr. Spindel every day after the bank closed. Mom was busy working overtime. Dad was either at a construction site or at home drinking. If they noticed my absence in the evenings, they didn't say a thing. We weren't really the sort of family that gathered for shared meals outside of special occasions.

Beau was still around but his approach to being an older brother was pretty easygoing. When I asked him how to pick a lock on a gate, he eyed me with suspicion for a moment, then laughed, ruffled my hair, and taught me a trick with a pen knife. I think he liked to encourage the mischievousness in me. It made him feel like we were alike.

We weren't. Not really. But I had hoped that would change with time because I couldn't think of anything better than being just like him—larger than life, exciting, fun.

Mr. Spindel was none of those things. More like the exact opposite.

Every day after the bank closed, he walked home. On Tuesdays, he stopped at Mrs. Lee's to collect his dry-cleaning—the shirts' see-through casings flapping in the wind like plastic sails. On Wednesdays, he stopped by the library, usually getting two or three thick hardcovers. On Fridays, he got groceries at the market. Two large bags, no more, no less. I bet he bought the same things every single time.

Weekends he didn't seem to go anywhere. I watched him cut grass, wash his windows, clean his gutters.

On occasion, he brought one of his library books out to the old wooden rocking chair on his front porch and read. For hours.

And sometimes he went for walks around the neighborhood.

I watched him for two weeks and found no deviations in his patterns. But then, I imagined, smart criminals must have strict routines and tight schedules because of the inherent risks of messing up and giving themselves away.

Meanwhile, I practiced with my pen knife until I got really good at picking locks. And once I did, I decided to take a peek at Mr. Spindel's backyard.

It was surrounded by a fence, about my height. Of course, he would have a fence. To protect all his secrets.

I got the primitive lock to unlatch easily enough. What lay beyond was an utter disappointment, a space as plain and bland as the rest of Mr. Spindel's life. Grass, a few spindly trees. Remnants of an old fire pit.

My imagination had morbidly served me up a picture of Mr. Spindel burning the remains of his victims in there, but no, he wouldn't do that. The neighbors would have smelled it. They were right there, so close. I hoped they weren't looking at me, wondering what I was doing there, contemplating calling the cops and reporting me for trespassing.

I walked to the back of the house and peered through the windows. All I saw was an orderly clean kitchen.

I looked around some more. There was a shed at the far corner of the property. It looked large enough to hold a person or two.

I furtively ran to it, hoping no one was watching, and fiddled with the lock until it sprung open.

The shed was just as neatly organized as the kitchen; with one wall taken up by a pegboard with hooks and outlines of the tools that were meant to go on them. There was a lawnmower too—one of the older models— and a rake and a shovel. I examined the latter for traces of blood, using the tail of my T-shirt as a glove. It was clean. Everything about Mr. Spindel was clean. Too clean.

It had to be the basement, I thought. *Whatever secrets the man kept had to be in the basement.*

That meant taking my breaking-and-entering thing to a brand-new level. I checked my plastic knockoff Swatch. Mr. Spindel wouldn't be home for hours. All I had to do was …

It's easy enough to think yourself out of something. Overthink the details and you lose the grand picture. I didn't let myself do that. Instead, I carefully locked the shed back up and sprinted across the yard to the back door. That lock had proved more of a challenge, but my pen knife had many handy attachments, and one of them worked. Just like that, I was in.

Mr. Spindel's house didn't have a distinct smell. That in itself was unusual. In my experience, most places had an indelible olfactory presence of their own. The way our kitchen usually smelled of burnt toast, our bathroom of Mom's perfume, and our living room of Dad's cheap beer.

Mr. Spindel's house smelled of clean abandon. No dust on surfaces, almost no pictures on the walls. His furniture was nicer and newer than ours. It looked just like a store's showroom display. The wooden floors had rugs, real ones, not cheap carpeting. There was a tall open shelf with some books on it and a few toy models of classic cars. I looked closer—the titles appeared foreign. I didn't know the language.

Upstairs, his bed was made perfectly, tight corners and all. The way I thought was only possible in movies. Or hotels. It seemed like such a strange thing to me then, to spend the time and effort in the morning getting all the corners tight and the top sheet smooth, only to mess it all up later at night. Waste of time, if you asked me. Beau was of the same opinion. Our mother wasn't, but she seldom won that one.

There was another room with a desk and another bookcase with some documents. Taxes, insurance, all sorts of tedious adult things. Nothing interesting. Certainly nothing that screamed serial killer. But then again, I hadn't seen the basement yet.

Bravely, I descended into a surprisingly finished space. It looked just like any other floor of the house. I hadn't known basements could be made to look like that, even though Beau had haphazardly converted a part of ours a few years ago.

Mr. Spindel's was well-lit and meticulously clean, much like the rest of his house. There was a corner with laundry machines and a drying rack. Some shelves along the wall with neatly labeled clear plastic storage containers. Winter clothes. Christmas things. Things like that.

A few old chairs stacked, presumably until his guests might need them. If he ever had any guests. An old record player he was probably not quite ready to get rid of, perhaps thinking of repairing. A framed artwork with a damaged glass front. Nothing else, nothing suspicious at all. Certainly no bodies. I didn't even know how one might bury a body in a place with finished floors.

I wasn't ready to give up just yet, and there was one more potential place.

I summoned the rest of my courage and rushed back upstairs. The attic door was in the same place it was in my house—the ceiling just outside the bathroom. Leaning against the wall in the corner, there was a stick with a hook on the end to pull the door down. It unfolded as stairs. I scrambled up.

The attic was empty. Nothing, not even storage boxes. Definitely no girls.

Dejected, I climbed back down and left, locking things behind me.

It felt like I was holding my breath until I was a few blocks away. Then I let the air rush out of me with a great whoosh. Deflating like a balloon, I let the disappointment wash over me.

But then I started thinking about it rationally. There was a phrase I heard in one of the movies Beau and I watched about the absence of evidence not being the evidence of absence. Something like that.

Basically, just because Mr. Spindel's house was model clean, didn't mean he was innocent. All it meant was that he was smart enough to commit his crimes off-premises. He was, after all, a bank manager, and presumably had loads of money. Perhaps, he had another home somewhere. A lot of people did. Even my dad had an old hunting shack he had inherited from his father. Only Dad wasn't much of a hunter, so no one had seen the place in ages.

All I had to do was stick to the plan and follow Mr. Spindel until he gave himself away. I only hoped he would do so before the summer was over.

There were still ongoing citizen searches for the girls. Neighbors with flashlights, wearing vests with reflective stripes on their backs and good intentions like hearts on their sleeves. Beau went once to the one for Alice. Afterward, he came home, his expression unreadable. When I tiptoed upstairs to our shared room, I heard him cry. Took me a while to figure out what the sound was since I had never heard my brother cry before. At least I had enough tact to tiptoe right back down and leave him to his sadness.

Our house was on the smaller side, with only two bedrooms. Beau and I technically shared a room, but a few years back he converted a part of the basement into his "man cave." Divided by some old bookcases from the storage and laundry area, it featured a mishmash of furniture discards from the street and upstairs that all together assembled rather nicely into a serviceable lounge area. The TV he had to buy brand-new—well brand-new secondhand—but the couch, the coffee table, the TV stand, and the easy chair all came with history and stains, some unknown and best not speculated upon. He even rescued an only-slightly-rickety pool table from a curb one day. All in all, it was by far my favorite space in our house. It was there I sat around and made my plans.

One evening, Mr. Spindel joined in on a search party. I followed, at a distance. Kids weren't supposed to go on those things.

I watched him, hoping the entire time he'd veer off somewhere, take a guilty turn, give himself away somehow. But no, he toed the line, went along with the others, even made small talk in that weird accent of his.

Did the others not see him the way I saw him? Did they only perceive his human suit and not what lay beneath?

Even Beau wouldn't listen to me.

"Do you not like him because he has an accent?" he asked me. "Cause dude, that's messed up."

I assured my brother that definitely wasn't the reason, but I don't know if he believed me. He shook his head with something like disappointment and told me to leave it alone. I wish I had.

If time still existed, it was no longer linear. It was no longer time at all. She didn't get her period, but that might have just been due to malnutrition. She didn't think it was a reliable method of telling time. And she had thought of so many ways. From measuring her leg hair to the length of her fingernails. But in the end, it didn't seem to matter much. Time only mattered when you were going somewhere, and as far as Amanda Teller could tell, she was stuck at a dead end.

If time didn't matter, then reality shouldn't count for much either. Her sense of it was slipping these days. She felt her existence sliding to the periphery, entering some strange liminal state of being where nothing seemed quite solid.

There was no longer a clear delineation between sleep and wakefulness.

Some days she thought the room was different, some days she thought the man was. Did he even sound the same? Everything was changing. Malleable. Unsteady. The shapes of things were smeary, blurry, unsettled. There was a perpetual sense of disorientation.

Was it the same window? Did the spider weave a master web over it and change the meager view for her?

The man came less and less now. Leaving more food each time. The food she had to budget and ration, uncertain of his next visit.

Most of the time he remained silent. Once, she imagined she heard a whispered apology, but that couldn't have been right.

Out of sheer desperation, she had tried talking to him, but he seldom answered, only stared.

Once she forgot herself and yelled, flat out yelled at his face, "What are you going to do with me?"

The man took a deep, deep sigh, let it out, and said quietly, slowly, "I don't know. I don't know what to do."

Of all the things he could have possibly said or done, somehow that had scared her worst of all.

A life of suspended animation, caught in the trap of an ambivalent villain. If he didn't want to kill her and couldn't decide to let her go, what was she? A Schrödinger victim? Someone who existed in both states and no state at all?

When they studied the cat experiment in school, it seemed like a silly hypothetical. Now it had become terrifyingly real to her.

"You can let me go," she whispered. "I never saw your face; I never saw your house. I'll say nothing."

He knelt down and studied her face, dark eyes eerily peering at her through the mask. If not for that layer of plastic, she would have felt his breath on her face, he would have felt hers. Maybe it would be a saving grace, a way to become real to him. Not just another girl in the room. Not just another victim.

But then the moment passed. The man straightened out and left. The finality of the door slamming shut reverberated through her entire body.

She pulled her knees up until she could rest her chin on them. Bone on bone. Always slender, she had become emaciated in here. And yet her body, malnourished and exhausted, was clinging on. Refusing to just shut down. Maybe it knew something she did not. Maybe it was merely stubborn.

Either way, one day soon she was bound to disappear from this place. With the wind, with the rain, like the fly, like the web. Gone, gone, gone.

I missed my best friend, Mike. Mike Russo. We've known each other since second grade. His parents divorced the winter before, and his dad moved all the way to Alaska, which he joked was as far as he could drive away from his harpy ex-wife without falling into the ocean. I never thought Mrs. Russo was a harpy, but then again, I wasn't quite sure what the word meant either. Now the Russos were doing shared custody, and Mike went up to Alaska for the entire summer. He sent me postcards every few weeks or so. Every one of them had a bear on it. I was beginning to wonder if the place had any people at all. It seemed unimaginably far.

Talking on the phone was too expensive, and I couldn't tell him what was going on in a postcard or a letter. Without Beau to back me up either, I felt all alone.

I told myself something about the going getting tough and the tough getting going, but that was superhero talk, and I was the farthest thing from it. When Beau crashed in the basement on the couch, I still slept with a nightlight. One I was careful to unplug and hide first thing in the morning to avoid embarrassment and teasing, but there it was.

"It'll probably be all over once the school year starts," Beau said to me one day.

We were in the kitchen, sharing a readymade pizza that had come out of our notoriously moody oven surprisingly unburnt.

"What will?" I asked.

"Everyone will stop looking, you know. I mean, they don't even do search parties anymore. It's like everyone just gave up."

"What about the girls?" I said, pulling apart a second slice, using my fingers to separate the burning hot cheese tentacles.

"What *about* the girls?" Beau shrugged. He seemed so adult to me just then, as if something had changed, some profound personality shift had occurred. Like when he emerged from puberty, all tall and deep-voiced and shaving.

"Well, they are somewhere, aren't they? They need to be found still."

"Johnny boy," Beau said with a sad smile, "they are likely dead by now. Crime statistics say so."

The delicious, melty, cheesy goodness in my mouth turned to cardboard.

Crime statistics? "Did Mom tell you that?"

"Dad, actually. It was in one of his mystery novels."

I looked at our dad through the archway that connected the kitchen and the living room. I couldn't remember the last time we had a conversation.

Beau followed my sightline, then walked up and plucked the almost empty beer bottle from our father's hand, before it fell and spilled on the carpet the way his drinks so often did. The sleeping man didn't even stir. All the way from the kitchen, I could see a trail of saliva on his cheek. It glistened in the ambient light of the TV.

"Is Dad … is Dad okay?"

"Same as always, kiddo," Beau replied. "Don't worry. You worry too much. Gonna get premature wrinkles right here." He rubbed at the spot between my eyebrows with a meaty pizza-warm thumb. "Look like a little old dude."

"I just think maybe he's been drinking more lately …"

"It's the war. Some days it's with him more than others."

I nodded, but the war didn't mean much to me. Not really. It was over before I was born. Just a chapter in the history textbooks. Something that happened unfathomably far away.

I could never imagine my father with a weapon, my father taking a life. It just didn't make sense. I changed the subject.

"But doesn't it drive you crazy that Amanda is just gone?"

Beau looked at me with that "drop it" expression. "Yeah, it does. Yes, it sucks. But there is nothing to be done. Life … sometimes it just doesn't make any sense. At all. It's like a game where you don't know all the rules and some of them are completely bonkers, but you still gotta stay in it anyway."

I tracked my brother's metaphor and thought about Amanda, a valuable player being taken off the field through no fault of her own. It didn't seem fair.

I said it out loud.

"It isn't fair," Beau agreed. "But it's all we got."

We finished our pizza in silence.

I couldn't stop thinking about what Beau said. The beginning of the school year was approaching, and that would be that. The end of the search. Mr. Spindel would have gotten away with murder. Three times. I couldn't stand the thought.

Even if life wasn't fair—especially if life wasn't fair—I wanted to do anything in my power to shift the balance to the right side of things. The good side.

I followed Karl Spindel dejectedly as he did his errands, spinning my wheels, trying to come up with something. Some brilliant idea that would materialize above my head like a light in a cartoon and solve everything.

One morning, Mr. Spindel was waiting for me outside. I was so surprised I almost fell off my bike. Outside of a few joggers and some sleepy dogwalkers, the streets were usually empty when I did my paper route.

Of course, there was a chance he wasn't waiting for me at all. He was holding a book, so ostensibly he was merely taking advantage of the quiet morning to catch up on some reading, or— my dark imagination whispered—he was just now getting back from doing who knows what who knows where to the missing girls.

He waved and beckoned, so pedaling away would have been rude. I cringed, laid my Schwinn on the sidewalk, and came up to his front porch, a rolled-up newspaper in hand.

"Good morning, young man," he said cheerfully.

"Good morning, sir," I responded with conditioned politeness. "Here's your paper."

"Ah, thank you. Nothing like the written word to start the day." He patted his book.

I didn't know. I wasn't much of a reader back then and had never read a newspaper outside of the occasional funnies, so I just nodded.

"You never came by with a parent to set up your bank account," he said, peering at me through those thick lenses of his.

"I … I changed my mind."

"Ah, of course." He did that weird smile thing of his. "There's always the old *sticking it in the mattress* trick."

"In the mattress?"

"Yes, a tried-and-true manner of keeping one's finances close at hand. Favored by distrustful old people and bank skeptics everywhere."

I nodded again. At this rate, Karl Spindel was going to think I was a dummy.

"Well, I nevertheless salute your enterprising spirit and economic acumen, and I wanted to give you a tip for your excellent service. Here."

He took out two crisp twenty-dollar bills and handed them to me. I had gotten an occasional tenner from my grandparents and once a twenty from Beau for my birthday, but never a largesse of this kind.

I reached for it without thinking. "Thank you, sir. That's … um … very generous."

"I, too, had a newspaper route when I was a young boy. I had just come over from Sweden, and it was the only job I could find to help support my family. At night, I used old newspapers to teach myself English. Seeing you on your bike takes me back to those days."

I didn't know what to say, so I thanked him again. Sweden seemed as impossibly far away and foreign as Alaska to me back then.

"What is your name?" he asked me.

"Johnny. Johnny Walker."

"Like the alcohol?" This time Mr. Spindel's smile almost made it.

"Yeah, like whiskey."

"Well, Johnny Walker, if you ever need anything, my door is open."

There was a chasm of unspoken things between us just then. Did he know of my intrusion? Did he catch me following him? Was he merely being nice? Was he lining me up as the next victim? Was he buying my silence?

My head spun.

I mumbled something about having to get back to my route, thanked him again, and rushed back to my Schwinn, pedaling away at double time. The twenties burned guiltily in my pocket. My heart pounded just as guiltily.

I couldn't keep my eyes on the road and ended up in a ditch. Skinned knees were a small cost to pay for the morning I'd had.

There wasn't much time left, and she knew it. She barely even minded it anymore. All she wanted was to leave this room. She'd take freedom any way she could get it.

The last time the man was there, he said nothing for a long time. Merely sat there with her. Then he reached out and touched her cheek, her arm. Gently, with butterfly fingers, as if to make sure she was there, she was real.

Perhaps, his sense of reality was slipping too. Amanda had some time ago begun hallucinating the girls talking to her from beneath their tarp. They didn't say the nicest things, but who could blame them. She'd be joining them soon enough.

Then, in that strange, thrown-off voice, he said, quietly, almost wistfully, "I didn't think I was much of a man. So, I wanted to see if I was a monster instead. And now I'm not so sure of anything anymore."

Is this why I'm here? she thought. *Am I a part of some twisted personality experiment?* Most people took quizzes in magazines, maybe saw a shrink. Perhaps, the man was a monster indeed.

It was nice to feel that spark of rage for a moment. Nice to feel anything. But it fizzled out like a cigarette in the rain. There was nothing left in her; nothing to fight him, to argue with him, to accuse him.

She lifted her eyes to the window, to the murky light out there struggling to get through the thick dirty glass. The spider never came back. The spider knew he was a monster and didn't care. The fly knew it too and it didn't matter. This was how the world worked. And it went on and on and on …

I sat on the edge of the tub with my feet in and poured hydrogen peroxide on my knees. The fascination of the fizzle took away most of the sting. Then I dabbed it dry with a towel and slapped some Band-Aids on. Not a perfect job, but it would have to do.

Dad was the only one home besides me, dozing on and off in front of the local news station report. The drink in his hand was coffee for a change, though whether he'd made it Irish was anybody's guess.

'What'd you do to yourself?" he growled at me when I walked into the living room.

"Fell off my bike."

"Ought to be more careful," he said, eyes returning to the screen.

"I know."

I looked at the TV. Right into a magnified photo of Amanda Teller. I had somehow forgotten how pretty she was. She simply became "victim number three," someone to find and rescue. Not a charming, friendly cheerleader I kinda sorta had a puppy crush on. The one who gave me a kiss on my last birthday, back when Beau and Amanda were "on." That kiss felt so nice I wanted to leave my cheek lipstick-smudged forever.

"All they talk about is them girls," Dad said. There was a heaviness in his voice. "No one can find them. Cops are useless," he'd all but spat out.

That kind of talk was why Mom never brought him to any of her office parties.

I headed to the kitchen to find some food. Because of the paper route, my morning started so early that most days I ended up having two breakfasts.

"Want some pancakes?"

The question threw me. I couldn't remember my father ever cooking.

"Sure."

As he clumsily got out of his permanently reclined chair, he managed to avoid spilling his coffee.

"I was gonna make some anyway, so …" Dad shut off the TV, shambled into the kitchen, and began getting out pancake mix, eggs, and butter.

"How's your summer been?" he asked me, stirring the ingredients together in a large bowl.

Butter sizzled in the skillet; birds were singing outside. The normalcy of the morning took me back to some earlier, more innocent time before all that's happened.

"I've had better," I answered truthfully.

"Don't let all this business get you down, Johnny," my father said. "Sometimes life don't make any sense, and you still gotta live it."

Same thing Beau said, more or less. Maybe it was what being an adult was all about. Knowing things like that. Believing them.

It was strange to be having this morning with my dad, almost surreal. He'd become the inert shape in the recliner, the snoring audio from the living room. A caricature more so than a real person. A nonpresence in my life, like a negative space. And now he was back? Just like that? It had to be some strange temporary thing, an anomaly. Maybe, I thought cynically, he was just out of booze.

My father poured the batter and flipped the pancakes expertly. Better than Beau, at any rate. Mom only ever ate yogurt for breakfast, and I usually opted for cereal. The brighter the box the better.

The smell of pancakes permeated the space, transforming it into one of those as-seen-on-TV kitchens.

"Got me a job interview this afternoon. A new construction company in town. Could be full-time." Dad winked at me.

I wanted to say something complimentary, something important. What came out instead was, "Dad, do you still have that cabin in the woods?'

"You bet, I do," he said. "There's value in real estate, you know. Why do you ask?"

"Are there other cabins there? Like cabins of other families who hunt?"

My father stopped to think, scratching the thick stubble on his chin. 'Hunt and fish. Yeah, yeah. A few of them. The Andersons have one, the Murrays, that banker fellow too."

For a second there, I thought my heart was going to jump right out of my body. "You mean, Mr. Spindel?"

"Yeah, that guy. Mr. RichiePants. I went to school with him, you know. We were friendly and everything. Now he won't even talk to the likes of me. I was gonna get a job at the bank once, you know. Would have done too if only he'd given me a recommendation. But no, he's too good for that. Made it about my drinking, but we all know …" My father drifted off into a rant. The last pancake burned, returning the kitchen to its usual smell.

I didn't care, I was starving and scarfing them down anyway, my mind whirring a mile a minute.

"Where are they?" I interrupted Dad's rant. "Those cabins?"

"Right by Route 7, there's a blink-and-you-miss-it turnoff. Used to be a sign, might have fallen off." My father cocked an eyebrow at me. "You lookin' to do some hunting, sonny boy?"

I shrugged. "Just curious."

"Well, don't go biking there," my father said, through a mouth full of pancakes. "If you're falling off on paved roads, you'll kill yourself out in the woods."

Of course, I went biking there. It was a clue I'd been waiting for this entire time. Like the light going on. "The big break" as they said on the cop shows.

I left a note for Beau because it was another thing I learned from those shows. You didn't just go off on a hunch without letting people know where to find you.

I packed my rucksack with everything I thought I might need, from my trusty pen knife and a flashlight to snacks and a bottle of water. I checked my supplies and added a hammer because one could never be too well prepared.

Once ready, I peddled to Route 7. The day was hot. August in full force, all too aware it was on its last legs and trying to make an impression.

My knees stung with every revolution of the pedals, but I persevered. Fueled by pancakes and a desperate need to know, I pushed on and on, sweat dripping down my face, my palms slippery on the handlebars.

It was a long ride, even for me, and I biked just about every morning. The sign wasn't there. I nearly missed a turnoff. Definitely would have, had I not been looking for it.

My father was right. There was no way to ride my Schwinn through the overgrown path. I laid the bike on its side, away from the road, and covered it with some branches for security purposes. Then I proceeded on foot.

I'd never been much of a hiker. The woods scratched me, towered over me, dizzied me. To be completely honest, the woods scared me.

I wished Beau was there with me. Or Mike. He'd probably come back all sorts of tough and rugged, having spent the summer in the land of bears. But maybe, just maybe, I'll have a better story to tell.

I followed the path; what I could make out of it anyway. I should have thought to bring a compass. That was stupid of me. At least the canopies of the trees provided a nice shade from all the sun.

Everything around me looked exactly the same. I refused to get discouraged. This was easy, I told myself, this hiking business. As easy as putting one foot in front of the other.

I couldn't imagine someone doing this for fun, but stranger things …

Eventually, I came upon a clearing. A miniature lake, a pond really, surrounded by some old-timey-looking small wooden cabins on three sides like the letter U. The other side had more trees, densely packed together, like soldiers standing shoulder to shoulder.

I counted seven cabins. Made an educated guess that the neatest one would belong to Mr. Spindel. Then I decided to be thorough and search them all. I'd come this far, and there was no going back.

It did occur to me that the search parties must have come out this far. But I had this idea that perhaps they missed something, Something crucial. The infinite hubris of youth had made me think that mine was the exact fresh pair of eyes needed to solve this case. After all, no one saw Mr. Spindel the way I did.

I started at the farthest one, deciding to work my way counterclockwise.

The last cabin on the left was merely a ghost of a building. If it ever had owners, it had been long forgotten by them. The building was in shambles, barely hanging on, still standing seemingly out of sheer stubbornness. It was unlocked, and there was nothing in it, but some decrepit camping supplies.

The next cabin obviously still had owners who cared. The door was secured with a heavy-duty lock, but my penknife made quick work out of the old window, and soon I was boosting myself up and over the sill. Inside, the air was stale, the space was clean and spare. There was a bunk bed against one wall and a makeshift kitchen against the other. A porta potty-like setup behind a curtain. More importantly for my purposes, the place was empty.

The cabin after that was roughly the same. Well-kept and waiting for its owners to come back during the next hunting season.

The next cabin had nothing in it at all. Solid and in good shape, but completely empty as if awaiting new owners.

I knew the fifth cabin belonged to Mr. Spindel before I even set foot in it. You could tell from the outside. From how neat it looked. With a newer door and windows. I couldn't pick the locks at all. Giving up, I did the only thing I could: picked up a good-sized rock and broke the window. The sound of shattered glass echoed in my bones.

It felt like committing a crime more than breaking and entering into Karl Spindel's house ever did. I don't know why. Maybe because it felt so much more like violence.

I used the rock to knock down all the loose bits of glass from the window frame before climbing through. I don't know what I expected. I guess I thought I'd bust in triumphantly like a video game hero to save the day. Fanfares. Something.

I didn't expect silence. Dust motes dancing in the light streaming through the windows. Nothing but a neatly appointed tiny space, almost like a small self-contained apartment. With Mr. Spindel's customary clean impersonal touch.

There was only one thing on the wall. A photo of a man and a teenage boy. If I squinted just right and used my imagination, I could recognize the kid as Karl Spindel. The man looked too much like him to be anything but his father. Both of them were grinning, holding a large fish. *So once upon a time you did know how to smile*, I thought with sadness.

And then a deep cloud of shame descended upon me. I had for the second time invaded the privacy of a man who'd likely done nothing wrong and had been nothing but kind to me. And why? Because I didn't like his face? His voice? What the hell was wrong with me?

I left, feeling chastised. Guilty. Almost ready to turn around and make the long, exhausting ride back. Almost. There was still that feeling deep inside me, that engine humming and driving me on, the need to know.

I recognized the next cabin as ours. I had never spent much time here. Dad used to take Beau, but by the time I was of camping age, he had mostly lost interest. Neither of us had ever taken to hunting or fishing. He must have been disappointed.

Strange how places leave their mark on you, even places you figured didn't matter or those you had nearly forgotten all about.

I ran my hand over the wood of the door, and a vivid memory washed over me like a tidal wave.

It's summer. Just the three of us, Mom must have gotten stuck at work. Beau is probably about my age, so I'm just a kid. Dad is yelling at him. Beau, this was years before he sprung up half a foot, is small and shrinking beneath our father's ire.

But wait, as I tune the memory's dial like it's radio, focusing on the signal. Dad isn't yelling at Beau, he's just yelling. Drunk and angry, he's screaming at the shadows. Something about the jungle, something about the war.

I had forgotten how bad he used to get. Anything could set him off. Gunshots. Even the crackling of wood in the fire that sometimes sounded just like a gunshot. Once he yelled at an Asian man at the movie theater, and we were asked to leave. When asked why, Dad simply said he reminded him of someone. When my exasperated mother asked who, he told her, "A ghost." And all those nightmares he used to have, waking us up with his screams.

After these episodes, he always seemed smaller and sadder. Oftentimes apologetic. In my memory, he takes us both for ice cream on the way home, letting us have any toppings we want. Smiling, he ruffles our hair. He even allows us to mess with the car radio, and then sings along to the tunes we find, deliberately messing up the words to make us laugh.

Whatever happened to all of that? Was it just my father on one of his rare, good days?

The memory left me breathless. Even then, I remembered feeling much too young to be so removed from happiness.

And I remembered one more thing, too. The rock under which my father kept the cabin key. It was still there. Wrapped in a piece of oilcloth to prevent rusting.

I let myself in. Finally, after so many trespasses, I was somewhere I had a right to be.

The smell hit me first, as potently as a fist to the face. I instinctively threw up my hands to cover my nose and mouth. Only then did I notice the state of the shack. It looked the worst kind of abandoned and neglected. Mostly empty. The few remaining things smashed up like my father had one of his episodes in there and strewn across the floor like oversized splinters. Some mess in the corner, too.

At first, I thought it was a pile of blankets. But then I looked closer and saw that the top one was a sleeping bag. The kind we used to keep in here. That's where the smell emanated from, so I figured things must have been left wet, piled instead of air dried, and they'd gotten mildewed and moldy. Or maybe an animal had made its way in there and died. Worse yet, maybe it was alive. I didn't want to get bitten.

It happened once when I was seven and crossed paths with a rabid dog. The shots afterward were even worse than the initial bite.

That's why I tensed up, ready to bolt. And then the pile stirred. Slowly, cautiously, a face emerged, and with a sinking feeling in my stomach, I recognized it.

"Amanda? Mandy?"

A couple of years ago, Beau took me to a visiting carnival. Most attractions were cheesy, a few kind of creepy, but the one that upset and unsettled me the most was funhouse mirrors. It wasn't a house, not really, just one large room, covered in reflective surfaces and none of them reflected me. Not the *me* I knew. Instead, they twisted and perverted reality in the most terrifying ways. I started crying and then got mad at myself for acting like a baby, which made me cry some more. Beau had to leave his friends and take me home, rolling his eyes, like, "Kids. What are you gonna do?"

But he didn't blame me and didn't shame me, and I loved him all the more for it.

The Amanda I saw before me wasn't the same lovely, lively girl that kissed me on my birthday. This was a funhouse mirror Amanda. Dirty-faced, skeletal, with bloodshot eyes and cracked-to-blood lips. Her hair was a greasy tangled mess. She looked at me like she didn't think I was real. Like she wasn't sure she was.

And then, slowly, so slowly, she opened her mouth, and a voice rusty with disuse, creaky like a haunted house door, said, "Johnny?"

I hated myself for a long time for what I did next, but for all our retrospective heroism and all our best intentions, we can't predict our reactions to unpredictable situations. Not really.

What I did was run outside. Into the sunshine and fresh air, into the world that made sense.

I retched, but nothing came up. And then, I sat down on the summer-warmed ground and thought about what it meant to find Amanda Teller in my father's shack.

I might have cried, I don't remember. I don't know how long I sat there.

Only her voice, still weak, but clearer now, calling my name, had brought me back to reality. I knew I had to go back. No matter what it meant for my family. It was the right thing to do.

I stood up, willing my leaden feet to carry me back in, and then I heard another voice calling my name. A strong, familiar one.

"Beau?"

He jogged up to me, beet-red in the face and panting. "What are you doing here, Johnny boy?"

"Oh, Beau." I just about collapsed into my older brother. "I found her."

"What?"

"Amanda. I found her. She's …she's here."

I pointed to the shack's door that stood ajar and waited for the shock to take him over the way it did me. Instead, my brother sighed the heaviest of sighs, rubbed his forehead, and said, "Yeah. I know."

Up until that moment, I thought I had heard the scariest thing there was to hear. I figured I'd maxed out on my adrenaline. But those three simple words broke my world. Cleaved it right in two.

"What do you mean you know?" I asked. Trepidation turned my voice into a trembly whisper.

"I mean …" Beau lifted his arms as if in surrender then let them drop heavily down at his sides. "I mean, I saw her."

I could not believe this. "When?"

"Just the other day. I decided to come out here, do some thinking, and I saw her."

"But …but why … why didn't you say something? Do something? Tell the cops?"

"Because kiddo …" There was that adult voice again, all sad and resigned. "Because she's in our father's cabin. Because he's a drunk with violent tendencies. Because he's home most of the time and likely has no alibi for any of the girls."

Other girls. I had forgotten all about them. "Are they … are they all there?"

"I don't know."

"You don't know?" I echoed back incredulously.

"I didn't check. I don't think they are."

"But Beau …"

"Look, if our father was arrested it would ruin everything. It would break our mother's heart. She'd likely lose her job, too. And we'd be forever known as his sons. *Forever.* Do you know what that means? Do you know how long forever is?"

I thought about what he was saying, tried to follow his logic, but I just couldn't.

"But Beau, Amanda will *die.*"

"You saw her, Johnny. She's already as good as."

It was the single cruelest thing I had ever heard my brother say.

"Besides," he continued, "it's almost over. No more girls got taken. It'll just be done and forgotten. We can go back to normal lives."

"Normal," I repeated, dazed.

Beau put his arms on my shoulders and lowered himself so he could look me in the eye. "Yeah, little brother. Normal. Everything's going to be okay."

I wanted to believe him more than anything. I wished I was young enough to still believe like that, against all reason.

"But did he do this?" I asked. "Did Dad *do* this?"

Beau shrugged uncomfortably. "Maybe he did, maybe he didn't. I can't exactly ask. And you know how he gets when his mind's addled about the war. They call it post-traumatic stress disorder. PTSD. It's not … it's not his fault, you know. Even if he did this."

"So what do we do?" I said to my brother.

He shrugged again. "Nothing. Nothing's probably best." He went over and shut the door without locking it. We sat down, side by side, looking at the water. All I could think of was Amanda Teller's eyes. I didn't know then if I believed in hell, but she looked like she had seen the place firsthand and brought some of it back into this world.

That was how our father found us.

"Boys," he said, walking up. "Look at that, all the Walkers are here again."

He was wearing a nice shirt and chinos, with a bunched-up tie sticking out of his pants pocket, and I distantly remembered that he had that job interview.

"Dad." Beau got up. 'What are you doing here?"

"I was driving home after my interview, and saw your car, so I figured there's only one place you could be out here."

For a while no one said anything. The air buzzed electric with unspoken things.

"So, what *are* you doing here, boys?"

"Dad," Beau said slowly. "The shack."

"What about it?"

"You know." Beau looked straight at him and repeated. "You *know*."

Something changed in our father's face right then, crumpled right in front of us.

"Well, shit," he said, rubbing his forehead the same way Beau did when he got stressed out. "Well … shit. To be honest, I was kind of hoping it wouldn't come to this."

There was no menace in his voice, just sadness.

"Why'd you do it?" Beau asked.

"What else could I have done?"

"You could have told someone. You could have stopped."

"And risk our family? Risk your future? I don't think so."

I got a strange feeling listening to them, a distinct impression that they were talking at cross purposes.

"Dad," I said. "That's Amanda in there. Why her? Why Amanda?"

He shook his head at me, his lips twisting. "I don't know, Johnny. Ask Beau."

"What do you mean?"

"Yeah," Beau seconded me. "What do you mean?"

"I mean, I figured you must have been mad at her or something. She was always messing with your heart; the way pretty girls do."

"WHAT?" Beau screamed, spittle flying out of his mouth. "WHAT?"

"Don't worry, son. I was never gonna tell on you. Not ever. No matter what you do. No matter what you've done with them two other girls. You're safe. We're family."

"Wait, wait." Beau held up his hands palms out. "Are you saying you didn't do this?"

"No, of course not. Why would I do this? I've done enough killing to last me a lifetime. I figured you had done it. You're the only one who knew about the place."

"But Dad," Beau said very quietly. "I didn't do this. I thought you did."

They looked at each other, eyes wild. They reminded me of a video I once saw on TV of old cars in trash compactors—the weight of the horrific realization pushing down on them, crushing them.

I realized what their silence meant. For the girls. For Amanda. For our family. I understood then the terrible cost there was to pay for loving each other enough to commit and cover up crimes but never really talking about anything that mattered.

And then there was the other thing. The giant question that hung in the air like a foul smell. If not them, then who?

Karl Spindel came into the clearing, his long legs striding, clad in expensive-looking hiking boots. *Emerging like a villain*, I thought. *Or merely an innocent hiker.* My world had been turned upside down and nothing made sense anymore. Maybe the man was simply going to visit his nice cabin.

"The Walker family," he greeted us. "How very nice to see you."

"Karl." My father nodded.

"What brings you out here today?" the banker inquired, smiling politely, his accent as soft as the breeze.

A rasping sound emerged from the cabin behind us, once and then again, sounding more and more like, "Help." No one had ever closed the door properly, and Amanda must have heard all the voices and found the strength to call out.

We all turned to look at it the way guilty people do in movies. When we turned back, Mr. Spindel was still smiling. The only thing different was a gun in his hand.

I had never seen one up close before. It struck me how innocuous it looked for a killing machine. I used to imagine my father with a gun, running through the jungle, shooting people. It would have looked natural for Dad to wield a weapon with his large meaty paws. In Mr. Spindel's long pianist fingers, it looked all wrong.

"I must apologize," he said, polite as ever. "I'm afraid I have trespassed on your family property and used it for my own means. Though, to be fair, your family had trespassed first."

"What are you talking about?" Dad growled.

"Johnny, would you like to tell, or shall I?"

I forced myself to look up, but I could not control the shaking that seemed to have suffused my entire body. Even my words came out all jumbled up like clothes falling out of the dryer mid tumble cycle.

"I may have … might have … gone to Mr. Spindel's house. Just to look. Look around. I didn't take anything. Or …"

"Your son had also followed me around. For weeks. Quite an amateur detective you have there." If I didn't know better, it sounded like Karl Spindel was almost proud of me.

"He's a smart kid," my father said.

"Yes, very smart. Great instincts. Certainly better than the police. But it did make me somewhat concerned, so I ended up moving the bodies around. It was easier to do once the searches eased up. Perhaps yours wasn't the best choice of cabins—though a bit of poetic justice there—but it was only for a short while. And you never come up here."

"So the bodies weren't always here?" I asked. Then immediately shut my mouth, terrified at my old brazenness.

"No, of course not. The woods were searched and searched. I had used my basement at first."

Remarkable, I thought. I was there and never would have guessed. It was so clean, so neat, so … innocent. It was possible I had just missed Amanda.

"Where are the others?" Beau asked.

"The others have been—" Mr. Spindel waved his spider-like fingers in the air "—disposed of. Don't worry. They are not in your cabin."

"You psycho," Beau spat at him.

"Oh," Mr. Spindel said airily, "sticks and stones."

There was a question bouncing around my skull, screaming to get out like it was the only thing that mattered.

"But why?" I finally exhaled.

"Why?" Karl Spindel repeated back at me, his smile amused. "That is an excellent question, young man. One I have given a great deal of thought. I suppose I wanted to see …"

That was the moment my father chose to charge at Karl Spindel. It looked powerful, like a well-timed football tackle, only no one brings a gun to a ballgame.

The shot was stunningly loud, sending all the birds out of the trees with a resounding whoosh. Dad collapsed like a sack of potatoes; not all at once like a chopped-down tree but slowly and gracelessly.

Beau shouted and attacked, smartly grabbing Mr. Spindel's gun arm first and twisting it away from him. They fought with a viciousness I had never seen up close.

In the movies, the fights were always choreographed and strategic. What I saw before me were two people, neither of whom did this often or ever, fighting for their life. An ugly dirty fight. One I was sure my brother was going to lose.

I still don't remember reaching into my backpack or getting out the hammer. I don't remember waiting for the moment when Beau had the advantage, pinning his opponent down. And I certainly don't remember burying the hammer, claw first, into Mr. Spindel's temple. All I remember is the blood. So much of it.

I came back to reality at the sight of all the blood. A sea of red. Some of it, repulsively warm, had splashed onto my face and arms. Beau had scrambled back, panting. Mr. Spindel was still alive, though I could see he had but a moment left on this earth.

He locked eyes with me and through the blood bubbles on his lips, I made out his last words, barely above a whisper. "I did it to see if I could. To see what kind of a monster I am."

Those words have haunted me all my life.

Amanda Teller had never fully recovered from her ordeal. Her body did, eventually, but she had spent too much time that summer close to death and left too much of her mind and her spirit on the other side. I'd see her around town from time to time, always accompanied by her mother. Funny, I remembered Beau telling me how she used to hate her mom, but I suppose people change when they have to. Now the two of them were inseparable. I tried saying hi to Amanda, but I think my presence upset her. I didn't blame her; I knew I reminded her of things she longed to forget. I wondered if she ever managed to, even for a short while. I didn't think so. Her eyes looked like the windows of a haunted house. I learned to avoid Amanda whenever I saw her, keeping well out of her sight.

The remains of Sandy Morgan and Alice Chang were never found. Polaroid photos of their dead bodies were discovered during the search of Karl Spindel's house—a much more thorough search than the one I had performed when I was there. It was enough. Eventually, everyone stopped looking. The families buried empty coffins for closure and tried to move on.

Our father got a hero's funeral for dying while trying to stop a murderer. Beau and I had spun the story just right. Beau had gotten some attention of his own. There was even a newspaper article praising his courage. Nothing much was said about me because my brother had wiped my fingerprints off the hammer and put his own on it.

"You didn't do anything," he said, looking me straight in the eye, "It was all me." He repeated it over and over until it became a sort

of alternative reality, the one we both could live with.

All he wanted, Beau told me, was for me to have a normal life. I have done my best to honor his wish.

Beau got a football scholarship, blew out his knee in college, and came back home. Did physical therapy until he could walk and run again, then joined the local police force. Of all things. Some of Mom's work friends had suggested it, but I never thought it would take. I was wrong. Now he's the sheriff. Sheriff Walker. Married with three kids. He named his firstborn after our dad. And none of them after alcohol. That's progress for you.

I took a long time figuring out what I wanted to do with my life. All I knew was that I wanted to see the world. Eventually, I got a journalism degree and started traveling and writing about different places. It suits me, this peripatetic life. I'm good at living out of a suitcase. I like the changing scenery, the way the world looks through an airplane window. I make acquaintances easily but seldom friends. I did grow into my looks, after all, becoming the tallest Walker man in our family. A decent-looking guy all around. I get dates easily but can't seem to settle down. It's difficult to establish a long, meaningful relationship with someone if you're always looking for the monster behind their eyes. Trust issues, as a shrink might say.

Doesn't matter. I'm doing okay. Often alone, but seldom lonely. I stay busy. The world has much to offer a curious mind.

The first time I ever visited Sweden, I interviewed this charming family who owned a curiosity museum. They invited me into their home to share a meal with them. Mid-meal, their little boy, linen-blonde and blue-eyed, started screaming, "*Spindel! Spindel!*" and I had almost choked on my kroppkakor.

"What is he saying?" I asked, unable to keep panic out of my voice as I wiped the half-chewed remains of the thick meat and potato dumpling from my mouth.

"Oh," they said, smiling, "don't worry. It means spider. He is afraid of spiders."

Aren't we all, buddy, I thought. *Aren't we all.*

Blues for the Soul

On Wednesday and Saturday afternoons, Martha Sutton read stories to small children at the local library. She found she could no longer stand being around adults, not for long, not after what happened, but kids … kids were fine.

It was a volunteer position, unpaid. Her qualifications were few: free time and willingness. The library did do a background check on her, but she supposed it was inevitable in this day and age for anyone working with children.

They never wanted to have any of their own, Martha and Sam; always joking about what terrible parents they'd make. How they'd forget their kids in airports, put whiskey in baby formulas. Their friends with kids would roll their eyes in that "just you wait" sort of way, like having kids was an unavoidable part of life, but they had never felt like they missed out on anything. And now, well, now, of course, it was too late.

Too late to feel much of anything, really. Martha went through her days in a cocoon-like numb state she had tried and failed to describe to her therapist. The therapist meant well, asking all the right questions, tutting sympathetically with a precise 'I'm-here-for-you' head incline angle. It didn't help. Martha stopped going.

Martha stopped going most places. Her friends were no better than the therapy, a different kind of useless. They alternated between smothering her with pity and valiantly cheerleading her on. They didn't get it. How could they? She didn't want to have to explain. There were barely words for it. No words to describe the vast emptiness inside her, to explain the way the world looked to her now.

Her friends still thought the world was an exciting and mostly safe place. Martha knew better. It wasn't just a peek behind the curtain either. The curtain was rudely ripped aside, and she was shoved forth, her eyelids taped open so that she couldn't look away. The ugliness she saw there made her want to curl up in a ball and never move at all.

Martha found herself retreating further and further inward. It was so easy. She quit her job—the life insurance money was plenty for her needs in the foreseeable future. Beyond that…well, beyond that she could not foresee. She sold the house. It was impossible to stay there afterward, no matter how thorough the cleaners had been.

It surprised her how quickly the house sold. Did no one care? Did no one read or watch the news?

Martha's new condo had all the personality of a sheet of printer paper. Sleek, white, modern, with gleaming appliances and zero character. She opted for the smallest unit and bought it furnished.

The furniture was unlike anything she would ever choose herself, unlike anything she and Sam ever had. Trendy, uncomfortable, low-backed, minimalistic, and bland. Relentless, personality-free aesthetic. Even the art on the walls matched.

Perfect, really, perfectly anonymous. Nothing about the condo said a single thing about her. In it, she could be anyone.

Martha never said a word to her neighbors. She forwarded her friends' calls to voicemail and eft her emails unanswered.

She waited, but time wasn't doing its healing work. Her heart still felt like an open wound. Her mind screamed, echoing through all its dark corners. She seldom slept and, when she did, nightmares found her.

She would have killed herself but turns out she still had enough leftover Catholicism in her to make that option a nonstarter.

Becoming a hermit was another viable option, but something about it seemed irreversible. Like the beginning of a downward spiral.

And so, Martha decided to reengage with the world, albeit within the very strict parameters: going to the grocery store instead of doing an online delivery, having a cup of coffee in the neighborhood café once a week where she sat outside on the patio and people-watched. And lately, the library thing.

She had never really liked kids, never got their appeal until now. Now, looking at their bright eyes, their guileless faces, their easy enthusiasm for the world around them, she got it. Sometimes, she found herself basking in the secondhand happiness of being around them.

If only Sam could see her now, surrounded by all these tiny humans and the rapt expressions on their tiny faces.

What would he think? What would he say? They were together for so long, longer than any of their other couple friends, that in many ways they've become a single unit. A solid unified WE being. It took her time to relearn how to be a single person, to remember her preferences, to figure out how to do all the things Sam usually did, to start cooking for one.

Loneliness was a wall she climbed every day. No, loneliness was a boulder she was forever rolling up a hill only to have it come crashing right back down. A truly Sisyphean labor.

For two hours every Wednesday and Saturday, the boulder of loneliness gave Martha Sutton a break. She sat in a low chair in the center of a brightly colored rug surrounded by kids. She read the stories preselected by the librarians, but she brought her own flair to the task, her once infamous penchant for doing voices and impressions. The kids loved it. Even some parents stuck around a few times.

Afterward, they tried talking to her and were perpetually surprised by the fairytale-like change of the outgoing and charming storyteller into a reserved monosyllabic person.

Martha didn't pay any attention to the parents, but she noticed the kids. How could she not? There were so many repeat faces from one week to the next. Some came both days. Most were cute. Some were obnoxious.

And then there was Darren.

Darren was the strangest, spookiest kid who had ever attended her readings. She felt guilty thinking this of him, but it was impossible not to. Her guilt made her overcompensate by trying to be extra nice to him. Darren wasn't having it. Probably didn't care for the pity the same way she didn't.

Skinny kid, all knees and elbows, he was small for his age; for the age she thought he was, anyway, and yet he had those all-knowing, wise-before-his-time eyes that put her on edge. His eyes followed her like the oversized peepers of those creepy kitsch artworks you found in retro thrift shops. Black eyes, so black, you could hardly see the white in them.

He had a mop of brown hair that looked like someone got exasperated and trimmed it quickly with craft scissors. Clothes that never matched or fit his tiny frame right. Cheap sneakers with canvas worn so thin in places that his socks were showing through. A giant old backpack he dragged around like a carapace.

Darren seldom talked to other kids, to anyone. He glared. Occasionally scowled. Martha didn't think he was stupid; there was a sort of feral intelligence behind his eyes. But how to engage it she had no idea.

When he wore short sleeves or pants, she spied bruises on his pale skinny limbs. Was he abused? She had no idea how to tell for sure or who to ask? Didn't want to get involved strictly past the minimum she had outlined for herself. Maybe the kid was just clumsy.

Then she started noticing other things. Caught him stealing from other kids, teaching them bad words.

When one of the kids made fun of Darren during a reading for falling asleep, he pretended to enjoy the joke. Later, Martha saw him in the library's parking lot slicing the tires on that kid's parents' car with an alarmingly sharp boxcutter. By the time she got to him, he was done and gone. Martha resolved never to leave her car in that lot again. Instead, she began parking on the street and walking a block.

She wasn't afraid of Darren, for how could one be afraid of a small child, but he disturbed her. Triggered her. In his eyes, she saw the calculated belligerent adult cruelty that she had been trying to avoid all this time.

Darren didn't need a reason to be cruel. Once, he spilled a drink all over another kid's favorite book and got caught by a librarian. They weren't even allowed drinks inside the library, and the entire act felt all too deliberate. Suppressing a smile, Darren managed an apology, but Martha could see how much he enjoyed what he'd done.

It shocked her. Outside of the horror movies that Sam and she occasionally watched around Halloween, she didn't think that kids had it in them to be evil. How could someone so young have the bandwidth for pure meanness for the sake of it?

That sort of evil—surely, that was the business of men, wasn't it?

The only time Martha interfered was when Darren almost hit another kid. She caught his arm, such a skinny thing, all bone, and stopped him. "We don't hit people," she said. Eye contact, firm voice.

He looked up at her from beneath his messy, uneven bangs. "Why not?" he asked matter-of-factly.

"Because violence is bad, Darren. If you have a problem with someone, you're supposed to use your words."

"But what if *I'm* bad?" There was a dare in his question, a challenge.

She sighed and steadied herself. This was definitely more than she had signed up for.

"You're not bad, Darren. You're just angry. Can you tell me why you wanted to hit Allie?"

He studied his feet for a while as if all the answers were there. "Because," he said eventually, "it's fun."

She reported him after that. The librarians could deal with it. The situation was well above her pay grade, especially considering she wasn't getting paid.

After that, he didn't come to the readings for a while. She thought she saw him in the library's parking lot a few times, but she was never sure. He was too small and too good at disappearing into the shadows.

The next time she saw Darren was in the supermarket. He was dragged around by a woman who had to have been his mother. She looked like she would have preferred to be dragging him around by the ear, but was sticking to the more conventional choice of hand for propriety's sake.

Martha peeked at their shopping cart. It was full of cheap foods in garish packaging.

Darren's mother looked as skinny as her son and smelled of cigarettes. Her age was impossible to place beneath the ravages of hard living and layers of makeup struggling to … well, make up for it. Her frizzy overdyed hair was of a chemical shade of blonde. She wore a ripped Sex Pistols T-shirt and a pair of distressed black jeans.

For all the world to see she looked like such a cliché, Martha thought.

She turned away, but not before Darren caught her eye and did that creepy scowl. It was difficult to blame the kid now, but that look still sent shivers down her spine.

Martha could never be sure why she did what she did next. It made no sense. What she should have done was finish shopping, pay for her purchases, take them to her car, and drive back to her soulless condo for another evening of pretending to read.

What she did instead was leave her cart full of groceries and follow Darren and his mom. She used all her best spy moves. In any case, Darren's mom didn't seem like an observant type. She shopped quickly and jerkily, tossing the items into the cart instead of placing them there gently. Whenever Darren tried to wander off, she yanked him by the hand the way mean dog owners yank on leashes. She paid for their groceries using crumpled up cash from the pockets of her jeans, then grabbed the bags, and made Darren carry some. The kid struggled with the weight of them.

They drove a Geo so old and rusty it defied the odds of being roadworthy.

Martha followed them discreetly in her Prius, feeling class-conscious and like a bit of a creep.

The drive took her to the part of town she had never visited before, only heard about. A trailer park sat amid the scraggly bushes. Barely a park, really, just a collection of beat-up old trailers rivaling the condition of the Geo.

She groaned inwardly at the cliché of it all.

The Geo stopped at the last trailer on the left. It looked like an Airstream knock-off whose bullet-slick aluminum body hadn't shined in decades. Darren and his mom took their groceries in, leaving Martha with no one to spy on.

Against her better judgment, she got out of her car and walked at the outer edge of the trailer park. A lot of people were home for a weekday afternoon, but then, so was she or should have been, anyway.

The place smelled like old soup. The ground was dirty, mud from the recent rain sucking at her shoes. There was an underlying soundtrack of yapping dogs and bass-heavy music. This wasn't a place anyone lived in by choice. The comparison to her sterile white condo building was startling.

She noted the series of mailboxes by the entrance mounted on wooden stumps that appeared to be slowly sinking into the ground. Which one belonged to Darren and his mom? She had never learned his last name. Alas, she didn't need to, the mailboxes—and presumably the trailers—were numbered, which with some basic calculations put Darren and his mother at trailer eleven. The name scrawled beneath the number was Dana Doyle. Someone was a fan of alliterative monikers, she thought, though the woman seemed hardly a superhero material. Either way, Martha committed it to memory and turned to leave.

This place was bringing up too much darkness in her mind.

Once home, she busied herself with other things: watching a quiz show, scrounging around for something to eat since her grocery trip was a failure. By the time she remembered to look up Dana Doyle, it was already late. Her computer was powered down, and she didn't want to use her phone for fear it would rip right through her already barely-there gossamer-like sleepiness.

A week later, a friendly librarian named Nancy stopped her for a chat. Martha steeled herself and stretched her lips into a friendly smile.

"Remember that Darren kid?"

"He's tough to forget."

"His mom wants us to let him back in. Says he's sorry."

"Does Darren say he's sorry?"

Nancy shrugged. "You know Darren. His sorries are about as sincere as my New Year's resolutions to lose weight."

Martha nodded, aware some polite protestations might be in order, but Nancy was undeniably fat and quite jolly about it.

"So, I just wanted to float it by you, since you'll be the one dealing with him."

"I appreciate that, Nancy." Martha thought of how to say what she wanted to say politely. "I don't know if Darren's presence is good for other children."

Nancy dropped her voice to a conspiratorial whisper. "He is a little shit, isn't he? And I know we're not supposed to say that about kids, but that one, he's just no good. With a mom like that, of course, what chance does he stand?"

"Is there no father in the picture?"

"None whatsoever. There's barely a mother in the picture. I mean, the number of times she came in here reeking of booze ..." Nancy trailed off, waving her hand.

Martha found herself torn, her curiosity overriding her studied reticence. "What does she do, the mother, do you know?"

"She sings, if you can believe it."

"Sings?"

"Yes. Like at nightclubs."

"Is she any good?"

Nancy guffawed. "I wouldn't know."

Martha felt a strange wish to find out. And no idea why.

She excused herself, telling Nancy she'd think about letting Darren back in. Then she Googled Dana Doyle. Dana Doyle Sings. Added the name of their town. And sure enough …

The bar reeked. After all these years, the news of the smoking ban must not have made its way to the owners of Calico. Was it named after the kind of cat? The fabric? The pirate? She had no idea, and the place gave no indication.

Cheap booze, cheaper décor, sticky floors, a small stage in the back. The sort of place Sam and Martha frequented very early in their courtship, mostly for novelty, and seldom since. If he were here with her right now, none of it would matter, not the shabby ambience, not the horrible smell she'd have to wash out of her clothes and hair. Her mind had nearly slipped into a reverie the way it tended to when she thought of Sam, but the place had a certain visceral immediacy to it that kept her steadily in the present.

She ordered a whisky. Took a tiny sip and found it serviceable.

Her watch said ten after nine. The posting she saw online said Dana Doyle went on at nine. "When does the performance start?" she asked the bartender, a large, gruff-looking man with full sleeve tattoos, close-cropped salt-and-pepper hair, and a full beard taking up the entire bottom half of his face.

"Whenever Dana gets her ass on stage," he growled, then did an eye roll. "She says you can't rush the talent."

Martha sipped slowly, suppressing the urge to chug the drink and order another. The bar was pushing all sorts of buttons in her psyche. This was the kind of place people who did evil things came to for fuel. It was in the smoke-choked air, thick enough to taste.

The men sitting on death row, the men who stole her happiness from her, they likely came to places just like this one. How many pitchers did it take, how many shots, to render another person's will, another person's life as immaterial, so easily discarded?

Martha closed her eyes. This was a terrible idea. She shouldn't be here. She shouldn't have come. There was nothing to learn, nothing to gain in this proverbial den of iniquity.

And then, she heard it. A voice so beautiful, so strong, cutting through the ugly miasma of the bar like water through mud.

She opened her eyes and saw Dana Doyle on the small stage. Same overdyed hair, same raggedy outfit, and yet absolutely transformed now, as if lit by some sort of inner glow.

"Make you wait, but she sure can sing, don't she?" the bartender grumbled with something like quiet awe in Martha's direction. All Martha could do was nod.

So far, the Doyles have been a cliché, but this … this blew the walls away. Dana Doyle sang the blues like her soul was on fire.

Martha had listened to her fair share of the blues—Sam was a fan. She had never heard a voice like that outside of the old recordings. Such splendid melancholy, such striking sorrow. She was only dimly aware of the musical accompaniment for Dana Doyle did not need it.

If the saddest, bleakest, most devastated corners of Martha's heart and soul had a soundtrack, it would sound like Dana Doyle's singing.

Martha didn't move until the set was over. She didn't even think she breathed.

Once finished, Dana sauntered over to the bar with a drunken swagger. "Hit me, Ricky," she tossed at the bartender.

Martha couldn't help but stare. Dana returned the stare. The world-weariness in her eyes matched that of her son.

"Do I know you?"

"No, but …" Martha stammered "… but you were wonderful up there."

"Yeah, well, thanks." Dana gave Martha a tired almost smile. "I like my compliments in liquid form, hon."

By the time Martha figured out what she meant, Dana was back on stage. Her encore was a song Martha didn't know.

"I danced with the devil on a moonlit night.

He said everythin' was gon' be alright.

But in the bleak light of dawn,

I woke up alone,

And he was gone, gone, gone."

The lyrics made Martha shiver. She ordered another whisky.

Dana came back to the bar and let Martha buy her a drink.

"You keep staring at me," Dana said, downing the contents of her glass in one. "You sure we don't know each other?"

Martha shook her head. "Where'd you learn to sing like that?"

"Learn it?" Dana laughed. "Girl, you don't learn the blues. The blues learns you."

"Do you write your own songs? That one about the devil. I've never heard it before."

"Yeah, that one is all my own." She grinned a crooked proud grin. "True story, too."

"How so?"

"That'll be another drink, hon."

Martha briefly wondered who was taking care of Darren while his mother is getting sloshed at a local dive but figured that must have been par for the course in Doyle's household.

She ordered another round.

Then another one.

She hadn't been drunk in years. Ages. Not like this. Not so drunk that she felt weightless and heavy at the same time. Not so drunk that her mind stopped playing the worst hits of her life on repeat and let itself wander. Not so drunk that she could let go of Sam, of all that guilt, all that grief.

"See, the Devil," Dana told her, "he likes the blues. Just like you do. Got good taste. Plays it in Hell even, I'm told. For all the demons to hear. Says the blues is as close as humankind can come to understanding him."

"So that's it? That's the Devil you danced with?"

"Nah, not me, hon. But here, lemme tell you a story."

They were sitting in a booth by then, old vinyl creaking, a scuffed Formica tabletop between them with all the glasses now empty and two still half-full.

Martha leaned in. She loved stories. Sam used to tell her stories, and now no one ever did.

"Once upon a time," Dana began, "when the world was young, there was a group of angels sent to watch over people."

Oh, Martha thought, a biblical story. She did not expect it and, frankly, Dana didn't look the type, but you never knew these things.

"The people, they were just going about their business, doing their best to make sense of the world, trying to figure out how everything worked. All they had to guide them was their desires." Dana smiled sadly and took a sip of her drink.

"The angels, they had rules, they had instructions. There were two hundred of them. The Grigori was what they were known as. Or just the Watchers. All they had to do was shepherd these new creations, so small and weak and different from them. Only they got too involved with those they observed, began to abandon their duties. The grass started to look greener on the other side, or some such thing. Maybe it was just loneliness. Maybe it was good old lust."

Dana did a playful thing with her eyebrows, then made her voice go all somber, as if recalling a lesson from a book.

"The Grigori gave mankind forbidden knowledge and took mortal wives. In doing that, they've gone too far for forgiveness. And so, they became the fallen angels. The second faction."

"Demons," Martha whispered, completely absorbed.

"Demons." Dana nodded. "But angels first. The eleventh of their twenty leaders was Armaros. He came to love humans. When he crashed to the Earth, he lost his voice, and nothing pleased him as much as human singing and human women. In return, he gave people early science or magic—the two were interchangeable back then. Eventually, he got tired of human affairs and retreated to Hell, but every so often he comes back up to roam the Earth in search of music and beauty."

The way Dana ended her story sounded nothing like the way she spoke and nothing like the way she sang. It's almost like she slipped into an entirely different personality. Martha found it fascinating.

"These Watchers, all their carrying on with women, their offspring were terrible," Dana said. "The Nephilim. They came out misshapen, hideous, monstrous. See, it was forbidden for them to have children with humans. But it was what they wanted and so, time and again they tried. Sometimes, the deformities were in the body and other times, they were in the mind. And sometimes, the wickedness of Hell came through in these children."

There was fire and brimstone in her words; not merely a lesson taught but a lesson learned first and all too harshly.

Martha suddenly felt like the floor was slipping from under her feet. A shift in gravity. A world realigning itself to make a new and terrifying sort of sense.

"Are you saying …?" She didn't, *couldn't* finish the sentence.

"I'm saying I danced with the devil," Dana grinned bitterly. "And he left me a gift. Although—" She took another hearty sip of her drink "—Darren isn't really much of a gift, is he?"

Strangers, Martha reminded herself, they were strangers. "Darren, what's he like?"

"Darren set the neighbor's cat on fire when he was four. That's what Darren's like. He hits me, he bites me, Sometimes, I have to grab him, restrict him, just to stop him. And then he bruises, and I feel guilty. Every damn time. Darren used to stand over my bed and watch me sleep. Occasionally, with a knife in his hand. I've had to throw out all the sharp objects in the house. All I've got now are craft scissors and plastic cutlery. Darren catches mice and tortures them. He hits other kids just to watch them cry. Got thrown out of every childcare place. Even from the library's reading circle." She shook her head. "You got any kids, hon?"

Martha said she didn't.

"Well, then, you don't know what it's like, do ya? To be afraid of your own kid. Every day."

Martha didn't know what to say. She drank instead.

"I've thought about it, you know. About just ending the kid. Kindly like. With mercy. But I can't. I just can't. I know he's gonna do terrible things: cut, kill, rape—" Martha shivered involuntarily "—when he gets older, but I just can't. He's still my kid, you know. I held him as a baby and had such high hopes for him. Now I'm scared to go near him."

They sat in silence for a while. Well, bar-at-closing-time silence which is really no silence at all.

Martha turned Dana's story in her head. It was crazy. And yet it made perfect sense. Or maybe it was just the alcohol talking.

"What about his father?"

"What? You think I get alimony from Hell?" Dana gave a bitter laugh. "He came to see me once since. Explained to me the way he could that the baby's got no soul. That's his problem, see, no soul. Because of how he was conceived. There's nothing to be done."

"So, he just needs a soul?"

"Yeah," Dana replied, sarcasm thick in her voice. "Just a soul. You got any of those lying around?"

The evening was drawing to a close one way or another. Ricky wanted to go home and watch porn before passing out the way he always did when he was too wired to sleep after a long shift.

Terrified to imagine the woman behind the wheel but too drunk to offer assistance, Martha watched Dana stagger to her Geo.

After Dana left, Martha climbed into her own car. She wasn't going to drive, not just yet, she needed some time to think. Sleep took her before any coherent thoughts came to mind.

The knock on the car window woke her up. Martha jerked up, her neck popping, and wiped the drool from her chin with the back of her hand. Tried to roll the window down before remembering the car had to be on for that. She opened the door instead. The brightness of the morning sun made her squint.

The figure in front of her only blocked out some of it.

She recognized Ricky, the bartender from last night.

"Well, thanks for not drunk driving, I guess," he said, grinning at her good-naturedly.

"Oh." Her mouth tasted like compost. "What time is it?"

"Nearly noon."

She couldn't believe she slept that late. Last night came back to her in dizzying flashes. The blues, the alcohol, Dana. That impossible story.

"You wanna come in? I'll make you some coffee for the road."

Martha barely managed a nod. She got out of the car, locked it, and followed Ricky.

Her hangover was attacking her with a pugilistic viciousness, throwing combination punches, one-two, one-two-three. Jab, jab, undercut. She shouldn't have drunk that much. She shouldn't have drunk at all. She was too old for it.

The bar during the day looked all wrong. Some places ought to be seen only during their hours of operation. Princesses turn into poor maids at midnight, carriages into pumpkins. And bars at noon turn into ghost haunts.

"Started doing early afternoons a couple of years back," Ricky explained, turning the lights on, and getting things set up. "For those who like drinking their lunch."

"Good business?" she asked to be polite.

"You'd be surprised." He looked her over, and she patted her hair down self-consciously. She must look a mess, she thought.

"Saw you really tying one on with Dana last night. Nothing unusual for her, but you just don't seem the type."

"I'm not."

"Well, good for you for pushing your boundaries then, I guess. Good for Dana, too. She gets real maudlin drinking by herself."

"She drinks like that a lot?"

Ricky sighed heavily. "If that girl didn't sing like Janis reincarnated, I'da thrown her ass out years ago. But she gets up on that stage and breaks my heart, every time."

"She is very good," Martha agreed.

Ricky got the ancient-looking coffee machine started. It reluctantly gurgled back to life.

The daylight, so bright outside, was barely streaking in through the few unbricked-up windows, creating a disorientating twilight effect. Martha watched the dust motes dance in it.

"You two know each other?" Ricky asked.

"Just since last night."

"She tell you that crazy story of hers yet?"

"She did."

"What'd you think?"

Martha gave a half-hearted shrug. "I think that's some story."

"You can say that again." Ricky placed a relatively clean-looking pair of mugs between them on a scuffed-up bar. "But then again, if you ever met her kid."

Martha looked up at him. A man like that, a walking image of pragmatism, a no-nonsense-through-and-through kind of guy, he couldn't possibly be saying …

"What do you mean?" she asked, watching him pour the coffee.

"I mean, the kid's creepy. Seriously creepy. She brought him by a few times. He just sat there, staring with those eyes. Kid's got eyes like they follow you around, like those old cat clocks, you know."

Martha said she knew.

"Made customers uneasy. And then one time, I swear he done something to people's drinks. I ain't never had any complaints 'bout my booze. It's cheap but good. This kid shows up, and people are saying things are tasting off. Suddenly, they are throwing up. Starting fights too. I dunno. Could all be just one of those things, but I didn't wanna take any chances. Had to ask her to stop bringing the kid by."

Martha took a sip of coffee. Much like Ricky's drinks, it was cheap but good. Good enough, anyway. Anything to cut through the havoc that alcohol had wreaked upon her.

"So you're saying Darren's the son of a demon?"

"That's right." Ricky snapped his fingers. "Darren, that's his name. I been trying to remember. Darren Doyle. You know my ma is Irish, County Clare, she always told me to stay away from any Doyle I meet. Says that name means a dark stranger. Says Doyles are *of the devil.*"

"Aren't there a lot of Doyles out there, though?"

"You bet. Ma's a superstitious thing, that's for sure. But I love her all the same. Did look it up one day, though. Turns out it's from a word that back in the day was used to describe the Vikings which were Danish from the Norwegians. Now, why back then the Danes were dark-haired, and the Norwegians were blonde I couldn't tell ya. They all seem pretty fair-haired to me, but that's the idea."

"Did you tell this to your ma?"

"I did, and she said that's all nonsense. What people meant, she said, was the Devil, only they were afraid to say so, so they talked around it. A dark stranger was as good of a euphemism as any, I suppose."

"Maybe they just equated the Vikings with the Devil because of all the pillaging?" Martha speculated.

"Yeah, sure, maybe."

Ricky shrugged then set his face like the conversation was over.

"Think you'll be okay to drive now, or should I call you a cab?"

Marth took stock of herself and found that the coffee really did the trick. The conversation might have helped too.

"I think I'm good," she told Ricky. "What do I owe you for the coffee?"

He waved her off. "On the house. But do come back, you hear?"

She said she would and left.

In the near-empty parking lot, everything felt exaggerated. The sun was too bright, too hot, the gravel too loud, even the birds sounded shriller than usual. Martha got into her car with all the eager immediacy of a prepper diving into his bunker just as the bombs outside were beginning to go off. She drove home, climbed into her bed, and passed out without so much as kicking her shoes off.

When Martha woke up, it was dark outside. She felt rested. The hangover was still there, lingering on the edges, but no longer ruling her.

She made herself a large meal of pancakes and eggs and ate every single bite. Her thoughts kept returning to Dana and her kid. There was nothing important or interesting enough in her life to knock those thoughts from their prime spot at the center of her mind.

The story's details were coming back to her. The names. The Biblical references. Martha booted up her computer and got to Googling.

A couple of hours and several spiraling episodes later, she was satisfied. The story checked out—if Dana made it all up, she at least did her research. What would cause someone to do that? Martha wondered. A religious upbringing? A horror movie taken too seriously? Why would a person make up such an elaborate story to explain a problem child?

Sure, there was something off about Darren. Probably several things. But odds were the kid just needed a good therapist. Not an exorcist.

And what it must be like for Darren to live with a mother who believes him to be a demon spawn?

Martha tried to feel sympathy or even pity for the kid, but it was difficult. Darren wasn't someone who engendered warm feelings. She felt something like shame, instead, for not being a better person. She resolved to get him back to her reading circle. It was the one small thing she could do.

"You're back." Dana sounded genuinely pleased to see her. She just got off the stage after doing another killer set. Tonight, Dana wore the same or similar pair of ripped jeans and a shapeless sort of thin sweater with a bleeding heart patch on its sleeve. Her hair was matted down with sweat; her makeup, as always, overdone. She plopped down on a barstool next to Martha.

"You know, I never got your name, hon."

"It's Martha."

"Ah." She nodded appreciatively. "You look like a Martha."

"What does a Martha look like?"

"Like you. All prim and proper."

Martha didn't think she was all that prim and proper, but looking down at herself, taking in her somber ensemble of pressed slacks, a modest cardigan, and sensible shoes, she couldn't argue either. She used to have clothes that were more fun, back when *she* was more fun. Dresses Sam loved, brightly colored blouses, trendy jeans.

She used to go to a hair salon regularly, too, and do her makeup. Now, her dark blonde hair was cut short, and her face left bare, except for some lip balm and eyeglasses.

Martha felt no longer comfortable dressing for attention, not after what happened. She boxed all those outfits and drove them to Goodwill. She took to wearing clothes no one would look at twice: bland, comfortable, plain.

"Got any requests tonight?" Dana asked her, downing a shot that had magically appeared before her the second she sat down.

Martha thought about it. She wasn't even sure why she was here in the first place, only that she wanted to be. It was either another night alone trying to distract her mind with the latest New York Times-recommended book or this. She didn't know if she wanted to hear another one of Dana's stories, but she did want to hear the woman sing. There was solace to be found in music. Martha longed to have those melancholy-soaked blues notes line up the grief-carved riverbeds of her heart and soothe her.

She asked for a song, Sam's favorite. There were tears in her eyes when Dana sang it, but she didn't feel them. All she felt was a sort of lightness, an easement of sorrow.

When Dana rejoined her at the bar, Martha bought her a shot. Then another one.

She resolved not to drink as much this time around. Easy enough, since Dana didn't seem to mind. All Dana wanted was to get blasted out of her skull, and she didn't care if her drinking companion matched her step for step and shot for shot.

"Kind of hot for long sleeves today, isn't it?"

Dana rolled up the right one, sticking her arm out for Martha to see.

"What *is* that?"

"You know those cookie-cutting metal shapes? The little devil heated one up on the stove and pressed it into my arm. Said he wanted to make me a star."

Martha shivered. The angry burn did have a star shape to it, she could see it now.

"I'm sorry, that must feel …"

"Yeah, and you know the worst thing? That's actually Darren being sweet. Cause, you know, it coulda been my face."

Martha downed the drink in front of her, forgoing her resolutions of moderation.

Dana spun her glass around on the table. "I take him to the library twice a week. So he can be around other kids. They sit around. Have some old biddy read them stories."

Martha laughed out loud involuntarily.

"What's so funny?"

"Oh, nothing, just that … biddy? Who says biddy?"

"Guess I do." Dana smirked. "Anyway, I don't think that's gonna last either. He was banned once already. Ain't no way he isn't sitting there planning to do something horrible to some of them other kids."

That was all Martha could think about next time at the library. And the time after that. She found herself unable to relax, get lost in the story and the kids' easy company, and just enjoy herself. All she could do was watch Darren. And he watched her back. She felt it. Watched her with those strange all-too-black eyes of his.

He didn't stab Stacey Alvarez until three weeks later. Martha was just beginning to relax, too, and then it happened. There was no provocation, no argument, nothing. One minute she was a happy little girl listening to a story about princes and dragons, and the next, there was a viciously sharpened pencil sticking out of her chubby hand. The screaming alone, Martha didn't think she would ever forget the screaming.

It was a huge deal. Of course, it was. They had to call 911 and the Alvarezes. There was talk of a lawsuit, of social services getting involved.

Martha sat there as if in a fog. The combination of the screaming, blood, and violence triggered her into a panic attack so profound, so all-encompassing, that she felt like she was underwater. Everything around her sounded distant, muted. Nothing as loud or as alarming as the deafening rush of her own blood in her ears. Her heart felt like a boa constrictor's lunch. All she could do was try to breathe.

Through the prism of her panic, she saw Dana. Of course, she'd have to come. Dana locked eyes with her, shooting questions like daggers, but said nothing. It was neither the time nor the place.

Through it all Darren sat perfectly still, eerily self-possessed. Politely and quietly answering the questions asked of him, discussing what he'd done with the same ease one might discuss a breakfast menu. A tiny terrifying smile played on his lips. Could everyone see that?

Eventually, it was over. Martha made it home. Close the blinds, locked the door, turned out the lights. And didn't leave again for days.

Days turned into weeks. Martha didn't go back to the library. Didn't answer phone calls or emails. She ordered some groceries but never seemed to be in the mood to eat.

She was tired, so tired, all the time. The panic never eased up long enough for her to rest and relax. She wanted Sam by her side. Sam always knew just what to do, just what to say. The kind of bone-deep knowledge you get from sharing your life, every bit of it, with someone for a long time.

Martha never knew how people managed to remarry, start over. How did one find the energy, the enthusiasm, the sheer glass-half-full optimism of rebuilding a life with another someone else? Learning another person? Of having them learn you?

What hubris, she thought, to expect that sort of connection more than once. What arrogance.

Her mind wandered. What did the angels see in humans that proved so irresistible? What was it they loved enough to fall that far? Only to get thwarted time and again. To have their offspring born ruined. To *be* ruined. Brought down so low. It was all too romantic. Too tragic. Did the two always go together?

What was the name of Dana's demon? Azimos? Armaros. Yes, that's it. He, who loved music so. Did he love Dana once? Or was it just a connection based on notes and chords and tones? The dynamic emotional and harmonic instrumentations, the slides and syncopations, the torn-down broken-down rawness of the singing? Why not? People have built connections on less.

Did the demon look upon his son in horror? Did the soulless infant remind him all too viscerally of how wrong he was? Of the mistakes he'd made? Did he feel guilty? Responsible? Sad?

Martha speculated until falling into an uneasy sleep. All of her dreams were nightmares. She was haunted by demons, real and imagined. She never felt rested.

She knew she had to do something. Reclaim some part of herself before it was too late. She tried to think of a single accomplishable thing she wanted.

"You again." Dana's tone was even. Not happy, not angry. "First time we met, I told you I knew you from somewhere."

"I'm sorry," Martha said. "I really am. Most of the time, I don't want to be me."

"I know how that goes," Dana said, the sadness in her voice palpable. "I kinda say that to everyone, anyway. So, are we drinking tonight or what?"

"Oh, we are definitely drinking tonight."

Ricky brought them a round. Then another.

"You gonna ask me what happened with Darren?"

Martha looked up from swirling the brown liquid at the bottom of her glass.

"I was going to, yes."

"Well, social services are useless so long as I'm not a junkie and ain't endangering him. Imagine that, what a joke. Me, endangering him. Ha. So, the Alvarezes were gonna slap my ass with a lawsuit, but then they realized I ain't got a thing they'd want, so they dropped that. Their little girl's fine. Nothing some therapy won't settle. Barely a scar left.

Can't put Darren in a normal classroom, though. Not now. Gotta be a special ed situation. Or homeschooling. That's another option, they told me."

"So what are you going to do?"

"Homeschool. What else? The little monster is mine. Don't seem fair to others to put him out there like that. Who knows what he'll do next."

"I'm sorry."

"Yeah, me too. It's a sorry situation." Dana drained her glass and signaled for more.

"Slow down, kiddo," Ricky growled. "Don't want you drinking yourself to death on my watch."

Terrifyingly, it occurred to Martha that perhaps that was exactly what Dana was doing. But what could she say?

They made it to a corner booth. A bottle between them to spare Ricky having to make the trip each time.

"So what's your story, anyway?"

"My story?" Martha pretended not to understand.

"Your story, you know. I told you mine. I know you got a story. I can see the blues in you. The way you cry when I sing. Somethin' cut you, cut you deep. You can tell me, we're …" Dana searched for the expression.

"Birds of a feather," Martha helped.

"Yeah, that's it. Birds of a blues feather." Dana smiled. "So, tell me."

"Two men broke into our house, raped me in front of my husband, and then killed him in front of me." She found it was easier to say it all like that: plain, matter-of-factly, in one sentence.

"Well, shit." Dana took a deep draw of her drink. "You just had to go and top me in the drama department."

Somehow, that was the absolutely perfect thing to say. The thing that sent them both roaring with laughter, albeit not of a happy variety.

There were tears in their eyes by the time they were done, but they didn't comment on it. Just wiped them away. Nothing to see here. Just two people, drinking their sorrows down.

"Tell me about him," Dana asked. And Martha did.

It had been so long since she got to just talk about Sam. Without an agenda, without any pretense. Being left alone with his memory had made her feel at times like none of it was real, like it was merely a wonderful dream she had once had. Speaking of it now, of all their years together—wonderful, fun, beautiful, not always but enough to make it shine, more than a handful, a heartful—it was like bringing Sam back to life. Making him more than the beloved ghost who haunted her.

"At least you had that," Dana said, a wistfulness in her voice. "Not a lot of people get that kind of love."

Martha nodded and bit her lip not to cry.

"He's gonna kill me one day, you know. He's bound to. Kid's like a wild animal, and I'm his keeper. No one likes to be caged up."

"You don't think he's got something in him that loves you?"

"I don't think he can, I don't think he understands love."

"I'm sorry," Martha said. What a stupidly inadequate thing to say it was.

"Nah. I watch a lot of nature shows. Animals. In the wild, they kill much more indiscriminately. The old cull the young, the young cull the old. Circle of life."

"I'd miss you," Martha smiled. "I'd miss your blues."

Dana shook her head. "Girl, you got the blues in you for days. You just don't sing it."

They drank to that. Closed out the bar once again. Outside, in the parking lot, Dana belted out a few lines that took Martha's breath away, then took a deep gravity-defying bow.

That was the last time Martha saw Dana Doyle alive. That was how Martha would always remember her.

She thought about calling in a welfare check when Dana missed two of her scheduled performances. Discussed it with Ricky. But in the end, she felt strangely obliged to go and check on her in person.

The trailer door was unlocked. The smell hit Martha like a ton of bricks. Nothing alive could ever smell like this or ever stand a smell like this for long.

The trailer was small and sad on the inside. Serviceable and reasonably clean, but obviously unloved and uncared for. The only personal touch seemed to be an old record player on a cheap stand with a stack of blues records on the shelf below.

There was no one in the living room. Martha said Dana's name over and over, gagging on the smell. She walked through the galley-style kitchen, past the tiny bathroom to the larger of two small bedrooms. The place was dominated by a bed. Old-fashioned wooden headboard and a small nightstand, a tall, wall-mounted mirror, and a free-standing rack of clothes. Martha's mind automatically clocked the inventory as if to distract itself from the nightmare in front of her, but eventually, she had to register it. You couldn't ignore that much blood.

Dana was on the bed. Naked save for a pair of plaid shorts. Covered in blood. There were bite marks on her. And cuts made by something small and sharp. Like a boxcutter. The deepest cuts were along her jugular. That's where most of the blood appeared to have come from. No one could survive a wound like that.

Going by the state of the body, it had to have been days.

Darren was perched on the nightstand, like a gargoyle. His skinny body contorted in half, his arms wrapped around his knees. He turned slowly to face Martha. She saw that his pale face was smeared with blood. His eyes looked like pools of black ink.

It turned her blood to ice, paralyzing her the way seeing a snake might. Amygdala screaming, something atavistic kicking in. The lizard brain, as Sam used to call it. With a terrifying certainty, she knew herself to be in the presence of pure evil. An apex predator. A killer.

"Father is coming," Darren said, barely moving his bloody lips. "Father is coming for me."

Martha bowed her head and backed away. Very, very slowly. It seems with both evil and royalty that was the only way to make an exit. One small step after another until she was out of the bedroom and then out of the trailer altogether.

It was still sunny outside, still bright, but it might have been the dead of the night. It *should* have been the dead of the night for a nightmare like that. She closed the door to the trailer. As if it mattered. As if evil like that could ever be contained.

She should call someone, she knew. She should reach for her phone, dial the numbers, give the address. Let the authorities deal with it. Let it be someone else's problem. Put it out of her mind. Wake up.

It was all she wanted, really, to wake up, to put this away into some dusty corner of her mind as a terrible dream she'd once had. To forget it eventually for it is the only power one has over their nightmares.

And yet, with every step toward her car, she wasn't reaching for her phone. She didn't make the call as she unlocked her sensible Japanese-made sedan and lowered herself into its comfortable ergonomic seat. She didn't make the call as she sat there for a moment shaking like a leaf, trying to get her bearings. Instead, she turned the key over, started the engine, and drove. And drove. And drove. Until she stopped recognizing the images in her rear-view mirror. Until the world made sense once again.

She kept the radio off, but she could hear the blues in her head as clear as day; like a movie soundtrack, rising in volume, threatening to sweep her away.

The Devil's Chord

"What do you call that thing? You know, when a song gets stuck in your head and won't leave?"

"Earworm," Mike replies without taking his eyes off the road.

"Gross," Peyton says, scrunching up her face the way only girls who have been told they are pretty their entire lives can.

"Earworm," I repeat as my mind serves me up an image of a slimy contracting body, wriggling its way inside through the unprotected … Ugh, makes me shudder.

"I heard people also say brainworm," Fish chimes in, pushing up his glasses. "You got one?"

I nod.

"What song?" Peyton wants to know.

"I don't even know its name or anything. Something my brother's playing in his car."

"Your brother is weird," Peyton says.

My gut instinct is to defend my family, my blood, but truth be told, AJ *is* weird. And has only gotten more so over the years. Granted, he's had some tough breaks but explaining it to the likes of Peyton would be a waste of breath.

I make a show of studying the road instead. There isn't much to see. It's all cars, billboards, and trees. We take the same route every time. Never even use the navigation app anymore.

"I like your brother," Fish says thoughtfully. "He's always been nice to me."

That much is true. AJ has always had a soft spot for the downtrodden and has fought more than a few bullies off Fish in his day. All the times I shamefully turned my head the other way, AJ had stood up for the count. I suppose that makes him a better man. But to be fair, he's also a solid half a foot taller than me, with swimmer shoulders and quarterback muscles. I don't know much about genetics, just enough to realize I got thoroughly screwed in that department. AJ takes after our dad, whose name still evokes the glory days of football for Lincoln High. I take after our mom, which is probably something no guy has ever wished for. Short, soft, with lashes like a girl. Thanks, DNA roulette.

AJ graduated last year. The bright future everyone's been predicting for him seems to be on hold. He's grieving, everyone says. His best friend disappeared. I may be one of the few people who knows Jeremy was more than a friend to AJ. So I understand better than most.

I get why AJ is still searching. Though I don't believe he'll find anything.

The entire case is just too freaky. And then there's that stupid cassette tape he left behind.

No one knows what to make of it. The local cops are baffled. As the sheriff's son, I know this for a fact. I see the lines that frustration has etched into Dad's face.

The tape is still in the evidence locker. The case has gone positively arctic. Unsolvable. But somehow, Dad made AJ a copy of the tape. I'm not sure he ever knew about him and Jeremy, but either way, it was a gesture of uncharacteristic kindness.

I wish he'd never done it. Now AJ won't stop playing the damn thing. Every time he drives me anywhere, I have to hear that unholy racket. It isn't even close to what I'd call music.

Twenty-five songs, each uglier than the next.

And one of them had crawled its way inside my brain. The earworm. It's been days now of having the songs spin their terrible symphonies on repeat and not being able to stop it.

I can't even tell you any of the lyrics. Or hum any of the melodies. All I know is that I'm hearing it when it's not playing, and it's driving me up the wall.

The discordance of it, the implied insidiousness behind the words. Imagine your worst nightmare turned into a song, and you'll know what I'm talking about.

Thing is, I never ask AJ to turn it off. I don't know much about grief, but I suspect he *needs* to hear the tape. All the time. And then there's the lamentable fact that I've failed my driving test three times now. So, I'm stuck. Whenever I have to go somewhere, I have to rely on others.

At least, with Mike driving, I can relax, knowing it's only ever going to be rap coming out of the car speakers. The songs do nothing for me, but at least they don't make me feel the nauseating pressure behind my eyes, like my skull might explode.

Rap is all predictable beats and lyrics, none of which does a thing to dislodge my stupid earworm.

I get lost in my thoughts, allowing the predictable monotony of the drive to lull me into something like a half-sleep.

"Here we are," Peyton announces, enthused like a game show host.

I snap out of my musing. Mike is parking the car in the gravel lot. Fish is double-checking his backpack, making sure he brought everything. The bag's enormous—Fish tends to overpack. So much so, Mike used to joke we should change his name to Turtle.

"Once a boy scout," Fish always says, shrugging good-naturedly. Of course, he's never been one, he just likes their motto about preparedness, but it isn't worth bringing up.

To an extent, every one of us creates our own narratives, then does our best to live up to them, as if rehearsing for the world to come.

We get out of the car and stretch. Not that the drive is long, but Mike's car is tiny, and he takes up a lot of it.

Hard to believe, but once upon a time we were the same size. Mike shot up two summers ago. Now he's on the basketball team and dating a cheerleader. At least he hasn't let it all go to his head. He still hangs out with his childhood best friends.

Peyton tags along like a good girlfriend. The first time we were all introduced, you could practically see her thinking "nerds." It was all over her expression, her barely concealed eye roll. But she's been decent enough about it since. If Fish and I get made fun of, it's strictly *behind* our backs, which is something we can live with.

The parking lot is gravel, those tiny pebbles that love getting into your shoes. The woods are looming high above us.

"What's the name of this place again?" Peyton asks, twirling a blonde lock around her manicured finger. I'm surprised she's actually dressed for the occasion. Normally it's all crop tops and short skirts, but today she's wearing a sweatshirt, blue jeans, and high-top hiking boots. Sure, the sweatshirt is bedazzled with a "Yas Queen," and her jeans are skintight and artfully shredded at the knees, but still.

Fish replies. Then, per her request, spells it out.

"Weird name," she says.

"Native American," Mike points out.

"Right, bae." She beams, leaning into him.

Fish sniggers. "Young love." He gets flipped off.

Mike grabs his bag, loaded for two. It looks small on his broad back. "Let's go."

For all our differences, we have always had one thing in common: horror. Coming together as friends was easy enough. As kids, geographic proximity alone did the trick, and we all lived on the same street. Horror is the glue that has kept us together through the years.

No matter how weird Fish got or how popular Mike became or how thoroughly mediocre I remained, we always had scary movies to watch and beat-up, luridly stylized paperbacks to trade. We pored over the well-thumbed issues of *Fangoria* and *Rue Morgue* and were the first to see new genre releases when they finally made their way to our tiny local movie theater.

Even Peyton made a valiant effort to keep up with us. She watched the screen in slivers, covering her eyes with her fingers and peeking through at the gory parts.

For the newest and freshest of horror, we browsed online forums and dedicated Facebook groups. And then there was The Treasure Trove.

With an awesome name *and* stylized to look like a pirate's treasure chest on the outside, The Trove was the best used bookstore around. Not that there were many of those left anymore. The owner knew us by name and would set aside horror, new and old, whenever it came in. His name was Ric, and he looked like he was in a death metal band. Truth be told, his band fell apart ages ago, but I guess he was still a rocker at heart.

Ric loved horror as much as we did and had a dedicated section for it, along with a small table featuring local authors.

That's where we discovered The Book as we have come to refer to it since. Ric didn't know much about the author, said it was left for him during the off hours.

A slim thing, just a novella, but it scared the crap out of us. No small feat.

Reading and rereading it, we recognized the woods in the story. The author had indeed stayed local. And once we knew where The Book took place, we had to go there. If only to pay homage. If only to reestablish the expertly blurred lines between fiction and reality.

In the story, there was a house in the woods. A strange, abandoned house in the middle of the hiking trails, covered in graffiti. And in that house, there was something evil. Waiting.

How could we resist?

None of us are really hikers, though Mike and Peyton are by far in the best shape. Fish is already huffing and puffing beneath the imposing carapace of his backpack. I do okay, but I'm not loving this. It's just like walking, isn't it? Only with all the leaves and dirt. In fact, I notice that my thoughts echo those of The Book's main character. I voice the observation to my friends.

"Hiking's supposed to be good for you," Mike says. "Relaxing."

"Do you feel particularly relaxed?"

Mike tightens his hand around Peyton's as they share a smile. "Sure, I do."

Fish groans.

"You know there isn't gonna be any house here, right?"

"I know no such thing," Mike counters with a grin.

"And if there is, what are you going to do anyway? Make wishes and see how that plays out for you?"

In The Book, it doesn't really work out all that well for the protagonist. I suppose the moral there is "Be careful what you wish for." Something like that.

"Nah, just take some photos, show them to Ric, post them on the horror group. People will dig it."

"I'll put it on Insta, too," Peyton says. "Get some more weirdo followers."

We laugh. Hydrate. Walk on.

After a while, I can't help but notice that my footsteps fall in time to the song stuck in my head. The terrible ominous thud of it has become my marching drum.

AJ's been teaching me to play guitar. Says it'll "help me with the ladies." I'm skeptical but what's the harm? Besides, it gives me more time to spend with my brother and offers him something like an outlet for his sadness.

I'm picking up the basics decently enough, but music theory eludes me. To AJ's credit, he's been trying to make it interesting, or rather he's been trying to tailor it to my specific interests.

Because if he just went at it talking about the triads or tritones, my eyes would glaze right over. But AJ knows me, so he comes up with Diabolus in Musica—The Devil's Chord.

Now *that* I'll learn. Flatted fifth, on the other hand, not so much. Though it's all the same thing. Only the names are different.

The basic concept here is an interval. Two notes played three full steps apart. It creates an ear-upsetting discordance. Striking but not to everyone's taste.

"How it happened," AJ explains to me, "was that Tony Iommi of Black Sabbath listened to some classical music by Holst, liked what he heard, and lifted the triad concept from there. Then he slowed it down to a crawl, threw in a trill to the flatted fifth, and added a vibrato to the rest for emphasis. And ta-da, the birth of heavy metal."

"For real?"

"Oh yeah." AJ grins. "Devil's music all the way." He makes a metal sign with his pinky and index finger extended like horns as he headbangs. "Churches used to ban the devil's chord, you know, back in the day. Couldn't take it. Now it's everywhere."

It seems like an oversimplification to me. No way an entire genre of music has been ushered in on a single chord trick.

I don't say anything, but I do my own research. Sure enough, in the Middle Ages, the churches were not fans of the technique. It was never officially banned but frowned upon severely enough to discourage anyone from using it.

And now it *is* all over the place from *West Side Story* to *The Simpsons* theme song.

I practice and practice until I master the devil's chord. Now that it's in my head, I hear it everywhere.

Is this what hiking does? Clears the cobwebs out of your brain? Weird. I don't know how it took me this long to recognize it, but now I hear it with every step—the Devil's Chord. That's the thing that haunts me with this earworm nuisance. The entire cassette is full of flatted fifths, but track five is a particularly egregious offender. Something about the quietude of these woods provides a perfect backdrop, a stage if you will, for the concert in my head.

AJ is right. The technique *is* effective. The way it screeches and slides from one chord to another, it makes your stomach lurch like a rollercoaster. You anticipate the dips and rises, and still it hits you.

It's a perfect day for a hike. Warm, not too humid. The tall trees are keeping most of the sun out of the path, so that there's a noticeable temperature drop once we're in the thick of it, but it remains comfortable. There's a creek or a lake or something. The water's clear, almost inviting.

But I remember all too well the way the woods are described in The Book, and it's difficult to view them now as anything but ominous. Something about the author's writing has really gotten under my skin. The way its *descent-into-madness* narrative is rendered so vividly, the claustrophobic sense of irreality, the slow creeping unease that steadily increases as the story progresses until it reaches its devastating end.

Even Mike thinks it's aces, and Mike tends to prefer the more in-your-face sort of horror, guts and gore and all.

I try to participate in the mindless chatter as we walk, but the song in my head is getting louder. I think I can even make out some of the lyrics now.

It's something like: "Pay your dues to learn the truth." Can that be right?

I suppose heavy metal can make anything sound evil. Though now I swear, there's also a "kill, kill, kill" chant happening. Or maybe it's "cull, cull, cull?"

Why is this happening now? I've been listening to that song, however unwillingly, for a while, and only now am I making out the words. It seems unlikely.

Is it the woods? Am I really freaked out by them?

Was it The Book that got to me?

Did I not eat enough for breakfast?

I get lost in my head, missing conversational cues.

"You okay, man?" Fish nudges me. His face is red and sweaty. His heavy-framed eyeglasses refuse to stay up.

"I'm good," I answer reflexively. "Just … creepy here, you know?"

He shrugs. "Looks like any old woods to me." Fish pushes up his glasses and squints at me. "You kind of look like you're nodding along to a song no one can hear. Is it that brainworm thing still?"

I didn't realize I was doing that. "Yeah." I smile, trying to play it off. "It's really wedged in there."

"I had an uncle who started hearing things no one else did."

"Oh yeah? What happened to him?"

"The family ended up committing him. He got really—"

Fish is interrupted by a shrill yelling.

We look up, then around.

Mike and Peyton have ended up a good clip ahead of us, and Peyton is screaming her head off. It takes a second to place the sound as excitement and not terror.

"There it is. There it is," she's saying.

We catch up as fast as we can. And sure enough, there's the house.

I suppose I didn't really expect it to be here. I've always had the ability to separate facts from fiction. After reading the novella, I looked the place up online extensively and found no information about any abandoned houses, so I just chalked it up to the author's imagination and left it at that.

Fish has always been more of a believer. The look on his face— it's like some Holy Grail business.

"It's just like in The Book," he exhales, awe in his voice.

"Creepy," Peyton comments, then proceeds to take photos.

Mike's the first to walk up the crumbling steps and into the front room. Fish follows him. I stand outside, taking in all the graffiti. Someone did all this, even the ones by the eaves and on the ceiling that appear to have required some acrobatics to accomplish.

I snap a few photos of my own. AJ might dig this.

It's strange, but now that my brother isn't quite himself, steeped in grief and muted anger, we're closer than we've ever been. AJ deferred his college acceptance, but he isn't doing much with his time. He mostly just drives around, listening to that horrible tape. "Looking," he says. But I don't think he really believes he'll find who—or what—he's looking for.

His car is actually old enough to still have a cassette player. A real clunker. Blue faded to grey, with upholstery worn thin, and a moody transmission.

I used to think I was going to inherit it once he went away to school and I passed the driving test, but now I'm no longer sure of what the future holds.

Even the present manages to surprise me. Just look at this house.

I skirt the perimeter, then tentatively set foot inside. The floorboards creak an unearthly welcome.

The music in my head amplifies, crescendoing into rhythmic pulses that feel like eye-bleed inducers.

I press my fingers against my temples and squeeze.

Nothing.

Mike's goofing off for the photos. Peyton's loving it, going into full paparazzi mode. Her phone is the latest model. She hands it to Fish, asking him to take some couples pics.

I realize I can't hear a word they are saying. The discordance in my head is that loud.

They gesture for me to get in on the photo. The phone is propped up on the disused fireplace mantle. I come near, get wrapped up in a sweaty group hug. The flash is blinding.

Suddenly, their limbs feel like clingy weeds pulling me down into a swamp. I shake them free and rush outside for some air.

I think my friends are asking me if I'm okay, but their voices are distant and muted as if I'm underwater.

The answer is no, I'm not okay. The devil's chord is riffing my mind to shreds.

Just as described in the book, the rear entrance brings you out to a steep drop. You can get down to the water from here, but you'd have to be really careful, grab hold of trees and rocks and whatnot on your way down.

I study the remnants of an embankment before me, thinking of how long the house might have before the river rises up and takes it away. Can a river come up this high?

The hand on my shoulder startles me. Track five running through my mind on a loop has ensured I hear no one's approach.

"Dude. Are you freaking out?" Fish says as I turn around. At least I think he says that; I'm not much of a lip reader.

I try to tell him, but the words won't make it past my lips. The pressure inside my skull is enormous. Even during the worst of the allergy season, it's never been like that.

And there it is again. That maddening interval. The chords skipped over and over and a murderous incantation overlaying it.

I don't mean to push Fish. I'm only trying to put some distance between us, get away from the concern etched in his features.

But I do push him. And of course, he loses his footing immediately. My friend isn't remotely athletic even on the best of days. In fact, he was so clumsy in gym class that he got teased for looking like a fish out of water. Hence the stupid nickname that stuck ever since.

Down he goes, tumbling through the anemic trees and medley of branches and rocks. Failing to catch hold.

The terrifying crack of his neck when he comes to a stop, landing awkwardly below, half in half out of the water, stops time. I can't breathe, I can't think. My heart is as still as a broken metronome. And then I realize, "Hey, I *heard* that." I can hear again. The song in my head has stopped.

The sheer relief of it floods my system, competing for supremacy with the horror of what's just happened. I'm breathing again, my heart has restarted, but I am paralyzed. Speechless.

The moment catches up to me as Mike comes outside, followed by Peyton.

She sees Fish first. Her screaming seems to rip apart the fabric of the world.

"What happened? Dude, what happened?" Mike asks me, but I can't speak. He shoves me aside, back toward the house, and descends the steep incline.

Numbly I watch him perform CPR. Peyton is hyperventilating, calling 911.

The song restarts. And just like being plunged back into the darkness after someone suddenly extinguishes the lights and finding it starker than ever, it's worse this time. Louder, more insistent.

I stumble, fall to the ground, wrap my arms around me. I cannot contain this. It's too much. The sound is larger than the world itself.

"KILL," it screams at me. Or something like it. And in a desperate need to appease it, I do.

I think I do, anyway. I'm not sure. I black out. When I come to, there's a blood-covered rock in my hand. Peyton is lying on the ground, right outside of the house. Her beautiful blond hair is red. Her eyes are gazing unseeingly at the sky. Both are the exact same shade of blue.

I'm just inside the main room of the house. Mike is nowhere in sight. I get up off the floor and look. I find him soon enough and wish I didn't. He'd fallen through a weathered plank railing down to the cellar. His body is twisted unnaturally like a discarded marionette. There's blood pooling beneath his head. So much blood.

I drop the rock I'm holding to the floor. My hands are covered in blood. I feel it, thick and tacky, in my hair, on my face.

I wipe at it, only making it worse.

Track five, my demonic companion, has slowed itself down into a background soundtrack. I can finally take deep breaths. I try it for a while but it's doing nothing to calm me.

Slowly, I make my way down to the creek below. Fish is still there. Still dead. All of it happened. All of it is real. I'm trapped in a waking nightmare and unlikely to rise from it anytime soon.

The water is refreshing, sun-warmed just enough to feel pleasant as I wash myself in the creek. Or maybe a lake. Or a river. Whatever this body of water is, it accepts my blood-red sins until I'm clean.

Then I make my way back. Through the house, through the woods. Retracing the steps of The Book's protagonist. Reflecting on our differences. Our similarities.

The sun dries me as I walk. Not a living soul here on such a nice day.

I try to think of something, anything, to distract me from the fact that the music is coming back. Beginning at the back of my mind and steadily getting louder, more prominent. Someone is turning up the volume dial inside my head, seeing how much I can take.

It occurs to me that I don't know exactly which woods Jeremy had been hiking in when he disappeared. At least I think that's how it happened. Was it here or somewhere very much like it? Was he hearing the same chords that are propelling my tired feet now?

Did he feel as weary, as broken as I do?

Where did he find the music on the tape?

Or perhaps I should be asking, "Where did the music on the tape find him?" Was it here, in these woods? In this house?

I march to the beat of this horrid drum of mine, out toward the parking lot. Upon getting there, I realize that I never took the keys off Mike, and even if I had, I still can't drive.

I'd call AJ for a ride, but my phone is dead. Besides, he might come blasting his music, and I don't think I can take the sound in stereo.

Walking home it is, then. My backpack feels like it's been weighed down with rocks. My heart is heavier still. My head is a concert arena—there's a show on. Only one song is playing but it's a killer.

When it gets too much, I suppose I know what to do for a reprieve, however temporary. Until then, I let the devil's chords sing me home.

STUMP

He dropped the gun.

The terrible weight of it hit the ground.

For a moment, the silence was absolute. He could hear nothing but his own breath, nothing but the swooshing sound of his blood like the ocean's rush caught in twin conch shells and held to his ears, nothing but the thudding of his own heart.

And then the screaming began.

Tobey.

Whenever it all—the bullying at school and the fighting at home—got to be too much, Tobey headed for the woods.

The woods might have been a misnomer. It was technically a park. At least, it had all sorts of park things in it: a couple of miniature ponds, some benches, a baseball diamond. There was a walking path, too. The moment you stepped off it, though, nature got wilder, less manicured and curated. The bushes and brambles got denser and unrulier. The trees got taller. Once you started walking off the proverbial beaten path, the park changed, and for Tobey, it became the woods.

Not that it was difficult for the trees to tower over him—he was the smallest kid in his class. Puberty was approaching, but from what he knew of genetics, looking at his short, athletically unremarkable parents, there wasn't much to hope for in that department.

Besides, he liked the feeling of being dwarfed by the trees. It felt safe and brought him comfort. Solace was the word he had for it. He got it from a James Bond movie he wasn't supposed to watch but did anyway, because his parents never really paid attention to what he was up to. It was a great word, Tobey thought, though not one he'd ever use in school. He was already picked on enough. For his love of books, for his jug-handle ears, for his unfashionable hair, and even more unfashionable clothes and off-brand sneakers.

His mom cut his hair when she remembered, never too concerned about doing a perfect job. "Perfect is the enemy of good," she liked to say. Not that her haircuts were good, either.

She was also the one who bought his clothes at a local Goodwill. The things she found for him were always the wrong size, mostly too large. Maybe she knew something he didn't. Perhaps there was a giant of an ancestor somewhere down the line, someone Tobey reminded her of, someone she thought he might turn into one day. Perhaps she just didn't care. She hated shopping, never wanted to take her time with it. Normally, she'd grab some things from the sales rack and shove them at Tobey, then tap at her phone until he picked what he liked best. At least his shoes were the right size. Ugly and bulky things Nike would never put their swoosh on or near, but they served their purpose.

Tobey didn't really care about what he looked like. He probably never would have given it a second thought had the other kids in his class not made such a big deal about it.

It was a nice school that he went to, his family's apartment just making the cutoff for the good district. Most of the kids came from money, some money at least. More than Tobey's family had.

Both of his parents worked, but their jobs weren't fancy enough and their hours were always getting cut. They had one car between them, which never seemed to be enough. And one kid that always seemed to be too much.

Tobey tried to be self-sufficient. He knew how to use all the major appliances at home, had known for years. Could make basic meals on the stove or microwave leftovers, could even do his own laundry. Most days he drifted through the apartment like a ghost, seldom seen or heard, though the place was always too small and the walls much too thin for a complete separation.

His parents argued about everything, it seemed. Mostly money. Sometimes alcohol. They liked to drink, then argue about drinking. It made no sense.

They were unhappy. Anyone could see that. Unhappy people who couldn't keep their unhappiness to themselves and let it spill over every which way, splashing every corner of their lives. Splashing Tobey most of all.

Times like that, when their two-bedroom apartment felt smaller than ever, Tobey would grab his beat-up backpack and head to the woods. For him, it was the best part about living where they did—all he had to do was cross the street, walk a little, and there he was. Among the trees.

The trees never shouted, never fought, never made fun of him. They were either exceptionally kind or majestically indifferent. It didn't matter. Tobey felt comforted among them either way.

He learned to recognize all the birds that lived there from the legend printed and posted on the path. There were six different species. And then other kinds that only came in the winter.

The pond had turtles. He only saw them during the warm months, sunning themselves like they didn't have a care in the world. He heard there were snakes there, too, but had yet to see one.

Tobey usually brought along food and books, setting himself up for hours of entertainment if needed.

Neither of his parents was a reader—their preferred form of entertainment was gluing themselves to the giant flat screen TV in the living room. Tobey loved books ever since he learned to read.

Loved the weight and the texture of them, the way simple words could add up and turn into wonderful adventures like plain bricks making up an impressive building. He didn't have many books at home but was steadily working his way through the local library's catalog. The ones he did own came from old Mr. Mooney, a neighbor who passed away three years ago, leaving Tobey a box of old hardcovers with age-yellowed pages and fantastical titles.

Mr. Mooney was Tobey's favorite neighbor—an old man who used to terrify him with his imposing height, giant curled-at-the-corners mustache, and a matching set of eyebrows. But then, they got to talking, and everything changed. Mr. Mooney, it turned out, had traveled the world, and his stories about it were as good as any you'd find in books. It was strange to think that after all those adventures, he ended up in the same unexciting place as Tobey and his family. Mr. Mooney's apartment had the most interesting things in it: objects from distant lands and cultures, menacingly-curved swords and scary-looking carved wooden masks. Tobey didn't know what happened to them after. Probably Mr. Mooney's son—a sour-faced man who never visited when his father was alive but came fast enough once the man was dead—inherited and got rid of it all. But he did leave the box of books for Tobey with a note from Mr. Mooney.

Tobey kept the note in an old cigar box under his bed, along with all his other treasures. The note read, "He who reads has the world at his fingertips." Tobey loved that idea.

Some of the books were too complicated, too dense, so he'd set them aside and read the others. Eventually, he worked his way through the entire box.

When one of the neighbors put out a small bookcase by the trash bins, Tobey dragged it into his bedroom. It was surprisingly heavy, exhausting to move, but at least it was solid and sturdy—he didn't know why anyone would throw it out—and accommodated all of Mr. Mooney's books. Tobey put the bookcase next to his bed, and it was the last thing he looked at every night before falling asleep, hoping his dreams would be as exciting as the stories on its shelves.

Sometimes, reading got in the way of schoolwork. When his parents remembered to check his report cards, they'd note the lower grades, never the high ones, occasionally cuffing him on the head. The general sentiment was that he better get his act together and manage good grades or he'll end up a loser. *Like them* was the unspoken end of that sentence, Tobey thought, though he never said it out loud.

Shrugging and mumbling apologies usually did the trick. His parents had too much of their own drama to focus on him for long.

It was always easier to deal with them. Adults were easy. Other kids at school, though … they seemed to have nothing better to do than to pick on Tobey.

Just that morning, he was given another swirlie. Tobey hated swirlies most of all. Such a cutesy name for such a horrible thing. His head was plunged into the toilet, and the water did indeed swirl and swirl. He'd have to wash his hair tonight. Again. The showerhead at home needed replacing. It spouted water every which way, making showers into something of an uncomfortable dance every time.

Tobey tried to shower daily. He didn't want the accusations of being stinky on top of all the other abuse he had to put up with, but washing his hair was an extra-tedious task. He could never tell if the funky shower spout got all the shampoo out, and the suds stung his eyes.

Oh well, he sighed, that was hours away. For now, he was in the woods, and he felt safe.

There was a tree stump he had found recently. He wasn't sure how he had never come across it before, but now he couldn't stay away. It must have been epic back when it was a tree. The largest one around by far judging by the size of the stump. It looked ancient, mysterious, like something out of a storybook.

It might have passed for a hobbit home had it been neater. Or, in its original form, it might have looked like The Old Man Willow tree from the books, the one that made the hobbits feel sleepy. As is, it made Tobey think of a magical castle that came to ruin, but in tree form.

The stump had a split in it, almost large enough to serve as a hideaway for someone Tobey's size. It was something he had never tried, though he liked to idly imagine what treasures might be hidden inside. He hoped it was treasures and not something like snakes.

Anyway, Tobey liked it. He liked it very much. He liked leaning against it and reading his books and imagining he was somewhere far away and somewhen infinitely more exciting than this time and place. Currently, he was working his way through all of the Tolkien books: large, heavy volumes from Mr. Mooney's collection that promised impossible adventures on every page. With their green leather covers that featured gold lettering and striking designs, the books even *looked* like magic. Tobey could get lost in them for hours on end.

He'd stop thinking about his home. About school. Only think about the world where being small didn't matter, where you can be a hero no matter how tall you were or what clothes you wore, where your courage and your mettle were measured by your character and your inner strength, not any superficial factors.

Tobey leaned against the tree stump, read his book, and dreamed.

Finn.

Whenever it all got to be too much—the whining customers at work, the nagging at home, the screaming baby—Finn tended to retreat into himself. A technique he referred to as turtling. Jenny found it cute once, but now she hated it. Said it took him away from them, from her and the baby. Made him separate.

That was the point, he wanted to say. He needed the separateness, if only temporary. To remember what it was like when it was just him, with none of the crushing responsibilities of adulthood that never seemed to have any upside.

When Finn was young, life was fun. Simple, uncomplicated, and fun. He did well enough at school to be left alone about it, he had friends, he was in a band. The future was something he didn't give too much thought to—he was always the live-in-the-now kinda guy.

Well, the future was here *now*, he was living in it. It was … underwhelming at best.

An apartment that was plenty for when it was just the two of them, but now, with the baby's arrival, seemed smaller every day. A job he never much cared for and lately was beginning to actively dislike. A job that now felt like a trap, one he couldn't leave because his family depended on it. Jenny had every intention of going back to work once the baby was older, but until then, Finn was the breadwinner. A stifling claustrophobic role, he found.

His parents loved to read and had named him Finn after one of their favorite literary characters. Probably hoping for a life of adventure for him. They never said either way. Divorced by the time Finn was starting elementary school and bitter about it, they never said much to him in the years since. He became the intermediary between two acrimonious adults, the shuttlecock they battered across the net in their game of accusations and recriminations. Each parent saw the other reflected in Finn, and it only seemed to fuel their anger.

Finn disengaged from that mad circus the moment he came of age and now, outside of the occasional Christmas and birthday cards, their relationship was pretty much nonexistent. Much to his relief.

Neither of his parents had seen the baby yet. They lived too far, they were too busy; that and a litany of other excuses. Finn didn't care. They sent some money for the kid, and that was good enough.

The kid, the baby. Finn seldom used her name. Alice. Another storybook character. Maybe once she was older, once she spoke, had thoughts, a distinguishable personality, maybe then Finn would feel that magic connection with her. The one everyone always talks about.

Right now, it was a small hairless bundle that liked to scream until it was red in the face. The bundle that turned his once-fun girlfriend into a mommy machine: sleep-deprived, irate, and irascible.

It seemed it wasn't that long ago when they were happy, or pretty happy at any rate. Having fun, living for themselves. The baby wasn't planned. The baby was, if you wanted to get technical about it, a contraception snafu. A drunken misunderstanding. A simple miscalculation. Crazy to think that's all it took to make a life.

If he was being perfectly honest with himself, he had hoped Jenny would opt for an abortion. Knew better than to press her about it, though. Knew enough to fake excitement when she decided to keep it. And now, well, now, he was a father. A provider. The man of the house.

He hated it.

The apartment had to be babyproofed. Jenny quit smoking and drinking and began to make him feel like a monster for not following suit. He sold his gaming console and his games to buy a crib and all the other things the books said the baby would need.

The baby—Alice—didn't seem to need anything but milk and undivided attention. At all hours of the day. And night.

Finn was exhausted. He dreamed of sleep, but when he slept, it was all nightmares.

Tobey.

He woke up to the sound of his alarm going off. The same alarm he'd had ever since he could remember. The other kids in his class all had cell phones, but he was still stuck with an old digital clock/ radio, the radio part of which hadn't worked in years.

Tobey shut off the annoying sound, stretched, and sighed. It was only Tuesday, the weekend seemed forever away. There was nothing to look forward to in his day, nothing he could think of outside of maybe reading more of his book.

He shuffled into the kitchen and fixed himself a bowl of store-brand corn flakes. Bland but he was used to it. His mom was sitting at their messy kitchen table, eating toast, and typing away on her phone.

"Morning," she said without looking up.

"Morning," he replied.

There was no room left at the dining table, which had long become a sort of catch-all of the household debris from keys to old receipts to mail. Tobey started for the living room couch.

"Come on, kiddo," his mom said, putting her phone down. "Let's sit and have a proper breakfast together." She swept the mail to the floor, clearing some space for him. A sort of comical grand gesture to showcase what a great and fun mom she was.

Tobey joined her, sitting down and stirring his corn flakes, waiting for them to become just the right kind of soggy.

She gave him a long once over. Without her makeup, she looked sleepy, pale, monochromatic. The darkness under her eyes appeared more prominent. She wasn't old, Tobey knew, in fact probably younger than most moms, but there was a permanent tiredness about her that seemed to age her beyond her years. Tobey never knew what it was she was so tired of. His dad? Her job? Her life? Him? He never asked.

"So how are you, kiddo?" His mom ruffled his hair. An old affectation that has long since turned into a tolerable annoyance.

"I'm good."

"Just good?"

"Just good."

"How's school?"

"School's good, too."

"Making any friends?"

He wanted to laugh. Instead, he shrugged.

"What about … what was his name … Jason?"

A while back during one of these impromptu face-to-face breakfasts, Tobey made the mistake of naming his chief abuser as a friend. His mom was prying, needing names, and it just slipped out. Now he had to hear about it. Somehow *that* was the thing she remembered.

"He's good."

"So, everything and everyone is good?" she summed up with a sarcastic smile.

"Pretty much."

She looked closer at his arm, sticking out of the short sleeve of his worn T-shirt. "Is that a bruise?"

"I fell in gym class."

"Oh." Their eyes met for a moment, then his mom looked away. No stranger to random bruises and made-up excuses herself, she found no words to offer.

She picked up her phone.

Ask me something, anything, Tobey thought. Ask me about my book. About my thoughts. About my dreams. Please.

His mom said nothing. They sat in shared silence for a while, then she got up before he was finished with his cereal.

"Gotta go get ready for my stupid job. Another day, another dollar, as they say. You be good, kiddo." Another hair ruffle, and she was gone.

Tobey finished his breakfast. He washed his bowl and spoon and left them in the cheap plastic drying rack with moldy edges. Had some orange juice, cringing at the acidity of the from-concentrate flavor. Waited for the bathroom, but his mom was taking too long, so he did his best to wash up in the kitchen sink and left for school.

"Whatcha reading, Tooooobeeey?"

He hated the way Jason stretched out his name. It was either that or Mopey Tobey, which wasn't even clever or rhymed, but that was Jason for you.

His tormentor had been kept back a grade, which, combined with some impressive genetics, resulted in him towering over any other kid in their grade. And most of the kids in the grade ahead.

Jason shaved his head to emulate his older brother who was in the Army. He wore lots of camo, too, presumably for the same reason. Today, he had a camo jacket on, though it was much too warm out for one.

Tobey found himself involuntarily shrinking into his school bus seat, making himself even smaller. He used to dream of having an invisibility cloak. Just wrapping himself up in it and going through life unnoticed. Everyone would leave him alone then.

Jason grabbed the book out of his hands.

"*Fellowship of the Ring*. Sounds gay."

Tobey knew you weren't supposed to use that word as derogatory but couldn't imagine correcting Jason.

"You gay, Tooooobeeey? Is that it?"

Tobey sighed and waited. Eventually, Jason was bound to get tired and move on.

"You sighing? You gonna cry next? Mopey Tobey gonna mope over his gay book?"

No, probably not. If there was one thing Jason and his crew had taught Tobey over the years is that you didn't cry. Not when someone could see you, anyway.

"Yo, Jace, we got that new game on Switch. You wanna check it?"

That was Drake, his inadvertent savior. Smaller than Jason, he was the only son of the wealthiest family in town and thus in possession of all the latest toys and an integral part of Jason's crew.

Tobey's book went flying to the floor, pages splayed, spine out. Like an awkward graceless bird. "Later, gator."

Tobey picked up the book. The bus' floor was dirty. He wiped his sweaty palms on his pants and smoothed out the pages crumpled by the fall. A book was a thing, he knew, and things felt nothing, but he thought it might have been as shaken by the violence as he was and so he cradled it like a baby for the rest of the ride to school.

Math went by, then history, then geography. While Jason and his friends always managed to single him out, the teachers tended to leave him alone. It was kind of like having an invisibility cloak that only worked part-time.

Tobey seldom raised his hand, though he often knew the answers. There was a satisfaction to be had just from knowing without showing off your knowledge.

At lunch, he found a seat as far away from others as he could. Peanut butter and jelly, he made them in bulk every Sunday for the week ahead. They never tasted fresh that way, but at least he didn't have to think about it or count on his parents remembering to leave him lunch money. Today he had an apple, too. A Red Delicious apple that proved to be both.

He ate while reading and almost succeeded at making the world around him disappear when Jason found him again. Flanked by Drake, Cody, and Alex, he leaned over and flicked the half-eaten apple out of Tobey's hand.

"What's up, Tooooobeeey? You don't wanna socialize at lunch? Still got your gay book going? Didn't I tell you to knock that shit off?"

Tobey tried to protect his book, but Jason ripped it right out of his grasp. He started reading from it, tripping up over the names.

"What is this crap? No wonder you're so weird."

"I heard of it. They made movies out of it," Drake offered.

Coming from anyone else that comment probably would have pissed Jason off. To Drake such liberties were often granted. After all, Drake had more pocket cash than the rest of them combined.

"So watch a movie, Tooooobeeey. Oh wait, you don't have a phone, do you? Whatsamatta? Your parents are too poor to buy you a phone? I've seen the car your dad drives, I'm not surprised. A losermobile for a loser. You a loser, too, ain't you, Tooooobeeey? It's like … whatchamacallit?"

"Genetic?" Alex suggested.

"Yeah, genetic." Jason grinned an ugly grin. "A genetic loser."

Jason's dad rode a motorcycle, a Harley-Davidson, that made a deafening noise whenever he came to pick him up from school. The man belonged to a motorcycle gang, according to local gossip, and had been to prison. He looked just like Jason, but older, with less hair and more fat than muscle.

Tobey said nothing. Could have been a mute, he thought bitterly, for how little he talked, for how much he held in.

Jason opened the book, held it by the spine with one hand, and ripped a bunch of pages with the other. Then he dropped the damaged tome and proceeded to rip the pages apart, throwing them at Tobey like some kind of terrible confetti.

Don't cry, don't cry, don't cry, Tobey thought, whatever you do…

What he ended up doing instead was charging Jason. He had no idea why or how; it was almost as if his body moved of its own volition without so much as consulting his brain.

He simply reached for the book, got kicked by Jason for his effort, and then he charged.

It was a failure almost from the start. The moment the initial surprise of the attack was over, Jason righted himself, grabbed Tobey, and threw him down. Must have been some kind of wrestling move or something. It knocked the air right out of him. Until then, Tobey thought that was only something they said in books.

Jason grabbed him by the ears. "What are you doing, stupid?" He said punctuating every word with a yank. "You wanna fight, stupid? You don't got a fight in you. You better learn to flap these giant ears of yours and fly away cause that's your best chance in a fight."

By the time a teacher intervened, Tobey's ears felt like they were on fire. It was the only way he knew for sure they were still attached.

The teacher, Mr. Marshall, reluctantly pulled the boys apart and sent them to the principal's office.

They were dealt with separately, one by one, like criminals on a TV show.

"Fighting, Tobey?" Principal Edwards sighed at him. Principal Edwards always sighed as if the job was weighing down on him too heavily.

Tobey studied his shoes. Their previous owner left a permanent marker design on the rubber toe part, something Tobey had never been able to decipher. "I wasn't. Jason started it."

"Jason says you did."

Tobey looked up, incredulously.

"Jason is a head taller and probably fifty pounds heavier than me. Why would I start a fight with him?"

"See. That isn't how we talk here, Tobey. No one likes a smart aleck."

You like stupid alecks well enough, Tobey thought.

"Jason says you had a disagreement about a book and then rushed him. He ended up defending himself. His friends confirm this version of events."

Tobey went back to studying his shoes. His ears were burning. He wanted to put a bag of peas on each to bring relief *and* to block out the tedious inanities the principal was spouting.

When it was over, he had a suspension. Two days. He didn't think Jason got any and didn't have it in him to protest.

All Tobey did was finish out the school day, gather his books, and go home. The injured volume made him feel like his heart got punched. All those years, the book was perfectly safe with Mr. Mooney, and now he'd managed to get it ripped. Ruined.

Tobey didn't cry, though he wanted to. He felt the tears burning at the very edges of his eyes and held them in as best he could. He skipped the bus home and walked. It felt like it took forever, but at least it was peaceful. Just putting one foot in front of the other and letting the mind empty of all thoughts. Like floating away into space.

His dad was home when he got back. Sitting in front of the TV with a beer in his hand. Watching the game. There seemed to always be some game on.

Dad loved sports. Used to play in high school until a torn ligament dashed all his hopes of taking it any further. Tobey didn't get sports at all. Another way there were nothing like each other.

"That you, T-dog?" his dad shouted over the TV without turning around.

"Yeah, Dad."

"You good?"

"Yeah, Dad."

That seemed to be the extent of their conversation most days.

Tobey went into the kitchen and made himself some ramen from a packet. Those things were cheap, and his mom always bought them in bulk.

One time Tobey saw ramen on a TV cooking show, and it looked nothing like the paltry too-salty noodles he consumed. He ate some peanut butter with a spoon while he waited. One could never eat enough peanut butter.

There was no point in doing homework, he supposed. Not without school to go to tomorrow. He ate his ramen and tried to read but the TV noise was too loud. He looked over into the living room. His father was passed out, a beer can perched in his lap. From experience, Tobey knew that shutting the game off or even turning down the volume would result in waking the man.

So, he took his backpack and went back outside. To the woods. To the stump. To where the much-needed peace and quiet awaited him.

Finn.

He woke up to the shrill screech of the alarm. Jenny had set that on his phone to the most annoying sound possible, claiming it was the only way he could be woken up. Used to be, not so long ago, that she'd shut off the alarm and kiss him, saying, "Wake up, sleepyhead" in that sexy morning growl.

It felt like that was ages ago.

Finn shut off the noise. Gave his notifications a quick once-over: nothing exciting.

The groaning pipes serenaded his shower. He finished quickly and got dressed in his ugly work uniform.

Jenny was already up, rocking Alice in the kitchen.

She grumbled something like "Good morning" or maybe just "Morning" without the false advertisement, shoved the baby at him, and went to the bathroom.

Finn looked at the tiny, wrinkled face and tried to recognize himself in there—but he could find nothing. Not much of Jenny, either. He supposed all babies seemed the same until they got older. Not that long ago, the one in his hands was a legume-looking thing on the ultrasound. Now it was a person. With needs.

"You sleep okay?" he whispered to the baby. He always whispered to it, thinking that adult voices at full volume must be deafening for its tiny ears. It was a theory that seemed incongruent with the amount of noise the baby produced all on its own.

Alice—Alice, he had to stop thinking of her as "the baby"—squirmed in his arms. He leaned over and kissed her head. She smelled like warm milk and pee. Finn hesitated. If he took the time to change her, he'd have to skip breakfast. And he was hungry.

Alice scrunched up her face and started crying. As shrill as any alarm. Finn's instinct was to recoil, but he powered through it and tried rocking her.

Jenny emerged from the bathroom; her eyes red like she was crying, but it might have just been sleep deprivation.

"What'd you do to her?" she asked unkindly.

"Nothing."

"Give her here."

He gladly did.

She went to change the kid. He poured himself a bowl of cereal. Store-brand, again. They had to economize. Being something of a cereal connoisseur, he missed his Weetabix and Kashi.

Jenny came back into the kitchen, Alice changed and cooing in her arms.

"You working a single or a double today?"

"A single as far as I know."

"See if you can pick up a double, will ya? With the rent due next week, it's gonna be tight."

Finn was sure *he* made the rent this month easy, the money had to be leaking out somewhere on her end. He briefly considered if it was worth an argument, risking a fight. Decided against it.

"I'll see what I can do," he said instead, rinsing the bowl out, and grabbing a banana. "Anything I can take for lunch?"

"There's leftover pizza."

They used to plan out their lunches together. Back when grocery trips were a couples thing and not something one of them did, hurriedly, whenever they found some free time.

He wrapped two slices of pizza in aluminum foil, trying not to cringe at the sight of the two-day-old, congealed cheese. Tossed it into his lunch pail, along with another banana and an off-brand granola bar.

"Don't take the last banana," Jenny said.

"You want me to work a double on nothing?" He didn't mean to say that; it just came out. She shook her head at him with disgust and left the kitchen.

He went to put on his boots.

"Finn, that thing we talked about, take care of it, okay?" Jenny threw at him like a parting gift. He pretended it was a "Have a great day at work, honey!" but didn't quite take.

Work sucked. Every day. So, at least it was consistent. He used to enjoy being on the sales floor way back when. There were different people to talk to all the time, new projects to assist with. He liked to get involved, imagining himself almost as a part of the family, part of the important decision-making process. People came to him looking to improve their home—put in new floors, repair the roofs, build decks--and he helped them.

Now all he did was shift boxes around from point A to point B. Had to get special forklift driving papers for the job. Yeah, it paid more, and Jenny insisted, but boy, was it tedious.

He missed casual interactions, missed being on his feet. All the sitting around was making him flabby. Then again, Jenny never lost the baby weight either, so neither of them was the lean youth they once were.

Finn wondered if she still found him attractive. She was never in the mood anymore. Does attraction fade from disuse? He could still see the pretty girl he met all those years ago beneath the tired matronly woman she'd become, but only briefly, only if he squinted just right, or caught her in a rare unguarded moment of pure joy.

The driving job left too much brain space available, and the thoughts that came to his mind were almost always drab, maudlin, self-pitying even. He wanted to think about other things, fun things like movies, music, and comics, but never seemed to have the bandwidth for it anymore.

The constantly interrupted sleep did a number on his attention span, affecting his grasp of popular things in media, in the news. It felt limiting, isolating.

Did he matter at all anymore? Was he visible?

There was a neighbor kid, a short, skinny thing, who walked around with his shoulders always hunched up, his giant backpack like a carapace, his eyes always on the ground. A turtle kid, Finn thought of him, not unkindly. A kid who looked like he just wanted to disappear. They never exchanged a word, but the kid looked how Finn felt most days.

Finn ate his lunch without reheating it, figuring there was no improvement to be had there. The pizza tasted as it looked but provided the necessary calories. His coworkers were discussing the game. He tried watching it on his phone last night but ended up getting frustrated with the tiny screen and falling asleep. There was nothing he could contribute to the conversation. He ate his banana slowly.

Checked the boards. No chance of a second shift that day. Signed up for the one a couple of days away. The singles wore him out; the doubles made him feel like a machine. And really, the only reason his job still required people to perform it was because the robotic advancements were not up to par. His was a robot's job if he ever saw one. Mindless, personality-less, tedious, repetitive. One day he shall be made obsolete, and then what? Hopefully, Alice will be older by then. Hopefully, Jenny will have a job by then. But what would *he* do? Who'd want a middle-aged forklift operator? Would he become useless?

Jerry, his boss, approached him, crashing Finn's train of thought to a sudden stop. They started at the same time, and Finn was technically older and more experienced, but Jerry knew how to play the game.

"Finn."

"Jerry."

They exchanged the prerequisite manly nods.

"You doing good?"

"Yeah, thanks. You?"

"Good, good. But I'll tell you, what would push that good into great was if everyone made their quota."

Finn frowned. "Did I not meet my quota this month?"

"Just barely, Finn, just barely. We wanna see you clear that hurdle, not almost graze it."

Finn wanted to choke that smarmy smile right off Jerry's face. He steadied himself.

"I'm sorry, I didn't realize, Jerry. I'll push harder. Got an extra shift this week."

"Yeah, see, we can't really do that now, can we? Give out extra shifts. Cause that would be rewarding the sort of behavior we're trying to discourage."

"Right, but I am making the quota. So, technically …"

"So, technically, we're gonna go with giving out extra shifts to people who are well above their quota, right? Like that makes sense, doesn't it? I'm sure you see that it does."

It was always something with Jerry. Every single time. If not an actual infraction to flag, then an almost one. He never seemed to leave Finn alone. A blood-boiling, nagging presence with all these small, meaningless displays of power.

Back in the day, whenever his temper got the better of him, Jenny used to tell him to count. Just count to ten before saying or doing something. Finn made it to five.

He could feel his fingers curling into a fist and forced himself to relax them.

"Sure, Jerry," he said. "I understand."

"I'm glad we had this chat. Come see me if you have any questions. OK?" Who knew a simple OK could sound so patronizing.

Finn nodded. Tried to smile, but who knows how that came out looking. Probably closer to a scowl.

Jerry tapped the table twice with his fingers, then walked away.

Finn imagined his receding figure as a target practice sheet. One bullet after another …

Long as it felt, the day ended eventually. Finn clocked out and headed home.

The drive was slow, the car as reluctant and moody as ever. As if it was doing him a favor getting him from place to place and never wanted him to forget it.

He walked in and was accosted by the baby wailing.

"Why is she crying like that?" he asked Jenny.

"I don't know. She's your daughter, too, why don't you go see?"

He went and looked. The baby was in her crib. Her diaper was clean. She appeared to be well-fed. No real reason to scream like that. He tried rocking her, it got him nowhere. The wailing dopplered in and out of his ears, making him nauseated, so he put her back down, and came back to the kitchen.

Jenny was making something that looked like spaghetti.

"You hungry?"

"Starving," he said.

"Finish this, will ya?" she shoved a wooden stirring spoon at him and went to see to the baby.

Finn stirred the concoction unenthusiastically, eventually putting the entire thing together. He was never much of a cook; the only thing he made well was pancakes. It used to be a joke between them, now it didn't matter.

The sauce came out burned, the vegetables underdone, the noodles rubbery. They scarfed it all down anyway, merely for the sake of calories.

Their conversation was stilted, halting. Mostly questions she asked and responses he grumbled.

"Did you get an extra shift?"

"Not yet."

"When are you going to take care of that thing?"

"Soon."

And then, an infinite number of things about the baby, though the baby did the least out of the three of them.

"I think I'll go for a walk," he said, pushing the empty plate away.

She looked at him with something like resentment.

"What?" he asked.

"I've been with Alice all day. You don't think *I* might want a walk? Some alone time?"

He shrugged. They've been down this road before, had the same conversation over and over, almost verbatim. Each thought the other had it easier. A neverending match, an unwinnable war. It didn't matter, he was going.

Finn left his dish on the table as a tiny act of rebellion. Changed out of his work clothes into a pair of old jeans and a hooded sweatshirt, stuck his feet into his sneakers, and left. He could feel Jenny angrily glaring daggers at his back. He told himself it didn't matter.

Finn went to the park across the way. It was the only decent thing about their apartment complex as far as he was concerned. The park was never crowded, not at the times he was there. A few walkers trying to impress their pedometers. Some people with dogs. Mostly quiet, though.

It was where he went to get high—his last remaining vice. What was the point of living in a state with legalized marijuana and not taking advantage of it? He would have killed for that sort of freedom as a kid when he first came to love weed. Jenny used to partake too, though she was too high (the wrong kind) and mighty about it these days.

Finn lit up a neatly rolled doobie and let the mellow settle into his bones. Nothing relaxed him anymore after a long day, not like this. There were places in the park he liked to frequent, a bench by the pond being his favorite. The metal signage proclaimed it was dedicated to the love of someone's life named Arnold. He liked to imagine the couple who shared a love worthy of a commemorative bench, but all that came to mind was Schwarzenegger and maybe one of his 1980s costars. Depending on how high Finn got, his thoughts wandered in different directions. At best, positively cinematic. At worst, straight-up weird. Either way, it beat reality hands down. Every single time.

The notion that these brief weed-induced reveries were the happiest moments of his life depressed Finn. He tried not to think about it. Just enjoy the peace and quiet.

Tobey.

He shut off the alarm and thought how strange it was that he had nowhere to go. What sort of a punishment was suspension, anyway? Most kids hated school. Being punished should include more school not less.

The morning sun was blasting straight through the cheap paper blinds of his bedroom window. It looked like it was going to be a nice day.

By the time he made it downstairs, both of his parents were gone. There were two wrinkled twenty-dollar bills in the middle of the kitchen table under the napkin holder. A pink Post-it note stuck to them read, "Buy some groceries. Only groceries. Bring receipt and change."

This was his parents' idea of teaching him adult responsibilities. The word "only" was underlined twice. Tobey tried to remember the last time he splurged their money on something other than food. There was that comic he bought a while back. Was that it?

He turned the Post-it over. There was nothing more. It wasn't even signed, though he could recognize his mom's jagged handwriting and even fake it pretty well for when he needed to.

Tobey made himself a large bowl of cereal and took it into the living room. Found a nature documentary on TV to get lost in.

According to television, the world was vast, magnificent, exciting. In Dolby surround sound and technicolor. Tobey would just have to take its word for it—he'd never been anywhere.

Well, there was the trip his parents took years ago in a rented Winnebago to see the Grand Canyon. He was there, but too young to remember. The photos showed them all smiling, they seemed happy. He wished he had any recollection of it.

Now his parents did something they referred to as staycations, meaning that on their days off they stayed put on the couch, flipping the channels and ordering takeout.

The nature shows absorbed Tobey completely. He was happily lost in the savannahs of Africa for hours, but it was difficult to relax completely, knowing that Mom or Dad could show up at any moment, and then there would be questions. They'd want to know why he wasn't at school. Or at least, why he hadn't gone to buy groceries if he was home all day.

With a sigh of regret, he shut off the TV, washed his cereal bowl, got dressed, pocketed the money, and set off for the store.

The sun was beating down on him like a schoolyard bully. He wished he still had his sunglasses, but they broke during one of the recent shoves from Jason and his pals. Squinting the entire way, Tobey made it to the store; a mile and a half took about half an hour to walk.

His purchases were simple: a loaf of bread, a jar of peanut butter, some ramen, a bag of apples, a hand of bananas, sliced cheese, pasta noodles and sauce his parents liked, a couple of cans of baked beans. He tried to stick to store-brand things or whatever was on sale.

Everything he bought fit inside his backpack, which he hoisted with some effort onto his shoulders. Back out into the sun he went.

There was an adorable puppy leashed outside to the biking racks. A blue heeler mix of some sort. Tobey knew all about dogs, different breeds and all that. He wanted one ever since he could remember. About the same amount of time as his parents had been saying no to the idea.

Tobey kneeled down, the weight of the backpack pushing on him like gravity. The puppy, grateful for the attention, came up to him shyly, then licked the extended hand with a warm tongue. Whoever owned this cute fuzzball shouldn't have left him outside in this heat. Tobey got his water bottle and poured some out into a cupped hand, holding it out for the puppy to lap up. Did it twice. Petted the little guy.

How nice it must be to have a dog; someone who looks at you with such love and kindness. Tobey let himself briefly imagine untying the puppy and taking him home. It would never work, of course, but what a lovely dream to …

"Oh, lookie here. It's Mopey Tobey, making new friends. Hiya, Tobes."

He didn't have to turn around, he would have recognized Jason's sneering voice anywhere.

Jason leaned over to pet the dog, who, demonstrating remarkably good judgment of character, moved away from him. Jason stuck out his hand the way you're supposed to, and the puppy gave a tiny snarl.

"Stupid dog," Jason spit. And then kicked the puppy. Not full force, but enough to make it yelp in fear and cower.

Tobey rushed to pick the puppy up, to try to calm him. The little guy was shivering. Unused to the violence, unlike the boy holding him.

"Lemme see him," Jason said. "Set him down."

Tobey intended to do no such thing.

He tried curling into himself, with his backpack as a carapace, hoping against hope to be left alone. Either way, he'd keep the puppy safe.

Strong hands pulled at his backpack, trying to pull him up by it. Then there was a kick. And another. Full force kicks this time, with Jason holding nothing back.

Tobey felt his ribs catch fire, but he didn't let go of the puppy.

His backpack was ripped away from him and tossed to the ground. He didn't dare look, mindful to keep his face covered—face bruises were always the toughest to explain away and lasted the longest.

The beating felt like it took forever, but it was probably mere minutes.

He heard footsteps, shouting, and then it was over. The kicking stopped. Jason was gone.

"You okay, kid?"

Tobey opened his eyes; it took effort. His eyelashes felt glued together by unspilled tears.

The man kneeling before him was eyeing him with concern. He seemed to be about his parents' age and wore bottle-lensed glasses and a brightly patterned Hawaiian shirt.

Tobey tried answering, but no words came out, so he settled for something like a nod.

The puppy came up and licked his cheek. His tongue was sandpapery, but it still felt nice.

"Were you protecting my dog? Did that jerk try to steal him?"

Tobey tried for another nod.

The man frowned. "Well, you took a hell of a beating there, sonny. Should I call someone for you?"

Tobey couldn't even imagine explaining all of this to his parents. He shook his head.

"I'm okay," he said finally. Looking around he saw that his backpack was torn, the groceries strewn every which way on the pavement. Some crushed.

"Can I give you a ride home or something?"

Tobey looked at the man. The man seemed uncomfortable, like he just wanted to take his dog and leave. Like he didn't want to get involved with some strange kid. So, Tobey let him off the hook by getting up—slowly, ever so slowly, his ribs screaming at him—and beginning to gather his things off the ground.

The man helped, collecting the now-bruised apples. Red Delicious had turned red and blue. Tobey was probably turning black and blue right now, too, he could practically feel the bruises forming.

The man handed him his groceries. "Well, thanks for looking out for my dog, kid. Take care of yourself." He patted him on the shoulder awkwardly and left. Obviously not a man who spent a lot of time around children.

Easier said than done, Tobey thought, this taking care of oneself. One of his backpack's shoulder straps was torn, so he shifted his balance to carry the entire thing on one side only. The walk back took forever.

At least his parents were still gone by the time he made it home. Tobey put away the groceries, left the change and the receipt in the same place he'd found the money that morning.

He went to the bathroom, lifted his now-dirty shirt, and tried counting the bruises that blossomed fiercely across his torso. Some of his ribs were likely broken. He'd feel it if he laughed but there was nothing to laugh about. He knew from reading that there was nothing one could do for broken ribs but wait.

He went back to the kitchen, made a sandwich, and ate it slowly, without appetite. Then put more water into his water bottle, grabbed his book, and went into the woods.

He didn't realize he was crying until he was safely ensconced in his favorite spot, leaning against the giant tree stump. For a moment, he thought the droplets on the pages were rain, but then he realized his cheeks were wet. Oh well, he thought, if he had to cry, this was the best place to do it.

One of Mr. Mooney's books was all about folklore, myths, and legends from around the world. It had this character in it, the Green Man, the wild man of the woods. The Green Man showed up everywhere, across times and continents, from ancient mythology to *The Wind in the Willows*. He was someone associated with spring and rebirth.

Tobey often fantasized about the Green Man living in these woods. What would meeting him be like? Did he grant wishes like a genie? Could he offer rebirth? Tobey thought that sounded like a great idea—a second chance to be someone better. Stronger. Happier.

Would they be able to have a conversation? Or a celebration?

It was Tobey's birthday today. An occasion no one but him seemed to remember or care about. So probably not much to celebrate there. No gifts. Nothing like that. His bruised body was screaming at him to lower it down onto the mossy ground and let it be. He obliged gladly.

From this perspective, the tree stump appeared even larger and more imposing. The opening in it looked like the mouth of a strange dark cave. Tobey didn't know what possessed him to reach up and stick his arm in there. He rummaged around the stump's innards and came away with a wrapped package. It was only about the size of a book and much heavier.

Tobey let himself imagine it was the Green Man's birthday gift to him. Someone remembered after all.

The wrapping was done hastily, using not gift paper but something like an old vinyl tablecloth. Funny, he would have thought the Green Man would use leaves or something like that.

Tobey held the bundle in his hands, speculating on its contents. Then he slowly unwrapped it.

Stared at it.

It was a gift he would never have expected. Or asked for. One he wasn't even sure what to do with. Maybe the Green Man knew something he didn't. The gift certainly wasn't something Tobey could bring home with him. Maybe he'd leave it there, in the stump. Maybe just knowing it was there, should he ever need it, was enough.

Finn.

The car wouldn't start in the morning. He tried everything, then gave up, and ordered an Uber, cringing at the expense of it. He was still late to work, mere minutes, but Jerry clocked it. Gave him that look, like, we'll talk all about this later.

Finn sighed. There was nothing he could do. Not about the car, not about Jerry. There seemed to be more and more things out of his control lately. Was that what adulthood was all about?

He wished Ty was still around, but no, his best friend of nearly two decades just had to fall in love with a California girl. A romance straight out of pop songs. Of course, he moved there, who wouldn't? The year-round sunshine alone was enough to convince anyone. He didn't blame Ty, just missed him. They tried staying in touch, but that sort of thing never worked. Long-distance friendships weren't meant to be; long-distance anything, really. Relationships were a thing of proximity. The out-of-sight-out-of-mind factor was too strong to override with sentimentality alone.

They still exchanged an occasional email, Ty and him, but those were fewer and farther between. Ty had no desire to come for a visit, and Finn had no means to. So that was that. And he was never any good at making new friends. Never had the knack for it, not even as he watched all his old friends drift away to marriages and fatherhoods and far-away jobs.

At least he had Jenny, but lately there was no talking to her. Even if he could afford it, he hated the idea of talking to a shrink, so that wasn't an option either. Nothing to do but hold his words in, hold his thoughts in, bottle everything up. Grin and bear it.

Jerry found him at lunch. Leaned over his table as Finn was trying to enjoy his sawdust-flavored granola bar. Sporting too much cologne and a bright white short-sleeve button-down with its lower buttons straining over his bowling ball gut, Jerry appeared to be in rare form today.

Funny thing was that Finn could trace this animosity back to high school. How stupid was it to hold on to a grudge for that long? Finn could hardly remember what it was even about back then. Something ridiculous, he was sure. Apparently, Jerry never forgot. And now, he never let Finn forget it either.

"Late again."

"Car broke down."

"And the dog ate your homework too, I suppose."

Finn wanted to wipe off Jerry's condescending smile with his fist.

"I'll make up the time by staying later."

"But that just isn't how time really works, is it?" Jerry's forehead was shiny with sweat. He always sweated too much when he got worked up, even in the rigidly air-conditioned warehouse.

"You know, this is a good job," he went on. "I have a lot of people applying for it. People who know how to budget their time."

Finn took a deep steadying sigh. "Look, I'm sorry. My car really did break down. I'm working my ass off, I really am. Check my numbers. I'm really trying here, Jerry."

The fat man steepled his fingers as if to signify some sort of serenity. "And yet we keep having these conversations, Finn."

"I need this job."

"I'm sure you do."

Finn held eye contact until the other man looked away.

"Get a haircut, too, will you? When you put on this uniform, you represent the company. You want to look your best. Makes sense, right?"

Finn's nails were digging bloody crescents into his palms as he nodded and said he would. He kept his fists below the table where Jerry couldn't see them. He thought that if he raised them and hit the man, he might never stop.

None of his coworkers ever interfered in these conversations. Finn couldn't really blame them; they weren't his friends, hardly knew each other. He was meaningless to them, just another body in the forklift's seat.

Eventually, Jerry left.

Eventually, the workday ended.

An Uber home was an expense too far. Finn walked. It took hours. At least, it seemed like hours. He was in no hurry. The simple thoughtless motion of putting one foot in front of the other was calming him, steadying him.

When he got home, the baby was crying. Jenny had a litany of complaints. Same as always. He tuned them out, went to the bathroom, and engaged the flimsy lock.

He'd do everything they wanted, he decided, everything they asked for. He'd do his best, even if, once again, his best would be judged and found wanting.

Finn picked up a hair trimming kit. A nice one Jenny got him for his birthday a few years ago, back when he was flirting with the idea of facial hair.

He stuck a plastic attachment on the main shaver tool, plugged it in, and went to town on his shaggy mane until all that's left was a uniform centimeter-long buzz.

When it was over, he took in a sink full of hair and the stranger in the mirror. The sink would have to be cleaned up, and the stranger's face would take some getting used to. He'd never worn his hair that short. The greys were gone from his temples and his ears appeared larger and more stuck-out. He couldn't tell if he looked younger, but he did feel lighter.

He reached up to shift one of the bathroom ceiling panels sideways. The spongy-feeling water-stained thing slid easily. Finn rummaged his arm up there until his fingers closed in on the object he was after.

His grandfather's gun. An old Colt. The man was long gone but his weapon remained, looking as good as the day it was made.

Finn loved his grandpa. Grandpa was a character. Only his parents said it with something like contempt, and Finn meant it genuinely. Grandpa got messed up by the war, had nightmares that sent him howling at the moon and searching for solace at the bottom of a bottle. But he also told the best stories, drove his Mustang the fastest, and was never skimpy with pocket cash.

The old man lived in a broken-down single-wide, worked on cars, and hunted when the spirit moved him. Taught Finn to shoot behind that trailer amid the untrimmed grass bordered by the encroaching state forest, practicing on the never-ending supply of empty beer cans.

When Grandpa finally drank himself into the next world, Finn's parents seemed relieved. Finn was devastated. The gun, this gun, was his only inheritance. One his parents were reluctant to pass on but did anyway.

Finn never fired it. Never wanted to. He took care of it, oiled it, kept it in good condition the way Grandpa showed him, but that was all. The thing was mainly of sentimental value. Jenny used to get it, but now that the baby was here, she wanted the gun out of the house.

Why? he'd argue. It wasn't like the baby was likely to find it or ever get to it. How would that even work?

But Finn was tired of arguing. He knew he was never going to win. The path of least resistance was beckoning, and he wanted things to be easy for a change.

Jenny had been asking him to take care of it for a while now. Okay, well, he was going to do it now.

The gun was wrapped in some old oilcloth. Only a simple bundle, only a family inheritance. Finn never even thought of it as a deadly weapon. Never considered how many lives it might have ended.

He came out of the bathroom. Plowed right past Jenny and to the front door.

"See, I'm taking care of it," he told her before leaving, gesturing to the package in his hands. "Just how you wanted."

She looked at him with shock. Maybe it was his new hair. Either way, he didn't stick around to find out.

Finn went to the car without thinking, before remembering it was dead. Where would he drive to, anyway? He didn't know the proper gun disposal protocols. Did it involve turning the weapon over to the police? Well, he was definitely not doing that.

If Ty was around, he'd ask him to hold on to it for him. All he needed, he thought, was a place to stash it. Not an ideal solution, but a good-enough one.

His feet carried him to the park across the street. He walked toward his favorite bench as if on autopilot. Sat there for a while. Just him, his grandpa's gun, and the ghost of Arnold.

The thoughts that came to his mind were all dark. Perhaps it was the gun in his hands making him contemplate a single easy solution to every problem he had. Almost too easy. That was the scariest thing about it. Squeeze the trigger and enjoy the silence, however brief, of no one telling you what to do, how to do it, or that you weren't doing it right. An unimaginable, terrifying sort of freedom at too high a cost.

Finn shook his head, forcibly clearing his mind like an Etch A Sketch screen.

Checked his phone.

It was his birthday. It seemed he was the only one aware of it. There were no texts. No emails. Nothing. He remembered how big of a deal birthdays used to be. The parties he had as a kid. The wild bashes of his misbegotten youth. The fuss Jenny used to make over the occasions resulting in anything from surprise parties to trampoline park trips. Now, there was just nothing—radio silence. If that wasn't a sign of getting old, he didn't know what was.

What did it matter, anyway? he thought. None of it mattered. Just another day, same as any other in a steadily soul-obliterating procession of them that his life had become.

Oh no, too maudlin. He caught himself. Changed gears.

Finn felt restless, so he got up and started moving aimlessly, his steps plodding and heavy. It had occurred to him that he must have done more walking today than in most of the previous days combined.

Some sort of a desperation-based exercise plan, he joked to himself, grimly. At this rate, he'd be fit in no time.

He'd have to go back home to deal with Jenny, to deal with the car, to deal with going back to work the next day and seeing Jerry's smug face again, but for now, there was just him and the trees, and he tried to let it be enough.

The tree stump, when he came across it, startled him. It was huge, for one thing. The tree it must have once supported would have towered over anything in its vicinity. It looked strange, ancient, prehistoric somehow. Like it has been there forever and knew every secret; saw others come and go and remained the same. Scarred by weather, time, violence, and yet still standing, its presence as solid as ever. Finn could only wish for that sort of resilience.

The front of the stump was split, the bark opening up like a hungry maw with only darkness behind it.

Finn shook his head. Of course, it was perfect. No one would look for it here. No one probably knew this place existed. The park was never busy along the beaten path, and off it, it was practically empty.

Finn kneeled, reached his arm into the stump, and placed the package inside. There, safe and sound.

He straightened out with his knees popping like firecrackers and brushed the mossy earth from his pants. The stump would keep his secret, he was sure of it.

Finn looked around, trying to commit the place to memory. It was nice here, peaceful, quiet. He thought maybe he should come back in the future, get high and think some thoughts. But then again, there were no benches in sight, and he felt too old to enjoy sitting on the ground.

He tapped the stump with his fingers---the sharpness of the bark nearly cutting him. Defensive by nature, he smiled to himself. A perfect spot.

He'd remember it, he thought, if he should ever need the gun again.

It felt like power. The weight of the thing. It's deadly purpose. It felt like a permission to never again be the subject of abuse. It felt like a way to say, "No. Enough!" and mean it.

The bastard was at it again. For no reason but because he could. Thoughtless cruel words, death by a thousand cuts, over and over again. But not today.

Today he was making a stand.

The mere sight of the gun made them go quiet. He thought it would be enough—this display of power. Thought he would just brandish the weapon, show that he meant business, and that would be it. But things didn't quite work out as planned.

Suddenly, there was shouting and posturing and threats. And more threats. The next thing he knew he was shooting. Squeezing the trigger not pulling it, the way they always said to do it in TV shows. And it was so loud. Deafeningly loud.

The bodies. The gun was turning people into bodies. Were they always that fragile? How could they have walked around the world throwing such force around when all it took to stop them was …

Blood had a smell. Like old pennies. Blood had a smell, and bullets had a smell, but that one he couldn't place. It made his eyes sting. Well, something did anyway. There were tears in his eyes, he could barely see. Just kept squeezing that trigger. Until there were no more bullets.

It got quiet for a moment. A perfect sort of quiet—like the sound forgot how to be.

And then the screaming began.

Flamingos

At first, I liked the plastic flamingos out front. Thought they were a nice homey touch. But then Kayla showed up with a housewarming cactus and told me the flamingos were a secret code to let people know swingers lived in that house.

So now, that's sullied. I can't even look at the front yard without the unwanted and unwelcome images of Chuck and Brandi Mitten spreading their love around.

I mean, ugh. The thought makes me want to take a shower. The Mittens are not a sexy-looking family. They are both perfectly round and cheerful in a way that makes me think of the Teletubbies. Same fondness for primary colors. Their last name is Mitten for crying out loud, a word likely never whispered in throes of passion.

As landlords, they are great. Not too fussy, not too invasive, easy to deal with.

I was reluctant to rent the apartment, initially, having never lived in a setup like this. They call it the in-law unit, though who'd want their in-laws that close is beyond me. It's basically a self-contained part of the house with its own kitchen and bathroom.

I had some privacy concerns, but then again, my old apartment building—a grey multi-unit box that was never anyone's house—was light on privacy too, owing to the paper-thin walls and obnoxious too-young-too-loud neighbors. So, I took a chance. Tried something different.

The Mittens advertised their apartment at a surprisingly affordable rate, and I managed to squeak past their rather relaxed credit and reference check, so now here I was. In a nice apartment that was part of a nice house that belonged to a nice couple … who were potentially swingers.

Mind you, I'm not a prude. I'm all about live and let live. I'm mostly just taken aback by this information. And also, how and why does Kayla know things like that?

"Because, stupid, I read," she tells me with a smirk.

That's a deceptive statement. Her ADD won't let her get through a book, but she tends to spiral into these insane online searches and spend hours looking up the most random things on the internet.

Without the invention of the world wide web, where would Kayla be? I sometimes think in my more spiteful moments. With it, she's a trivia genius, a master of useless information. She'd kill it if she ever got on *Jeopardy*, but she gets stressed out and tanks the online tests.

So now she calls me stupid. And I let her. After all, I only have one sister; besides, I'm pretty sure most days she means the epithet affectionately.

"I can't picture them swinging," I tell her.

"And I can't picture this cactus surviving your care, but stranger things …" She looks around and plops it on the kitchen windowsill. "Plus, I couldn't just show up empty-handed, so there."

This is officially my housewarming party. I got us some boxed wine and a supermarket-baked box of cupcakes. The wine was on sale, the cupcakes weren't.

"So how do you like it?" Kayla asks. She sits on the couch, grabs a sprinkled vanilla, and takes an enthusiastic bite. As if she needs more sugar. Her leg is already jogging up and down like she's winding up to take off.

"It's good. What? No. Seriously. It's good."

She nods and studies my décor. Which is to say she disapprovingly eyes my mostly empty walls and plain serviceable furniture. "Love what you've done with the place."

"Thanks," I tell her. "I worked really hard at it." There, sarcasm cuts both ways.

In my defense, the place came furnished, and what the Mittens have in here is way nicer than the things I used to own. So, I put up my crap on Marketplace, got a few bucks for it, and moved in here with one carload. Just clothes, books, kitchen things, etc.

But no, I've yet to figure out what to put on the walls and where. I have a few prints that I taped to the walls of my old apartment, afraid to use a nail and a hammer and bring the entire place down. Not sure they'd work in here. The Mittens' furniture is all real wood, not crappy particle board; seems like the art should be at least framed to hang in this apartment.

Needless to say, I haven't gotten around to it. Don't have a good excuse either.

I take a sip of wine and study the cactus. It's small and has a bright yellow bloom atop a squat green body. Kind of a cupcake shape, but also it reminds me of a knit hat I had as a kid. I like it.

"I like it," I tell Kayla. "What kind is it?"

"A Star cactus," she says, licking the wrapper the same way she always does. Waste not, want not, our mother would be proud. "Astrophytum Asterias, also known as a sea urchin cactus or starfish cactus. Just—" She takes a sip of wine to wash the cupcake down "—make sure it gets plenty of sun."

"I will."

She eyes me skeptically.

Kayla is the oldest, meaning she has known me my entire life. I cannot say the same; there were five years before I was born where my sister's presence is purely hypothetical, shabbily supported by a few snapshots. Our mother didn't like taking pictures. Kayla and I have always been the least photographed kids we know.

Age difference or not, we're close. She knows me the way one knows their own scars. It's mostly comforting, sometimes annoying. I wouldn't trade it for the world.

Letting yourself be known by others is an intimate art I can't seem to master. My ex used to call me China, because of all my walls. Kayla used to call him Greenland because she said it was like his brain—all this empty space with hardly anyone there. He thought it was because his last name was Green, proving her right.

Needless to say, the relationship didn't work out with or without my sister's approval.

But my sister knows me. And also has a freakishly good memory. So she likely remembers that time in elementary school when I decided to reinvent myself and made everyone call me Star.

The reinvention didn't work; I don't think those things ever do. It takes a lot of willpower and internal fortitude to change who you are. Most people just stay themselves. The path of least resistance may not be paved in gold, but those bricks are mud-soft, making it so you could just stay there forever, maybe take a nap too.

All to say that I appreciate the cactus gift and intend to do my best to keep it alive.

"How's work?" Kayla asks.

I groan. It works for zombies *and* most conversations about my nine-to-five.

"How's yours?"

"I met this homeless man who might have been a wizard."

Despite never reading books, Kayla works at a library. Not as one of those people with master's degrees who sit behind the desk all day, but as a lowly grunt who does checkouts and shelving. She enjoys being able to move around, it gives her boundless energy some outlet.

"Don't all homeless men kind of look like wizards who have fallen on hard times?"

"Chrys." She looks at me with mock horror, then guffaws.

"What?" I shrug. "They do. The ones around here anyway."

"Well, we get a variety of them at work. I swear I once saw one that looked like Jeff Goldblum."

"No, you didn't. No one looks like Jeff Goldblum. That's the quintessential appeal of Jeff Goldblum."

One of my unframed prints is a shirtless Ian Malcolm reclining seductively, mullet and all. That one I did hang up above my bed. It's only partly ironic.

Kayla winks and sips her wine. Growing up, these boxes with spouts were always around. Mom would call them her "juice boxes." I thought they were, so I tried it once. The taste was so nasty, I still remember gagging. Took me decades to try wine again; now it's just about all I drink. But I don't like the way it feels, like a cycle repeating itself, like some uncontrollable predestination.

Of course, neither Kayla nor I drink as much as our mother did, but still, it unsettles me. I wish life was nicer and kinder and easier to get through sober.

"So did he grant you a wish or something?"

"Who?"

"The wizard dude."

"Ha, no. That would have been nice." Another sip. "He just pissed the chair and left a couple of books with their spines damaged beyond repair."

That's big city libraries for you. That's why I stopped going.

The one near my new place is small, quaint. Quiet. It smells like books and books alone. I told Kayla all about it. She said it sounded lifeless.

You'd think we were these devoted urbanites, but no, we grew up in a trailer park thoughtlessly dropped into the empty space between the city's outskirts and its suburbs. It was some kind of an industrial zone with all these crazy alien-looking constructions lit up day and night, regurgitating white toxic clouds into the ether. Who knows what they allowed to seep into the ground or dumped in the anemic-looking creek that ran along the trailer park's edge?

It wasn't a nice place to grow up, but we didn't realize it until much later. As a kid, you sort of just accept your lot and make the best of it.

Which is funny, because as an adult you spend forever trying to figure out that very same trick.

I don't remember our dad; he took off before my memories began forming in earnest.

Kayla does, though. She says he smelled like cigarettes and machine oil, even after a shower. That he was tall and cooked perfect toasted cheese sandwiches. That he told wild rambling stories that often didn't have a point or an ending but were still fun. That he had a shaved head and facial hair like a Viking.

The man she describes is clearer to me than the faded image from the old photos, so that's the one I hold onto.

Kayla says Mom and him fought. A lot. Loudly. And then he left. He sent postcards for a while. Sometimes small gifts. His writing was indecipherable; his gifts random. When I was ten and Kayla was fifteen, he crashed his motorcycle and died. His new wife wrote to tell us.

Kayla says Mom drank and furiously ranted about getting ripped off. How this new wife must have inherited his life insurance money or something. Though we never thought he had any.

The new wife sent us some of his things: a leather string necklace with a metal pendant and an old lighter. There may have been more, but those were what we got to keep.

Mom got worse after that, according to Kayla. Angrier, more reckless. She drove drunk and brought strangers home. Our small trailer got dirtier and louder. We spent as much time out and with friends as we could. The moment Kayla turned eighteen, she left and took me with her.

From the trailer's ratty couch, our mother stared daggers at us as we packed, chain smoking and mumbling to herself something about our ingratitude. Next year, one of her cigarettes started a fire in her sleep. The trailer went up like a roman candle, which was about the only time a neighborhood like that saw fireworks.

Kayla did some paperwork, officially becoming my guardian. And here we are, all these years later. Still close.

In fact, renting out here was something of a bold move. Geographically speaking, this is the farthest we've ever lived apart. But I'm right by the train station, and the trains are surprisingly nice, much better than city buses. So Kayla can still visit.

She doesn't drive. Says she doesn't want to. Truth is, she likely can't afford to, but it doesn't matter so long as I have a car.

"Wanna walk around town, see the sights?"

'Sure." She grins. "We can count all the flamingos they got."

We're not drunk, merely pleasantly buzzed. The cupcakes have absorbed some of the wine.

"Your bathroom is nice," Kayla says. "You even got your own laundry."

"I know, it's totally luxurious. I can't believe I went all my life without it."

Growing up, I don't ever remember our washer working. I don't think we even had a dryer. When Mom cared, she threw our things into the bathtub and halfheartedly swirled them around in bath bubbles. She had these weirdly strong, ropey arms and she'd wring them out making audible grunts. For some reason, I remember that. Then we hung them all around the trailer to dry and for a while at least, the place would smell pleasantly of artificial strawberry or lemon. All of our clothes were always stretched out and misshapen in those days.

Afterward, it was a string of laundromats.

The sheer joy of having your own washer and dryer in one neat stackable unit right in your bathroom is incalculable.

Kayla slips back into her flats and fixes her hair in the hallway mirror.

"Come on, Chrys."

Most people don't know how to spell my name or that it's short for Chrystal. Our mother had named us both in a truly spectacular trailer trash fashion, but I definitely got the shorter end of the stick there. I even thought about legally changing it, just never got around to it.

I check to make sure the stove's off, and all the lights, and all the major appliances.

A friend studying to be a therapist told me once that it was a leftover from living with my mom; she used to leave things on all the time, all around the trailer. There'd be burners on, and lit cigarettes left lying around, forgotten. I guess I was an anxious little kid.

But these days I tell myself I'm just being a conscientious tenant and a responsible adult who minds their bills.

Though we both drink, at least neither of us smokes. A small mercy, that.

I can't stand the smell of nicotine at all. Kayla can tolerate it—and I figure it's because it reminds her of our dad—but she doesn't crave it.

Originally, there might have been a way to get to my floor from the main house, but the Mittens didn't show me it. For all practical considerations, there is a set of metal stairs, leading up from the ground to a small landing outside of the door that opens up directly into my apartment. So much more convenient than traipsing through their house. Especially if they *are* swingers.

Once we're on the street, I orient us toward the town's thoroughfare. It's where all the shops and restaurants are; I figure Kayla will want to see that.

I plan on showing her the local library, too. Just so she knows they are not all like hers. Or like the dumpy moldy one we could just about bike to from our trailer.

We only see one other set of decorative flamingos as we walk.

"Ah, the poor Mittens," Kayla says. "Not a lot of local choices."

"I seriously don't think they are swingers. I bet they just like the decorative aspect. I mean, I do. It's like … homey."

"Uh-huh," my sister says absentmindedly, studying the window at a real estate office. "Sheesh, look what it costs to live around here. And then I can't even imagine what the taxes must be. It's like you're paying for space *and* history. Madness. You know why you think that?"

Classic Kayla, not a hint of a segue, conversations perpetually set on shuffle mode.

"Why I think what?"

"Why you think flamingos are homey," Kayla clarifies. "It's cause Mom had them."

"She did *not*."

"Did too. I remember them. All half-broken and bent out of shape."

I strain my memory for the next few blocks until finally an image surfaces. It's blurry like a photo only halfway developed. Thin spindly metal legs, sun-faded plastic bodies, and … red beaks?

"Why'd they have red beaks?" I ask my sister, as always relying on her to clear the cobwebs of my childhood memories.

She gives me the strangest look. "They didn't have red beaks, stupid. They had normal beaks. Yellow with black tips."

"Are you sure?"

"Yes, I'm sure. Mmm, look at this candy shop. Should we go treat ourselves?"

It's like we didn't just split an entire box of cupcakes.

We go in. She gets some things in bright wrappers, but I can't stop thinking about the flamingos and their beaks.

Only once we're outside, does something else occur to me.

"K, I hate to ask, but was Mom a … you know?"

"Nah." Kayla laughs. 'Dude, gross. Besides, I think you have to be part of a couple for that, and she only got them after Dad left. Actually, I think she stole them from the Mulvaneys down the street because they told on her parking illegally or something. Yeah, that's it." She punctuates her point with a candy wrapper. "That's it."

"So she just stole them and then proudly displayed them in our yard?"

"Well, I don't know about proudly, and I wouldn't necessarily call that patch of dirt a yard, but yeah. It was like her "fuck you" to them. To all of them."

"Damn."

I don't know why we talk about the past so much. It's neither interesting nor exciting. Not even particularly nice, but it's like we're stuck and just keep returning to the same place, like moths to a flame. Like murderers to the scenes of their crimes.

"Now the Mulvaneys might have swung," Kayla says with a wink.

I try to remember them.

"Weren't they …?"

"Old as dirt. And fat as fuck?"

"Um, yeah."

"See, you do remember some things," she says, and we laugh. And then we can't stop laughing. Until we're red in the face.

People are looking at us like we've lost our minds. In a town as poshly polite as this, we seem like madwomen.

"Ah, good old Camelot." Kayla sighs once we're calmed down.

Yeah, to add insult to injury, that was our trailer park's name: Camelot Park. Arthur must have rolled over—and over and over—in his mythical grave.

I'm done thinking about it for one day.

"There's a Chinese place down the street," I say. "Wanna get takeout? "

"Takeout? Why don't we just dine-in?"

I shrug. "Let's dine in then."

"Ooh, fancy," Kayla singsongs. "You buying?"

"Sure."

"In that case," she links her arm through mine, "lead the way."

General Tso doesn't disappoint. "By far my favorite general," Kayla jokes, stealing my fortune cookie. She doesn't care about the corny predictions; she genuinely likes the taste of the cookies.

We stick around for a while. The place is nice, bougier than the one we used to go to back in the city.

Eventually, I pay, tipping precisely 20% under Kayla's supervision. She's the one who taught me all these small practical life skills. Now, funnily enough, the shoe's on the other foot. I'm the one with a better job living in a nicer place. I'm the one who pays for Chinese food.

Until I turned eighteen, we lived in a shoebox apartment above a pizza parlor. The place always smelled like cheese and not in a good way. Kayla juggled several part-time jobs including late shifts downstairs. Our diet in those days consisted primarily of forgotten or wrongly placed orders. My sister was tired all the time, but she made sure I had everything I needed to concentrate on schoolwork. Once I turned sixteen, I began helping out at the pizza shop too, things got a bit easier. Kayla wouldn't let me work too many hours, though.

"Don't be stupid, stupid," she'd say. "You're not gonna be serving pizzas all your life. You gotta study, get a scholarship, get a degree."

So I did all of those things. And then, it was like a huge weight was lifted off my sister's shoulders. She started to work less, go out more, party, date. It was like she finally gave herself permission to be her age while also making up for some of her lost youth.

Eventually, she slowed down. Got her library job. But I know she's scraping by, living paycheck to paycheck at best, too proud or maybe just too damn stubborn to ever ask for or accept help.

After we leave the restaurant, we walk around some more, but the town is rather small. It does have some great walking trails nearby but neither of us is dressed for a hike.

Besides, it's getting dark out.

"I should go," Kayla says. "Before I forget what the real world looks like and get stuck in this movie set."

"Ha ha, very funny. You know you like it here."

She shrugs. "It's okay," she says, drawing it out syllable by syllable. "You like it, though, right?"

Suddenly my sister looks very serious.

"Yeah, I do, I really do," I tell her.

"All that matters." She smiles and flicks my shoulder the way she's done ever since I can remember.

I walk her to the train station. The platform is empty, but it doesn't have those creepy city subway-empty vibes.

"Look," I gesture around me. "So quiet, so clean. You don't like it at all? You sure?"

"I like it enough to visit," Kayla prevaricates diplomatically.

"Well, good, 'cause, you know, I miss you."

"I miss you too, stupid." My sister envelops me in a hug.

Affection is hard for me, both physical and verbal. I have been told some version of this by every person who's ever left me. The flip side of that coin is that attachment is almost equally unobtainable, so I'm seldom crushed by their departure.

But to Kayla it comes so naturally. All this love. I never have to question it.

After she leaves, I walk to my new home slowly, enjoying the evening. People here smile and nod when they pass you on the sidewalk, sometimes they even say hello. Perfect strangers. I'm still getting used to it.

The Mittens are in their living room glued to something sitcom-looking on their TV. As I approach, Brandi gets up to draw the curtains. She sees me through the window and waves. I wave back. She disappears.

I look at the flamingos; I can't help it. It's like learning a new word and then hearing it pop up everywhere. Or maybe it's like being told not to think about elephants and then being unable to think about anything but.

What's …? Are their beaks *red*? No, that can't be. I look closer and of course, they are yellow with black points. Same as always. Must have been a trick of the light.

I shake my head and climb the stairs where a new (to me) bed and a delightfully comfortable double mattress are waiting for me.

In my dreams, I return to Camelot, but I don't know if it's the one I remember, or the one Kayla talks about. I can't tell if the two of them are one and the same.

My job is about as unexciting as they come but it's easy enough, I'm good at it, and the pay's decent. Essentially, I provide online support for a company small enough to still care about its customers but large enough to afford people like me to do that caring for them. I also do some bookkeeping and data entry. Fun, fun, fun.

The best part is that I have the option of doing it remotely. Now that I'm finally living somewhere quiet and spacious, it's an option I gladly exercise.

The desk that came with the apartment is old-fashioned and heavy-looking. It's certainly an improvement over the rickety secondhand dining table that pulled double duty in my old place. The chair isn't the best, but I tell myself it's likely good for my posture.

I take phone calls. I apologize in a smooth professional voice. It sounds like playacting. I answer emails, check figures online, perform some spreadsheet magic. It's all perfectly, mind-numbingly simple.

I play my music on low, pausing it each time a call comes in. It's amazing how many people in this day and age of digital everything still want to speak to a live person. Computers are great for so many things, but apparently, they are crap at apologies and calm reassurances.

ABBA gives way to Cindy Lauper then segues into Taylor Swift. I am unapologetically a fan of pop, irrespective of the decade.

Kayla makes fun of me relentlessly, but I've seen her tap her foot and sing along to some of my tunes when we drive.

Sometimes, I doodle when I work. Neither my sister nor I have any artistic skill, but of the two of us, I'm somewhat closer to making the drawing look like its subject. This is something we learned the hard way during numerous rounds of Pictionary.

It's one of the things we used to play during game nights. Kayla has always had way more friends than me. They got used to her kid sister tagging along. Now less so. I miss it occasionally.

Takes me a moment to realize what it is I'm drawing. At first, it looks like some sort of medieval weapon, but eventually, I realize it's a flamingo.

Ugh. Not those things again.

I wish Kayla had never told me about them.

I'm curious about the past *and* my poor recollection of it, but I don't like the way our reminiscences make me feel like I'm trespassing on some off-limits zone of my psyche. It's weird.

I tear off the notebook page, crumple it and bin it.

The day goes by uneventfully. By seven, I'm on the couch slurping soup and reading, a trick I'd never manage with a paper book but can do easily enough with my Kindle.

The soup is store-bought and microwaved, but it's the good kind, one of those low sodium, fancy flavor things that I have only recently convinced myself is worth the extra money.

For years and years, my diet was invariably crappy. It seems fair to try and make up for it now that I can afford to.

Eventually, my eyes get tired, and I switch the TV on. My rent includes cable and internet shared with the Mittens. Flipping through channels seems like a quaintly antiquated idea. I hit some buttons.

John Waters' voice comes on. Inimitable. Kayla's a fan so I've seen all of his movies. This one is, wait don't tell me, ah, yes, there's Divine—the one and only—as Babs Johnson, "the filthiest person alive."

That one's Kayla's favorite. I never understood the appeal, but I've seen it or been near it when it was on TV too many times.

I switch channels. It's the '80s now. The good-looking Dillon brother, young and cute in all his polo-shirted splendor, gets a summer job at a posh club. I've seen this one too.

Click.

Disney animation comes on. It's a classic, I can tell; the modern ones don't have the same look. It takes me a moment to recognize the movie. Odd since it's based on my favorite book of all time. A pretty blonde girl in a blue dress and white pinafore is playing a game of croquet with a technicolor-bright cast of characters. For clubs they are using …

Okay, okay, I get it. It's like some stupid cosmic joke. Or a maddening coincidence. I bet if I found a nature channel, it would show flamingos too.

Suddenly, they are all the rage. I can't unsee them. What I wouldn't do for something normal. A dog. A bear. Something. Anything.

I shut the TV off.

Pick my book back up. It's a thriller. I've been reading the same series for three books now, and I'm almost done with this one. There's just something about a middle-aged Louisiana detective that engages me. His life is kind of a mess both professionally and personally, but he just plows on. I read for a few hours and finish it. Immediately, I get advertised the next book in the series: *A Morning for Flamingos.*

Oh, for fuck's sake.

I shut my Kindle off. I'd toss it dramatically in disgust but I'm too practical and it's my favorite gadget. Besides, it's not its fault that I'm being pursued by tall pink birds.

It's so quiet out here. Back in the city, it seldom got this quiet and never at ten at night.

I look outside and there's no one around. My eyes are drawn downward to the front yard. If I didn't know any better, I'd swear the flamingos are staring right at me.

Swearing under my breath, I draw the curtain and go to bed.

The trailer park we grew up in isn't there anymore. The fire that killed our mother wasn't what did it in. It was just one of those things where the proximity to the power plants won over the proximity to the city. It's all an industrial wasteland now. The dream of Camelot is well and truly dead.

My sister and I have driven past there once. It was bleak, empty. No, more than that, *barren* in a way that not only forbids life but obliterates any imaginings of it, past or present. Like nothing was ever there to begin with.

I don't miss it. It was an ugly place with nothing but ugly memories. I'm not surprised I don't remember much—I can't imagine why I would want to. I like it this way, this tabula rasa of sorts. I've always considered it a random act of kindness my mind has granted me, a gift for surviving, leaving, and moving on.

Which is to say that I don't understand why I've been dreaming about it now. And I'm angry.

I thought we had a deal, my brain and me; it's hard not to feel in some way betrayed.

After a few days, I call Kayla. We seldom go for longer than that without speaking.

"How are the Mittens?" she asks. "Any weird noises? Any overnight guests?"

"Grow up," I groan.

We make small talk, but it feels just that: small, restricting. The things I want to talk about seem bigger. Prohibitively so.

Fact is, the Mittens are delightful. Just the other day, Brandi left me a plate of homemade cookies outside my door. Even her Tupperware containers are nice.

Mom never made cookies. Up until I was a teenager, any baked good I've ever had was store-bought. Usually with pilfered change. When I came to live with Kayla, she tried the domesticity bit. I remember the popping sound of those vacuum-sealed containers–tschpock–and suddenly the dough was falling out, ready to be sliced up and put in the oven.

But then, our oven was old and tended to smoke up the apartment enough to set off the fire alarm, and eventually, we went back to store-bought.

Brandi's cookies taste like happiness. Chewy delicious oatmeal raisin goodness. Whenever I take walks, I always peer into lit windows and imagine the lives led behind the glass. Specifically, I imagine sitcom-happy families. They love each other, smile often and genuinely, and all of their problems are always resolved in thirty minutes minus commercials. If you could put that into a taste, you'd know what Brandi Mitten's cookies taste like.

I don't know how to say any of that to Kayla. Instead, I tell her I keep dreaming of Camelot.

"Shit, don't do *that*, stupid," is her response.

"Seriously? Those are your words of wisdom and compassion?'"

"Um …" She pauses. "Every man's memory is his private literature."

"What the crap is that?"

"It's a quote, from that *Brave New World* guy. The library's been hanging up quote things, getting ready for some exhibit or something."

"Uh-huh."

"Well, I mean, I like it. Like it gives you permission to invent or rewrite your own."

"I'm not sure that's what he meant."

"You don't know that," Kayla counters. "The dude was so into mind-altering substances that maybe no one knows exactly what he meant."

"Un-huh," I say again, willing my sister to be helpful.

"Look, my point is that you probably got some unresolved issues about things you don't remember or whatever from that time and I'm telling you that it doesn't matter. Sometimes dreams are just, you know, dreams. Stupid mind junk."

"Well, mine are more like nightmares," I confide in her.

It's true. I dream of churning earth, hungry worms, fire, blood, and, of course, flamingos. Those spindly-legged bastards are haunting my sleeping hours.

"Same dif," Kayla reiterates. "Mind junk. Just don't think about it too much. I mean, I get nightmares."

"You do?"

"Sure, yeah, want me to tell you all about them?" She laughs. "Kidding. I'm not gonna be one of *those* people."

Which to me sounds like I shouldn't be one of *those* people.

"Let's talk about something fun instead."

"Like what?" I ask.

"Well, since your swinging neighbors are off the table, did you know that Huxley is credited with the first use of the words *snooty* and *bitchy*?"

"For real?"

"Yep. "*Nymphomaniacal*, too."

"Awesome." I'm the one who's actually read *Brave New World*, but my sister's the one with the random trivia.

We talk about nothing important for way too long and by the end of the conversation I do feel better. Kayla was always good at dispelling my dark clouds, from the time we were kids. She's a total one-trick pony, and her main trick is distraction, but hey, it works.

By the time I hang up, my heart feels lighter. Or maybe it's my mind.

I look through the window—the world seems as peaceful as a postcard. My apartment is clean and quiet. The Mittens heavily favor beiges and browns when it comes to décor. At least, up here in my unit. The place is color-coordinated but it looks like the inside of an old man's sock drawer.

The dark wood matches the chocolatey couch upholstery. Even the walls are some sort of khaki shade. It is surprisingly comforting.

I read until I begin dozing off. Micronaps. Strange brief snippets of dreaming every time. I wake up in the dark, jarred and briefly disoriented. My Kindle has long since auto shut off, and without its glowing screen, there's no illumination.

It's darker here at night than in the city. Not as much neon, barely any passing cars. There's just barely enough ambient light to see by and I make my way to the window. I shouldn't, I know, but sleep has weakened my reason. I'm a fool. Like Orpheus, desperately seeking confirmation, reassurance.

The flamingos in the front yard stand still. As they are meant to. I let out a heavy breath I didn't know I was holding in. And just then, the plastic birds tilt their heads up and glare at me with an undisguised look of menace in their plastic eyes.

I let out something between a gasp and a sob. Their gaze is snake-like, mesmerizing. And then, without taking their eyes off me, the flamingos begin to slowly, ever so slowly, lift their wire legs out of the ground. When the first one takes a step toward the house— *toward me*—I jerk away from the window and stumble. My foot catches the rug, and I fall on my ass into a sea of light brown shag. Trembling. I half-scoot, half-crawl backward all the way through the small apartment, until I hit the bed. Then I climb in and pull the covers all the way up, creating a duvet-soft safe haven. A refuge. Just like I did when I was younger. There, there, safely hidden away where no monsters can get me.

I'm shaking like a leaf. Blood's thudding in my ears. I wonder if I'm having a panic attack or a heart attack. I can't seem to remember how to tell the difference.

I try deep breathing, but it sounds ragged and choppy and not at all like my own.

Tap-tap-tap. I think I can hear them. Their feet are just metallic points. Sharp, so sharp. Tap-tap-tap. They are coming.

I don't scream. I don't cry. It's too late. I know it, I know, I …

I wake up. The morning is bright with sunshine and promise. I think back in panic. Last night was … What? What was that? Another nightmare?

I feel almost cheated, like when the main plot twist of the story is that it was all a dream.

Some dream. Sheesh. I rub my face with my hands. My palms sting.

I look and see the outlines of tiny crescent moons carved into their flesh. The moons are bloody, my nails had pierced the skin. I used to clutch my hands like that as a kid. Always had to keep my nails trimmed to the quick to avoid doing more damage. But I haven't done that in ages. My nails are longer these days, practically ladylike as Kayla jokes. Sharp enough to cut straight through, apparently.

Leaden feet carry me to the window. The flamingos in the yard look as innocent as any plastic bit of décor. I shake my head and shuffle off to start my day.

That evening and the following night the flamingos stay put. In my nightmare, my mother screams recriminations at me, spittle flying. She looks angry and … afraid? I can't quite tell. I know we're in our trailer. I can tell by the way the sound echoes off the tin can walls. But I can't make out a single word.

"What?" I keep asking her. "What are you saying? What are you saying?"

I never get my answer.

It goes on like this. My new pattern. Terrified evenings, restless nights. Kayla's lighthearted reassurances and nonsensical distractions over the phone are increasingly useless.

I want to take a train and go see her, but the distance seems insurmountable these days. Besides, I don't want to have to go past the flamingos.

I order my groceries delivered. Despite my precise instructions, the bags are left at the main house entrance.

Chuck brings them up, good-naturedly, asking if everything's okay.

I thank him, tell him I twisted my ankle and haven't been going outside much because of it. He asks if there's anything he can do to help. "Yeah," I want to say. "Take down those stupid flamingos before they kill me."

Instead, I tell him he's very kind, but I'm good, and my sister will be visiting me soon. And she better, because I don't know how much longer I can do this on my own.

I haven't asked Kayla to come up. Guess I was hoping she'd just do it, but it seems this new geographical distance between us is putting a strain on her sisterly intuition.

I don't want to be a baby about this, I really don't. She's babied me enough. I know it's not fair to her. The older we get the more I think about it: how tough it must have been for her to be stuck raising a teen at such a young age, of all the normal things she had to miss out on, of what it did to her.

Kayla won't address it ever, not directly, but she never talks about having kids or even a husband. Her relationships don't last either; she blames them on trust issues. We're both bad at letting others in, albeit in different ways. At least, she knows how to share her heart. Even if it doesn't work out, even if it never works out.

I know she loves me. I love her back by not asking for help.

Until something happens.

A night like any other but marred by rain. I'm curled up on my couch with a Scandi Noir and a cup of tea. A perfect evening. Or so it should be.

I used to love the rain. The way the steady drumbeat on the trailer's roof eliminated all the ugly ambient noises, the way Camelot always felt just a bit cleaner afterward. The memory comes to me as clear as day. I can hear the falling water, smell the petrichor.

When did I stop? At some point, I must have. Because now I hate the rain. How strange. I make a mental note to ask Kayla about it.

I read and read, getting deeper and deeper into the plot, until I hear something. Faint at first but it's the sort of thing you can't unhear once it registers. A steady tapping. Like rain on a tin roof.

I shouldn't, I mustn't, but I go to the window and look. The rain's sheeting, curtaining the world, and through it, I can just about make out the flamingos out front. They are digging at the ground with their beaks. I don't know why it makes a tapping sound. Shouldn't the earth be softened by all this rain?

But of course, the noise really isn't the main issue here. They dig as steadily and as mechanically as excavators, in alternating motions. Up and down, their neon brightness slashes through the night. It's hypnotic.

And then, they stop, as if on command. Tilt their plastic heads and look up at me. I know there's no way I should be able to see this, but logic has left the building a while back.

In the dark, in the rain, I swear the tips of their beaks are red.

Kayla is always good at talking me off the ledge, always has been. Just hearing her voice sometimes is enough to release some calming chemicals in my brain.

Right now, her voice is irate, and I can tell the timing of my phone call is crap, but I'm having a panic attack the size of Australia and not thinking rationally.

"Dude, do you know what time it is?" my sister all but growls into my ear.

"Um…" I check the digital clock readout. The glowing red digits—I'm surprised the Mittens didn't find one with brown ones—are telling me it's late, too late for a phone call. "Sorry. Were you sleeping? Or in the middle of something?"

"More like some*one*. What's up?"

Well, now I just feel stupid, which compounds my inability to draw a proper breath in the most unpleasant fashion.

"I'm, I'm just …"

She cuts through my stammering. "You're having a panic attack, aren't you?"

"Yeah. Sorry."

"It's fine, it's okay. Hang on." She sighs. I can hear her say something to someone but very quietly like she's talking away from the phone's mic. When she comes back on, her tone is gentler, more soothing. "Hey, I'm here. You don't have to be sorry, okay, just talk to me."

I want to tell her about something—anything—else but all that comes out are my flamingo nightmares.

To Kayla's credit, she doesn't laugh or call me stupid. She just listens, occasionally asking for small clarifications, and by the time I'm done, I feel like I can breathe again.

"So what do you think?" I ask her, spent and tired now, but calmer. "Am I losing my mind?"

I'm expecting a reassurance of no, either sincere or humorous, but what Kayla says instead is:

"Ever hear of Pythagoras?"

That throws me. I dig around my mind palace and come up with: "The triangle guy?"

"Yeah, that one. Well, I read this thing online that he was weird about beans."

"Beans? Like legumes?"

"Yeah. Don't interrupt. Like he had a phobia of beans. So, this one time some people were after him and he was actually getting away but then he came to a field of beans, and he couldn't make himself cross it."

Kayla does a dramatic pause.

"And?"

"And then his enemies caught up to him and killed him."

"What? Shit. Wait, is that true?" I ask. Kayla's been known to over-rely on online sources, forgetting that old "trust but verify" nugget.

"Maybe. Who knows. The dude lived centuries ago; the records were shit. Anyway, that's beside the point."

"What *is* the point?"

"The point is that most fears are unreasonable, and you can't let that crap run your life."

"Uh-huh." Yes, my sister's view of psychology is rather reductive, but there is something reassuring about it. Like maybe things *can* be as simple as that. Like if I just figure out how to live with the same pragmaticism, I can crack the code to the universe and live happily ever after or something.

"Go and look out of the window right now, will you?"

Reluctantly, I do. Quiet, sleepy small-town idyll. Nothing out of the ordinary. Nothing sinister. Even the rain has tapered off.

"Report your findings, soldier."

"Um, all's quiet on the western front."

"Everything's in order, including yard décor?"

"Yeah," I tell her. The relief floods my system, better than any alcohol. It's almost euphoric.

"Do you feel better now?" she asks.

"Yeah, I do," I answer, meaning it. "Thanks."

"Are you gonna go to sleep and have pie dreams?"

I smile. That's something from our childhood. Whenever I was upset, Kayla would tell me to think of a pie before falling asleep, so that I could dream about it. Apparently, pies were the happiest thing we could imagine back then.

To this day, the notion largely holds true. Try having pie and feeling sad at the same time—it just doesn't work.

"Wait. Who's there with you?"

"None of your business, stupid." Kayla laughs. "But I am going back to what I was doing."

"Eww. Gross."

"Oh, shush." More laughter. Then serious all of a sudden. "You're gonna be fine, kiddo."

"Thanks, K."

"Lurv you."

"Lurv you back."

We hang up.

I fall asleep thinking of pies as hard as I can, but by the time I wake up, all I remember are flamingos eating them, their beaks gleaming red.

And so it goes. My days now have a pattern to them: they get worse at night. The flamingos outside are my enemy, the field of beans to my Pythagoras. Whenever I force myself outside, I strategically avoid being near them. They merit no more than a glance, like a scary movie that's intriguing but too scary to watch.

I keep waiting for Kayla to visit again, but things keep coming up and getting in the way. Her work or social life or whoever this mystery person she's seeing is. On the phone, she doesn't go into too many details. To be fair, it won't last. Empirical evidence and all that.

But for now, she's having fun. And I'm happy for her. Well, I try to be, but I miss her. This is exactly what I was afraid would happen if I moved out of the city. And exactly the sort of thing Kayla said wouldn't.

The distance that seems nothing on paper is proving borderline insurmountable in person. And of course, I could go visit too—the train goes both ways—but I have the strangest feeling about leaving this town. Like if I do, it'll just disappear. Like it'll become one of those cheesy "it was all a dream" scenarios.

So, we're at this weird standoff, my sister and I. Waiting for something to change.

Meanwhile, I feel like I'm slowly losing my mind.

Oddly enough, what makes it worse is that sometimes everything's perfectly fine. My mind is quiet, the flamingos stand still, etc. Just long enough to think I must have imagined anything was ever off.

And then something happens, and my world gets thrown off its axis. It's a shock to the system. Every time.

I can't tell if my psyche's being kind or cruel. Imagine sitting in the darkness for a while. Your eyes will begin to adjust, you'll start getting comfortable. Then someone puts the light on, briefly, blindingly. Afterward, the darkness is so much worse, black as night, impenetrable. Makes you question how you could ever see in it at all.

That's where I'm stuck. Darkness, momentarily illuminated. Madness, with short intervals of sanity.

Should I talk to someone? I can just imagine—for some reason cartoonishly—the sirens going off while people in white jackets are bundling me off and away, joking with each other about how it was the flamingos that got me.

The other option is moving, but I'm not sure it would solve anything. Besides, I love my new home.

Just gotta buck up.

Ha, haven't thought about that expression in ages. Our mother used to say it. I can still remember her inebriated sneer. "Buck up, buckaroo." Which was usually followed by a drunken rant about some sort of injustice or another.

To hear her tell it, life had dealt her a rough hand, and she never let anyone around her forget it.

That's probably the main reason Kayla and I are the way we are—emotionally buttoned-up. It's easier that way. Mostly.

I think it would stay that way for the duration, perhaps indefinitely so, if not for what happened next.

That night comes back to me in glimpses and flashes. It's as if the strobe lights of my psyche can't figure out where to focus or what to shoot. The full picture takes a while to rebuild.

I remember waking up to a noise. It sounded like crying or screaming. It sounded like it was coming from the outside.

In socked feet, I padded to the window and peered through the glass. The flamingos were staring right back at me, some of their necks twisted at impossible angles. Their plastic beaks were open, another impossibility, emitting mournful wails.

The scene was hypnotic. Terrifying.

Then one of them took flight.

Embarrassingly enough, I had no idea flamingos could fly. I'd never seen them fly. Figured maybe they were like emus or something. And certainly the plastic ones should have stayed put no matter what.

And yet …

In flight, the flamingo's profile is nearly a straight line with an outsized fin of a wing. With its neck and legs stretched out unfathomably long, the bird is as graceful as it is strange-looking. Evolution's trajectory undeniable, there's something of a pterodactyl about it.

It would be beautiful—majestic even—on one of those nature shows. In-person, as it flies kamikaze-style at me, the effect is distinctly more horrifying.

Its plastic beak smashes into the window and I can see the glass starting to slowly crack around the impact site. The cracking's audible, unsettling, like nails on a chalkboard.

The flamingo perched on the window ledge outside as if waiting. If the creature could grin, it would. And its grin would be evil.

Following instinct more than logic, I run outside.

Apparently, that's where the Mittens found me some time later. Wearing nothing but fleece pajamas and fuzzy socks, digging up their front yard with my bare hands.

Apparently, the only thing I told them that made any sense was not to call 911.

They did the next best thing and phoned Kayla, listed as the emergency contact on my rental agreement.

It takes her just under an hour to get here, by which time, I've calmed down just enough to stop crying and wash my hands. The dirt under my broken fingernails is wedged in so tightly. I don't feel like they'll ever be clean enough. Going to have to cut them off.

I'm still picking at them by the time Kayla arrives.

The Mittens have been the picture of kindness, but I can tell they are relieved she's there to take me off their hands. I've interrupted their night, worried them. Scared them. They are probably thinking about reasons to break my lease right now. Get a nice *normal* tenant to live above them.

Kayla thanks them profusely, going into full customer service mode, all apologies and gratitude. Then she takes me upstairs.

"I didn't know the trains even ran at night," I say numbly.

"Owl service, baby. You're looking at an Owl rider. Who-who!" Kayla grins, but her expression quickly turns serious, as she sits down next to me on the couch and takes my hand. "What happened, kiddo?"

I shake my head. "Don't wanna talk about it."

My sister sighs. "I think we have to, though, don't we?"

"Oh, I don't know. I figured I'd just keep that fact that I'm losing my mind as a private matter."

My voice carries more bitterness than I realize I was holding on to. Kayla picks up on that.

"Look, I'm sorry I haven't visited."

"It's okay, I get it, you're busy. I mean," I tell her. "I mean, I haven't visited either."

"And I'm sorry if I haven't taken your … concerns seriously."

"Yeah, no, it's plastic flamingos, so it's difficult to …"

"No," Kayla says, "don't do that."

"What am I doing?"

"You're doing that fake toughness thing. You know you are."

I rub my face and exhale. "Isn't that like our family specialty?"

"That and deflection." My sister grins at me. "Now you wanna tell me what happened?"

"Not particularly," I say, shaking my head. "They are gonna kick me out, you know."

"Who? The swinging Mittens?"

"Stop it."

"They are not gonna kick you out, and even if they do, you can always come stay with me."

These days, Kayla's apartment is a swirling chaos set to a heavy metal soundtrack. I love her but I'm pretty sure I'd rather sleep in my car.

"Have you been getting out? Going for walks or whatever?" my sister asks me, her forehead wrinkled with worry.

"Yeah, sometimes," I say. "Oh, I forgot to tell you, I saw the funniest thing the other day. These people had peacocks in their front yard."

"What, like live peacocks?"

"No, K, not *live* peacocks."

She shrugs. "Dude, you live in a bougie little place. I wouldn't put it past these people."

"They were metal, I think, like sculptures. Like art."

Actually, when it happened, when I first saw them, my stomach contracted in fear. For a moment, I thought they were flamingos. Then I saw how different they were in all their glowing iridescent splendor.

"So if flamingos are for swingers, what would peacocks be for? An orgy?"

"That's exactly what I thought."

We both crack up. It's such a relief to be doing something normal at last like sharing a laugh with my sister over a joke that's likely only funny to us.

"Like a proper Roman emperor-style orgy," Kayla adds fuel to the fire. "Togas and hand-fed grapes."

When we calm down, Kayla makes us tea. Decaf, but it doesn't matter, I doubt either of us is going to sleep anytime soon.

"Look, Chrys, are you okay?" My sister asks me. The question hangs suspended in the steam rising from our tea mug. "Seriously?"

"No," I answer honestly. "I don't think that I am."

She sips her tea in silence for a while. "Yeah, I was afraid of that," she said. "Do you remember Mr. Woogles?"

Oddly enough, I do. Mr. Woogles was a little stripy tabby that we had for about five minutes as kids. He wandered off from one of the other trailers and stuck around. I remember the M shape on his forehead, he liked it rubbed. I can't remember why I ever named him that.

He strayed into the road and got crushed beneath the wheels of one of our neighbors' trucks.

Kayla didn't tell me about it for the longest time. Instead, she made up stories about friends he went to see and the adventures he was having. Only I kept looking for him and calling for him and eventually, Mom sat me down and said, "That kitten's roadkill. He ain't coming back, so stop making a fuss."

I cried for days and never wanted another pet again, but, in a way, it was a relief to know.

"Yeah, I remember."

Kayla puts down her tea. "Well …"

Something about the way Kayla says it makes the world around me slow down and my heart speeds up. It feels just like the beginning of a panic attack.

She sees it, takes my hand, and rubs my palm in slow circular motions.

"It's okay, it's okay, don't freak out. Just listen. It's nothing. Nothing that'll affect anything. Just something from the past."

Both of us have always tried to live like the past had no effect on us. We carried our scars on the inside and kept our memories in a storage box in the basement of our mind palaces. It worked too. Mostly.

"I've always known we'd have this conversation someday," my sister says. "Actually, I'm surprised it took us this long. And the funny thing is that I never quite figured out how I'd say it, so I'm just gonna go for it, okay?"

I nod slowly.

"Here goes. Dad died when you were five."

"No," I automatically correct her. "I was ten."

"No," Kayla counters emphatically. "I was ten, and you were five. After he died, both Mom and I lied to you for years about it."

"What? Why?"

"It's … it's complicated." She rubs her forehead. "Shit, no; no, it's not. Dad was a piece of shit. You don't remember so take my

word for it. He drank, he beat us, and, when it came to you, he …
he tried worse. And then something happened."

"What?"

"Mom and I were out, and he was at home watching you. When
we came back, he was on the living room floor, pants down, in a
pool of his own blood. There was a huge gash on his head where it
hit the corner of the coffee table. Remember that awful ugly thing
we used to have? The corners were so sharp, we were always hitting
ourselves on them."

I don't remember. But I do remember the hideous orange living
room shag rug we used to have and then one day didn't. I guess now
I know what happened to it.

"So, wait," logistics set in as if to keep the panic at bay. I feel
preternaturally calm, one of those quiet-before-the-storm things.
"You knew he was abusing me, and you left him with me alone?"

"I never knew. I don't know if Mom did; she swore she didn't.
But I mean, that day his pants were down, his dick was out. And you
told us that Daddy touched you, and you pushed him, so …"

"Fuuuuuck."

"Yeah, that."

"So what'd you do?"

"Well, that's the best part." Kayla's smile is bitter, like she can
hardly believe what she's saying. "We didn't do things the … um …
normal way."

"Meaning?"

"Meaning we waited until dark and buried the bastard in our
yard."

"You did *not*."

"Did too."

"Why?"

"I don't know. I think Mom was worried they'd think she did it or they'd take us away or something. She just figured it'd be easier not to get the law involved."

"And was it? Easier?"

Kayla shrugs. "It sucked at the time, but in the long run, yeah, maybe. The weirdest thing is that you just went to sleep, and then woke up in the middle of the night and came outside when we were digging. You were all calm, like freakishly calm. You asked us what we were doing, and Mom said we were gardening. And you brought up your little plastic shovel and started helping."

I close my eyes, and I can see that shovel. It's as yellow as a cartoon sun. Part of a beach toy set I never really got to use because we never went to the beach. I've no idea why I even had it.

"We just didn't say anything and let you help. Figured maybe you were sleepwalking or having some sort of dissociative episode." Kayla shakes her head, thinking about it. "It was such a mess. And then it started raining too. He was huge, heavy. And there was so much blood. It kept seeping through the rug we wrapped him in. Even got on those stupid stolen plastic flamingos. We didn't notice until the next day when you asked why their beaks were red, and we had to clean it up."

One by one all the missing puzzle pieces are falling into their places. Soon, I'll be able to see the entire picture. And then, I know, I'll never be able to unsee it.

"But Kayla, how did I forget all that?"

"That's the weirdest thing. I have no idea. I've never seen anything like it. You just, I don't know, *erased* it from your mind. We told you Dad left, and you seemed okay with it. Mom and I took turns writing you postcards for years until we figured you were old enough to tell you he was dead. You didn't even have that much of a reaction. I mean, you seemed fine. We thought you *were* fine."

Kayla sighs.

"Mom just got worse and worse, though. Her fits, her drinking. I took you away as soon as I could and we were good, weren't we?"

"Yeah," I tell her. "We were."

"And you just … I dunno. Memory's weird. You know how they say it rewrites itself with every recall? Well, I think yours erased itself instead. And it was a good thing too, like a blessing. You just got to live your life without any of this shit hanging over your head."

"Until now," I say grimly.

"Until now," Kayla echoes.

Something occurs to me. "Did they ever find the body?"

"Nah, not that I know off. I used to have nightmares about it, but nothing ever … I mean, after what happened to Mom, no one came digging around or anything. Who would? It's trailers, you just plop them on the surface, no foundation needed. And then Camelot closed down. And now I think the entire place is just buried under a layer of toxic sludge from the waste plant, so …"

"Right."

We sip our tea in silence for a while. It has lost all of its heat, but the ritual alone is calming. It's something Kayla and I picked up from her one-time obsession with BBC movies. And it's stuck around, like her crush on Colin Firth.

"So now what?" I ask her.

"You tell me. I mean, how do you feel knowing all this?"

"I'm not sure," I say honestly. "It explains everything, but it doesn't quite … feel real, you know? And also, in a way, it doesn't change anything."

"Are you mad at me for lying? For not telling you sooner?"

"No. No," I assure her. "I'm grateful. Seriously. For everything."

She puts her arms around me and kisses the top of my head. "You're welcome, stupid."

I hug her back as tightly as I can.

Then together we walk to the window, which is of course perfectly fine and uncracked, and stare down at the flamingos. They ignore us, exactly as the yard décor is supposed to.

"What happens next?" I ask her.

"We bake the Mittens a pie and apologize and assure them that nothing like that will ever happen again, and then we get on with our lives," Kayla says.

"That simple?"

"Maybe," my sister replies quietly.

We stand there and watch the world go by. The only things that move are the ones that are supposed to: traffic, clouds. I take my sister's hand and lace my fingers through hers, something I used to do as a kid, when it was just us against everything and everyone. It still has the power to make me feel safe and secure.

Of all the things I have forgotten and all the ways my memory has betrayed me or saved me, I hope I can hold on to this moment.

Together we watch the sun come up.

THE TRUNK

1.

There was a large park stretching out right across the street from the condo development. The kind of park you don't find in the city—an unkempt slice of wilderness, Mother Nature's greeting card, with only a simple walking path through it to remind you of civilization at all.

None of the manicured and curated city parks with their matching tree layouts and paved exercise corridors that he was used to.

This park made him smile. This park made him feel like the place they were about to see would be home before he even set foot inside its walls.

And sure enough, the condo turned out to be spacious, updated if not brand new, with all the modern conveniences they were hoping for and even a storage unit in the basement for whenever their possessions crossed from the current bare minimum into excess.

Bogdan looked around the place, trying to imagine him and Aimee living there. He pictured their meager furnishings punctuating the rooms. He visualized the two of them side by side in the kitchen cooking—their current efficiency setup allowed no such luxury. The sheer joy of never having to trudge down five flights of stairs to the basement to do laundry flooded his heart with happy warmth.

The ceiling fan whirred softly above his head, lulling him into a pleasantly relaxed state. Aimee was talking details and logistics with the realtor in the bathroom, acoustics echoing, as Bogdan leaned on the living room's windowsill and looked out. A park view would have been ideal, but most of the condos, it seems, were designed to look out onto the evenly mowed grass divisions and parking lots.

It was all so … peaceful. He dug around his mind for a better adjective and came up with tranquil. English was his second language (third technically, for anyone counting), and he never missed an opportunity to work on it.

After two decades of city living, how did one deal with such tranquility? How did one sleep at night without the cacophonic soundtrack of sirens and shouting drunks and irate horn-beeping drivers?

He guessed they were going to find out. The place, despite its convenient location and overall nice shape, was—surprisingly— well within their budget. He knew they still had to talk about it, but he also knew this was the one. He met Aimee's eyes and recognized the excitement there.

At last, their search was over. They found their home.

The logistics of buying real estate were a nightmare, an expensive one. There were inspections and lawyers and all the official things that still gave Bogdan such anxiety even after all his time as a legal, passport-carrying citizen. All-in-all, a grueling but mercifully brief process. Soon they were moving in—an exhausting process despite not having much. And then, they were home.

"Time to nest," Aimee declared. Bogdan was only too happy to oblige.

They promised themselves no more used furniture, no more trash-day-salvaged couches, and Craigslist's secondhand finest. Instead, they made a budget and slowly, methodically hunted down the best deals on new, if discounted, things for their home.

Slowly but surely the place was taking shape. The walls gained art, the couch throw pillows. The blandly white kitchen got colorful accents to liven it up. The bathroom got matching towels.

At last, their place looked like a proper grown-up home.

"Ah," Aimee would say looking around, "look how well we are adulting."

Their working definition of adulting until now usually restricted itself to making sure they had enough toilet paper.

City living had the strange effect of perpetually infantilizing its dwellers. It traded stability for convenience. And there was much to be said for the convenience factor, but at some point, not having to rent a small temporary box crammed alongside others just like it began to outweigh being next door to a 24-hour beer deli.

For Bogdan and Aimee, that time came later than for most, but then again, Bogdan always felt like he got a late start in life. He didn't come over to this country until he was almost an adult, thus forever retaining the accent he was shy about. He left behind a war zone and crossed over into a world so startlingly different that it gave him whiplash.

"It was like going from Dunkirk to Disneyland," he'd joke later. He learned to joke about it, because his new country valued levity and glib jocularity and, more than anything, he wanted to fit in.

He practiced carefully in front of an old tube TV for hours to improve his English and ameliorate his accent. He learned to carry himself with the ease of his new compatriots, who walked around like the sky was never going to fall down. Lightness, there was lightness all around, often artificial but no one seemed to mind so long as it was there.

He started going by Dan. He passed his citizenship test with flying colors. He teared up at the ceremony. The first question anyone ever asked him after hearing him speak was still, "Where are you from?" That narrowing of the eyes, the instinctive distrust of the proverbial other. The barely disguised disappointment or confusion at not being able to place his answer on their mental map.

Bogdan has never met a population so generally ignorant of geography. He figured it had to do with the size of the country they lived in—maybe a place that large made people in it feel like they were the only thing that mattered. Back in the day, people thought the Sun orbited the Earth; now here was a nation so hubristically proud that it had thought itself to be the center around which the entire world revolved.

None of it mattered. Not when Bogdan's past was scorched earth and death, and his future was stretching out ahead of him so brightly.

He knew cars. His father was a mechanic, and Bogdan liked to joke that he was raised on engines and motor oil. And so, he worked on cars here; a career path that slowly but steadily culminated in being the co-owner of a used car dealership. How's that for living the dream?

Decent if unspectacular income. Honest work for honest pay. Something to be proud of. Bogdan liked to think that if his family could see him now, they would be.

That's how he met Aimee, too. She came in to buy a car and ended up with a husband. Your classic *opposites attract* scenario that romantic comedies thrive on, and yet it worked.

She was the perennial sunshine to his low-key gloom. Unlike him, she smiled without thinking.

He'd joke with her about white privilege, and she'd point out that he was whiter than her. She had her Midwestern tan on at least six months out of the year.

"I'm paler," he'd point out. "There's a difference. The sun doesn't love me as much."

The sun—most things, in fact—favored Aimee more. He could relate. She was lovely. Lovable. Easy to love.

Bogdan could think of a million things that attracted him to Aimee and was never sure of a single one that attracted her to him. And yet there they were, mostly happily married for nearly a decade.

In their first home, one they had so diligently saved for. Life, as the T-shirts said, was good.

They had all but forgotten about the storage space until Christmas season. It was the first time they lived somewhere spacious enough to accommodate a Christmas tree and not just a decorative wreath they would normally put up in their old apartment.

Aimee, a lifelong tree-hugger, couldn't stand the idea of cutting down a living tree for a month of merriment, so they went with a near-life-size artificial one. A good investment too, something to use for years to come, but unlike their old wreath, much too large for a closet.

"What about that space in the basement?" Aimee suggested. And so, upon unboxing the tree in late November, Bogdan took its large cardboard box down to the storage unit. He figured he'd bring it back up the first week of January to put the Christmas tree away until next time. A neat and practical solution—his favorite kind.

The box was light but awkward and nearly as tall as Bogdan's six-foot frame, meaning that standing upright, both were grazing the low basement ceiling in an overall claustrophobic effect.

Their storage unit was marked with the letter A corresponding to their unit. It reminded Bogdan of a cage, specifically the sort of cages he heard people were put in during the war back in the old country. The thought made him shudder.

The basement was lit with bare bulbs hung from the ceiling—bright punctuation marks amid the cobwebbed darkness. Without windows, the place seemed timeless and airless. Oppressively so.

Not somewhere he'd want to spend an extra minute if it could be helped.

Bogdan set the box on the floor and got out the key for the unit's lock. They hadn't used it since the realtor gave it to them. There was rust on the metal gate, but the lock itself looked shiny and new. The key turned easily, and the door opened with an ominous creak that rippled eerily throughout the basement.

Prepared for darkness, Bogdan brought a small flashlight with him, but it turned out the unit had a working overhead light. Well, a bare bulb, but still, it provided enough illumination for the small space. When Bogdan reached up and pulled the string attached, the lightbulb buzzed to life.

It was then that he noticed a trunk against the far wall. A decent size, sturdy-looking wooden trunk that put him in mind of a bygone era of steamships travel but nowadays would likely end up as a millennials' retro furnishing affectation.

After moving the Christmas tree box into the storage space, Bogdan went over to get a closer look at the trunk. It appeared in good condition, with dark wood and silver-like metal banding across and on the corners. The locking mechanism seemed to be crafted out of a darker, time-tarnished metal.

His better angels told him to leave the thing well enough alone, but curiosity overrode those instructions. Bogdan tried the same key as the storage unit—it didn't work. Didn't even fit.

He tried moving the trunk and found it surprisingly heavy. It had to be real wood, not some cheap MDF. He idly wondered why the previous owners would leave behind a thing so obviously well-made.

The locking mechanism looked a bit like a puzzle. Bogdan used to like puzzles as a kid. He still remembered his first Rubik's Cube fondly. Then he remembered the way it looked amid the burned-down ruins of his old house, a bright flash of color against the canvas of devastation, and he shuddered and willed the memory away.

Maybe this was a puzzle he could solve. Bogdan fished his house keys out of his jeans' front pocket; his keychain was a small multi-tool. Aimee got it for him a while back, calling him her Mr. Practical.

It was indeed a thoughtful and handy gift; one he would put to good use now. The lightbulb above him flickered, and he tapped on it a few times until it resumed its steady if less than impressive fight against the surrounding darkness.

The lock was tricky but not impossible, and soon, Bogdan heard the tell-tale click. He set the multi-tool and his keys on the floor, took a deep breath, and lifted the lid.

What he saw inside made him jump back, crashing down on the dirty concrete floor and bruising his hands trying to arrest his fall. He didn't cry out—he was too naturally reserved for such displays of emotion. His shock was a thing of quietude.

Still, it *was* a shock. Bogdan could hear his heartbeat, deafeningly loud in the sepulchral silence of the basement. His hands, he noticed, were shaking. It took a moment to steady himself enough to get up and approach the trunk for a second look.

Even in this gloomily illuminated space, there was no mistaking what he was looking at. Something all too familiar to him from his past life, left behind so many years ago. Something entirely incongruous with his new life here in the new world. A dead body.

2.

Bogdan closed the trunk. Slammed it shut, in fact; then cringed as the sound echoed loudly as it bounced off of seemingly every wall in the basement, hoping no one heard it but him. It was an ostrich reaction at its best—the *out of sight out of mind* solution. It wasn't going to work long-term, but it gave him some breathing room, some thinking space.

The thing was, he knew what he *should* do. Knew it with overwhelming clarity. He *should* walk up the stairs and tell Aimee all about it. She would say to call the cops, because it's the sort of thing a person like Aimee would say. She was a middle-class Midwesterner through and through in her values, brought up to view the police as the servers and protectors they proclaimed to be. For her, it was the first and only recourse for a situation like this.

For Bogdan, it was more complicated. No matter how Americanized he thought himself to be, there was still a strong underlying immigrant mentality deeply ingrained into the very fiber of his being.

It wasn't so much the way he always finished his plate, abhorring waste, or the way he bargained every chance he got, always looking for the best possible deal, or the way he tended to distrust people, especially those in positions of authority. Bogdan *feared* the law. It was irrational, he knew, but he couldn't help it. He could recite the Pledge of Allegiance with his hand on his heart clutching an American passport, and yet there was always that precarious feeling of tiptoeing an invisible line and being a mere misstep from having all of it taken away.

It would be like being rudely awakened from a nice dream you were never sure you deserved to dream in the first place. Something to fear indeed.

It wasn't a predominant thought on his mind most of the time, more like a steady but distant hum —a program operating in the background of his consciousness, but his recent discovery had amplified that hum into a deafening crescendo.

He stood stock-still, trying to steady his breath, trying to steady his heart. When he felt in control again, he locked the storage space and went back upstairs.

"I was going to send out a search and rescue team for you," Aimee said from the kitchen.

"Sorry." He thought quickly of a plausible excuse. "The lock didn't work."

"So you couldn't get in at all?"

"No, I did. It just took persuasion."

"Ah, my man, the lock whisperer." She smiled and kissed him as he approached.

"Smells good."

"It's the caramelized onions." Aimee turned back to the stove.

Bogdan looked around their homey kitchen, taking it all in. It seemed impossible that this place and that basement existed in the same building. In the same world.

He hugged Aimee from the back and pressed his face into her hair. It smelled like coconuts. He willed it to be enough.

"I'll just go wash up."

"Okay This thing—" Aimee gestured at the concoction in the frying pan "—got about ten more minutes before I'm too hungry to care if it's done."

Bogdan closed the bathroom door and locked eyes with his mirrored reflection.

Everything was normal, everything was fine, everything was under control. In reality, nothing had changed since yesterday. Not in any way that mattered. The body was always there. It's likely been there since they moved in. No one saw him just now. No one knew. There was plenty of time to decide what to do. Or do nothing at all—head in the sand and all.

The food was delicious. Well, it smelled and looked delicious, but to him it tasted like cardboard. So did the dessert. Bogdan knew the fault was his alone—his psyche suppressing his taste buds.

He made small talk the best he could, helped wash up, and then stared unseeingly at the TV screen beside Aimee, unable to follow the plot of their latest show.

That night they kissed goodnight but didn't make love. Secretly, he was glad of it. He couldn't imagine getting his head into the right mindset for it and didn't want to have to conjure up excuses. Bogdan never lied to Aimee if he could help it, but he wasn't above omitting the truth, especially when he thought it might upset her.

He listened to her fall asleep in the dark silence of their bedroom. In the city, there would have been noises to distract him— drunks stumbling home late, neighbors arguing, passing cars showing off the potency of their sound systems. Here there was nothing. His thoughts were much too loud for the night, and none of them were good.

Sleep wouldn't come, he could tell. No rest for the wicked.

Bogdan got out of bed as quietly as he knew how and tiptoed out of the bedroom. The sheer act of moving around made him feel calmer. Things always seemed worse at night when sleep wasn't an option.

He sat on the couch, their first brand new couch—so cushiony and comfortable it still felt like a showroom display piece, not yet broken in with butt grooves and saggy give—and put his head in his hands.

Thought after thought raced through his mind until one won out. And he knew it was right. The head in the sand approach wasn't going to work after all. This evening was merely a preview of all the days and nights to come, performed on autopilot and barely enjoyed. It was no life, no life at all. Bogdan had to do something about the body in the trunk.

3.

The basement, he knew, would be even creepier at night, but at least it all but guaranteed privacy. Plus, Aimee was a sound sleeper, and this saved him from making up excuses.

Returning to the storage unit was like reentering a nightmare—a strangely familiar fear suffusing his mind.

The trunk was still there. He had kind of hoped against all hope that he'd hallucinated the entire thing.

He took a deep steadying breath and opened the lid. The body was still there. Bogdan trained his flashlight on it, waited for the terror to subside into something more manageable, and looked, *really looked,* at the body.

Straight away, he noticed certain incongruities. First off, there was no smell. Bogdan knew all too well the smell of death; it never left your memory. Olfactory triggers were supposed to be the strongest. And yet, this body emitted no odor whatsoever.

Come to think of it, there wasn't much in the way of putrefaction in general. The body had more of a mummified look to it. Skin too tightly stretched across the bones. Gossamer wisps of hair still attached to the scalp that put Bogdan in mind of a sea creature undulating beneath the ocean. The expression on its face was strangely peaceful. You could almost imagine this was someone curled up in a tight ball, sleeping. Except, of course, this person was dead and in a trunk.

The longer Bogdan looked, the calmer he felt. By all appearances, the person looked like they'd been dead a long, long time. Way before the two of them moved here. Surely there was no way anyone could blame it on Bogdan. Even if the trunk was in the storage space that now belonged to him. Right?

The dead bodies he saw before, in his other life, in his other home, never looked peaceful. Their expressions were twisted in anger, in outrage for being victims of the conflict that had nothing to do with them. For finding themselves at the bloody crossroads of destiny, casualties of geography and politics and mindless hate spilled over.

He remembered seeing dead bodies in the streets. The smell, the blood, the fear.

Boys as young as he was at the time going away to fight in the war they were sold like a video game, frothing at the mouth with jingoistic pride, coming back too soon in body bags, or never coming back at all. It's what happened to his best friend. It was a fate Bogdan himself so narrowly avoided.

It all came back to him still, at times. He knew what it was and the acronym for it but didn't feel like dragging it into the light. Ever. Not with Aimee, not at work, certainly not with some random therapist. Post-traumatic implied that the trauma was left in the past. Assuming time was accommodatingly linear. Assuming memory accommodatingly placed the memories on the farthest shelves of your mental palace's library.

Some days, the recollections hit him so vividly, so potently, that the intervening decades simply faded away. And some days, it was as distant as a movie he saw ages ago.

How strangely the mind worked.

The discovery of the body was bringing up a lot of things Bogdan preferred buried. He wondered if burying the body would push the things back down. At least, there was a nice symmetry about it.

That's it, he thought, *depersonify it*. It's just a body, not a person. Just a problem waiting for a solution. Solve it and move on, so that one day this too can be a traumatic but distant memory.

The body was clothed. Or covered. Something was on it, some spiderweb-thin remains of fabric stubbornly surviving the ravages of time. It was impossible to tell age or gender.

Aimee dragged Bogdan to an anthropological exhibit once. They had real Egyptian mummies. The strangeness of seeing someone's dead body—once lovingly, carefully preserved for centuries, and now crudely displayed in a glass box—jarred Bogdan. There was a certain callousness about it all. Death wasn't meant to be a spectacle. Buried bodies ought to be left in peace.

"I'll give you peace," Bogdan whispered to the body in the trunk.

"I know you will," replied the body as it opened its eyes.

4.

There were pivotal moments in life. Sometimes you recognized their arrival, awed and cowed by the knowledge that nothing would ever be the same again. Sometimes you could see them coming and get a chance to steel yourself in preparation. Sometimes—*usually,* in Bogdan's experience—they snuck up on you, like a clown in a haunted house attraction.

There was no question in Bogdan's mind that he was in the presence of one such moment. It was an almost physical sensation of having a rug woven of sanity and reason pulled out from under his feet; a sudden shift in gravity.

A trunk in the basement was explainable. A body in the trunk in the basement was tragic but plausible. A talking sentient body in the trunk in the basement was simply a step too far.

Bogdan slammed the lid of the trunk shut and backed away. He willed his bladder to stay strong, though his body shook like a leaf in the wind. He told himself over and over again that he was hallucinating as he tried to slow down his gasping into breathing.

He read once that time was an illusion. That seemed like a stretch. But sanity, now *that* was illusory. A hat you wore, a purely performative thing, a fake-it-till-you-make-it bit all the way.

He had lost it once in a place where madness took over, became a barely recognizable version of himself, a survivor, but that time had long passed.

Here in this comfortably cushioned country, in this comfortably cushioned life, sanity was easy. The rules were laid out clearly, and you followed them to the best of your ability. Success wasn't a guarantee, and the system wasn't perfect, but he felt that it was designed well enough to maintain at least a credible presentation of stability.

Then again, so many felt that way about his old country before the war.

There were things you did in wartime that peacetime wouldn't condone, wouldn't even understand. You'd talk to corpses, sure, you'd talk to anyone who'd listen or was simply there, you'd pray to any power just to get through the night. Bogdan remembered it all too well.

But here, in this technicolor-bright advertisement of a country, such things were unimaginable for a sane person. Madness was for people in the city who huddled on park benches, muttering to themselves. Madness was for a young boy named Bogdan who had seen too much. Not for a middle-aged man named Dan who had engineered a brand-new life for himself in a country so obsessed with happiness, it enshrined the pursuit of it as a basic right into its constitution.

Bogdan may have found a talking body in the trunk, but Dan would have most certainly only *imagined* such a thing.

He rocked gently, steadying himself, repeating his mantras with a penitent's dedication until he believed in them. Enough to go back upstairs. Enough to resume his perfectly normal life.

5.

Christmas was a quiet affair. Aimee's parents weren't up for making the trip all the way from Florida. Aimee's sister was spending the holidays with her in-laws. And so, it was only the two of them. Just as they liked it.

The tree was decorated, the cookies were baked, the presents were wrapped. Every year they agreed on gift limits, both out of cost and space considerations, but this time they had made an exception. And why not? They were homeowners at last. It was worth celebrating.

"I wish there was a fireplace," Aimee said, cuddling up against him on the couch.

"Next home," he promised.

"Next one?"

"Well, you know, after a while."

"Probably be a long while."

"Probably," he agreed, kissing the top of her head.

Truth was, they were both perfectly content here, as the fireplace video softly crackled on YouTube.

Bogdan patted his new amp lovingly. "You think the neighbors will mind?"

"Not if you play well."

"You mean, not if I play during reasonable hours?"

"Suuuuure." She laughed. "That's what I mean."

"I'll have you know I'm an excellent guitarist."

That was a stretch, and they both knew it. Playing guitar was more of a hobby to him, a way to relax.

"I know, I know. It's like Jimmy Page, Eric Clapton, and then you."

"Exactly. And for this, I am eating the last cookie."

"Rude." She playfully swatted his hand.

"Rude? I'm not the one who burned the first batch. We would have had twice as many."

"Well, at least now we know the fire alarm works."

Bogdan nodded, his mouth full of oatmeal raisin chewy goodness.

Moments like these, it was all too easy to imagine that life was perfectly normal and the body in the trunk was nothing but an ugly dream. At night, he clung to that notion for dear life. During the day he found plenty to distract himself from thinking about it. Whatever it took, from work to domestic chores. Even dusting, which he normally hated, was now a task worth performing.

Aimee noticed and figured it was part of the new pride of ownership mentality. Bogdan never corrected her.

New Year was a quiet affair once more. Years ago, there used to be parties, or they'd go see the fireworks by the river, but now they were happy if they managed to stay awake until midnight. The fireworks on TV were nowhere near as good as the real thing but cuddling up on their new cloud of a couch in the warmth of their new home beat—hands down— huddling amid drunken strangers on a winter night and then having to make their way back across town.

They kissed as the clock struck midnight and then promptly passed out while watching strangers do the same on TV. The New Year was successfully ushered in.

There was no art to distracting oneself, only the number of tasks you could find and the single-mindedness you could bring to tackling each of them. You had to hone that razor focus until the world around you fell away.

Dan went to work and cheerfully sold cars. Dan came home and happily spent time with his wife. Dan did chores, paid bills, watched movies, played guitar, shopped.

Bogdan lay awake at night, wrestling with his mind. Bogdan avoided the basement, avoided even saying the word. Bogdan fought decade-old nightmares when the sleep did come, whispering mantras to himself upon waking. Bogdan held the flood of memories at bay, for he knew should they come, they'd bury him under.

The split was perfect, it was reasonable, it worked. All the way until January sixth.

"You know I once had a cashier at Walmart named Epiphany."

"That's funny. As in, her mom had an …"

"Right."

"Well, don't try to talk your way out of this. The tree is getting taken down."

Bogdan knew the day was coming and dreaded it, but there was nothing to say or do, just grin and bear it.

Returning to the basement took all his resolve. He went about it quickly. The lock cooperated. He grabbed the Christmas Tree box, ignored the almost-certainly-heard whispers emerging from the trunk, and hurried upstairs.

Aimee helped him pack the tree up and away until next Christmas, and he took it back down.

Once more, please, please, in and out, nothing out of the ordinary, please. Not this time.

The storage space door slammed shut as Bogdan was situating the Christmas tree box. The overhead light flickered and went out. Bogdan prepared for this—brought a flashlight but didn't dare reach for it. Didn't think he wanted to see what the illumination would show him.

In the absolute darkness, a creak told him the trunk lid was being opened. In the echoing silence of the basement, it sounded like someone cracking a spine. An endless spine.

"I knew you'd come back," said the voice, nails on the chalkboard of Bogdan's mind. "I've been waiting."

6.

Sanity could slip away as easily as a dream at the sound of an alarm. Sanity, in Bogdan's experience, was a skittish thing.

All that he's done in the past weeks to calm himself, to convince himself his mind was merely playing tricks on him, merely tripping him up with flashes of PTSD the way people get acid flashes years later—all gone.

The whispering corpse chased away all the sanity in him.

"What do you want? What do you want from me?" Bogdan, at last, found his voice.

"I want peace. You said you'd give me peace." If dust had learned to speak, it would sound like this.

"You want me to bury you?"

"Not quite."

"Then what?"

"I want you to feed me."

"Feed you?"

"Yes, I am hungry."

"What do you want? A sandwich, some pizza?" Bogdan heard the note of hysteria slipping into his voice and stopped speaking to get it under control.

"Not quite," the voice repeated, infusing the words with a sinister undercurrent.

An ominous silence ensued, just deafening enough to let Bogdan's mind spin the worst-case scenarios into life. *It'll be better in the light*, he told himself, the way people have been saying for centuries, and turned on his flashlight.

He was wrong. It was better in the dark.

Bogdan didn't need to see the eerie mummified visage before him, leering at him hungrily. The random thoughts of the CryptKeeper—a skeletal horror show figure of screen and comics fame—came to his mind, but this was nothing like it, not really. Nothing cheesy or hokey about the creature before him. This was a nightmare come to life. It was like pulling back the veil of reality to glimpse at the hell beneath. *This was death*, Bogdan thought, *death personified*. He had seen so much death, he had willed himself to forget so much death, and here it was once again, staring at him malevolently, daring him to look away.

Its eyes were all black, like an abyss gazing back, and just as magnetic. Bogdan didn't think he could look away if he tried.

The creature stuck its tongue out as if to taste the air. The tongue was much too long and, Bogdan noticed, bifurcated. It made the sound of sizzling flesh. Brief but terrifying.

"I can taste your fear. You have so much fear." The creature shook its head and rearranged its features into something like a smile. Bogdan felt that smile in his spine like nails.

"It's delicious," the creature continued in that sibilant whisper. Its lips didn't quite move to articulate the words, but then again, it didn't matter. Bogdan could hear it in his head with the piercing quality of the fire alarm. "But I want more. Bring me blood."

There were no arguments to be made. No objections to be raised. Those were all things for the sane world, something for Dan to use in his daytime life. Nothing Bogdan could use at night. The night had its own logic.

He stopped by the supermarket after work and bought some fresh meat cuts. He hid them until Aimee fell asleep, then snuck into the kitchen at night and squeezed the blood out of them into a Tupperware container. He considered throwing away the meat, but on a second thought, he packed it up too, and took the entire thing to the basement.

Years ago, Bogdan used to have a co-worker named Jose who couldn't stand the sound of other people eating, said it sounded like a knife scraping a plate. Grima was the word he used. A useful word in Spanish for a thing that had no name in English. A sound so repulsive, so awful, so unpleasant. Jose could never go out to eat or be comfortable at work parties. At lunch, he'd always sit by himself and as far away from everyone as he could. *Such a peculiar thing*, Bogdan thought at the time. Then Jose married a woman and moved to Albuquerque, and Bogdan never thought about him again until now.

The sounds the creature from the trunk made while enjoying its gruesome meal—slurping and chewing and lightly moaning in pleasure—were definitely grima. The grimmest grima of all.

Bogdan couldn't look, so he trained his flashlight downward and studied the rough floor around his feet.

"Ah, yes," the creature hissed at last. Bogdan involuntarily looked up and immediately wished he hadn't.

Blood glistened around the creature's mouth, dripping down. The forked tongue flicked in and out licking up the dregs.

"Not bad, but I want something fresher," it said. "You can barely taste the fear in this long-dead thing."

"How am I supposed to …?"

The creature cut him off. Those eyes were staring right into his soul, it seemed.

"I know you," it whispered. "I know all you've done. I've tasted your nightmares."

At this, Bogdan shuddered so powerfully that he dropped the flashlight. He fell to his knees to find it like his life depended on it.

"You will bring me what I need," said the voice in a tone that brooked no argument. And Bogdan knew with a terrible certainty that he would oblige.

7.

Bogdan never told Aimee why he loved their condo's location so much. The truth was, it reminded him of the very first apartment he lived in after coming to the US. Sure, their present nicely updated and manicured accommodations were nothing like those old-fashioned boxes with ancient appliances and paper-thin walls, but the location was similar. Those apartments, too, were right across from a park. A park very similar to this one.

In fact, back in the old country, Bogdan's family had also lived near a park, albeit an entirely different kind—a vast, Central Park-like affair with lake-sized ponds that people, too poor to get away to the sea, eagerly mistook for beaches come summertime. The water was dirty, but no one seemed to mind.

Being firmly of a box-up-the-past-and-store-it-away mentality, Bogdan tended to avoid dwelling on those years, although, curiously enough, the memories of them did give him a certain sense of comfort. He liked these similarities, these parallels. Something familiar in a life demarcated with such monumental changes and upheavals.

And now there was something practical about the park's proximity, too.

There were animals living there, Bogdan knew. He just wasn't sure which ones. Beavers or groundhogs or woodchucks. Something like that, he imagined. Squirrels, certainly.

He had never been a hunter. Nor a trapper. He wasn't sure how to go about catching an animal, and his research left him more bewildered than prepared.

In the end, he had to buy some cage traps. Things usually sold for residential use, to get rid of the unwanted critters in basements and attics.

Bogdan wished he could just go for mice, but their condo was the first place he had ever lived in America that had none. Was it irony? he wondered idly.

He stayed away from the trunk until he could catch something. The traps were not cheap, and he resented the expense, but what could he do? He only hoped no one would disturb their locations—he went for the wilder, least traversed areas of the park.

During the day, he put on a performance. He was Dan—the most easy-going, likable version of himself. He didn't want Aimee to see the strain behind his eyes, to know the depth of his despair. He was glad that her work had kept her busy enough not to notice.

You could love someone and not know them, not all the way, not like the romantic stories told you one ought to. Some secrets were good for the relationship, some things were meant to be kept private. Bogdan had only ever given Aimee a heavily edited version of his past and never regretted it. It was much easier to love Dan, the abbreviated version, he believed, so why not make life easier for a loved one whenever possible? Wasn't that the point of love?

At night, the nightmares came. They were different from his usual ones. It felt like someone— specifically, the creature from the trunk—had unearthed all the footage from Bogdan's past, recut it into the worst possible selection of home movies, and played them back while curating the experience in a voice that sounded like a haunted house door opening and closing.

Not the sort of nightmares one could wake up from or stay awake avoiding—these were inevitable, like fate. Every night, as soon as his head hit the pillow, they came.

He knew the creature was sending him a message. Obedience in a timely manner was expected. No, *required*. Bogdan could only hope his traps worked.

The first victim was a squirrel. Bogdan had no love for the creatures; a city-emboldened one got into his old apartment once and wreaked absolute havoc. Still, he didn't kill it then—merely waited for it to get out—and had a tough time killing one now. In the end, he hit it with a sharpened stick, then slipped the dead body into a heavy-duty reusable plastic bag.

That night, the creature feasted, complimenting the freshness of the kill. Then it requested another. Something larger, perhaps.

It didn't want to hear about Bogdan's qualms or excuses. It just wanted to eat.

Bogdan knew about that kind of hunger but never let himself think about it. Some memories were better locked away. He remembered just enough to never let himself go hungry in his adopted homeland, not even for a moment. Not ever. There was always a snack around, power bars in the car, fruit: apples or bananas. Bogdan never let their kitchen cupboards go empty or even low, restocking before they were out completely.

Aimee would laugh at him and call him a prepper.

He'd shrug and carry on. He packed his own lunch so that he never had to wait for someone to prepare his food. Hunger is a terrible thing—the way it can take over you until nothing else matters.

Bogdan could almost sympathize with the creature in that way. But then again, of course, he couldn't.

He did notice that the creature was getting fuller. The blood and the meat were changing it, altering the previously skeletal appearance into something more like mere thinness. There looked to be flesh now between the skin and the bones. The effect should have been normalizing but instead, it made it all the more terrifying.

Otherworldly creatures, Bogdan believed, should have the decency to look otherworldly. For if they should look like us, how can we tell the monsters apart?

One day, Bogdan trapped a groundhog. Or a beaver, he wasn't sure. Killing it wasn't the same as with the squirrels. Bogdan cried while killing it. It didn't make sense, but he felt tears on his cheeks. He couldn't remember the last time he cried.

Then he brought it to the basement.

The sated, self-satisfied look on the creature's face haunted Bogdan for days. If not for the ghoulish complexion and demonic expression, the creature could almost pass for a person now. How soon until it would *want to?*

Bogdan couldn't stop thinking about it, but so far, the creature appeared to be comfortable enough in its trunk.

Its appetites satisfied, the creature made the nightmares abate. It was a small mercy, a scrap, and Bogdan hated how much he was grateful for it.

Days passed; weeks passed. The sharp duality of Bogdan's life became his new normal. He turned into an expert at compartmentalization, but it didn't feel like a personal improvement. It felt like lessening. Like he was losing himself, more and more each day.

He wasn't giving his best to Aimee or to his work. He was surviving. Merely surviving. Which was as far from living as one could get while still being on the right side of the dirt.

Life was careening out of his control, and he was adjusting to it, but it was all reactionary, passive. He was no longer a master of his fate.

When the creature made its next demand, Bogdan acquiesced once again, as he had come to do so well. He wasn't sure how he'd go about acquiring something that was loved and would be missed, but knew he'd figure it out.

8.

If Aimee had noticed the changes in him, she never mentioned it. It made Bogdan wonder what it said about their relationship. There was a difference between alone and lonely, more than a subtle linguistic shift. Between work and home, he was seldom alone, but he did feel lonely. There was no one he could talk to about the madness that was taking over his life, no one who could understand or believe him.

Fortitude, he told himself. *Forbearance*. His internal dictionary was full of qualities he aspired to. The men in the old country were like that, with strength favored over most other attributes. His father had been like that. The man seldom smiled or shed a tear, just made his way through life with a sturdy, almost grim, determination.

Once upon a time, Bogdan wanted to be just like that. But that was long ago and far away. Now he found himself in a sort of hybrid mode—some old-world notions, some new-world ones. He still disliked crying but knew it was okay to. He was suspicious of psychotherapy but not unaware of his feelings.

Aimee cheerfully and unselfconsciously emoted all over the place, be it over a silly movie or a cute puppy. She would think him a monster for what he was about to do, he feared. And yet …

Mrs. Woolworth, their downstairs neighbor, didn't need the square footage of a two-bedroom condo. It was just her and Lentil.

Pampered and obsessively groomed, Lentil thrived as the sole object of her affection; his status somewhere between best friend/confidant and a beloved child.

In that peculiar way that pets come to resemble their owners or perhaps vice versa, Lentil and Mrs. Woolworth were both short, stout, and dramatically overweight with slightly bulgy eyes and small, pressed-in features.

More than anything, in Bogdan's opinion, it made Mrs. Woolworth appear pug-like, since Lentil the pug still looked distinctly like a dog, albeit terribly overindulged.

They didn't know her first name. Former librarian, she stood firm on formalities, although out of consideration for their age difference, she did start referring to her younger new neighbors by their first names— Aimee and Daniel.

Bogdan never corrected her.

Mrs. Woolworth had to be in her seventies, although the extra weight gave her a sort of timeless appearance, like one of those people who had never looked really young and, as the years progressed, never got to look really old either.

Lentil had to be on his last legs. Most of the time he got around by being pulled in a children's red wagon. Walking made him wheeze terribly, and most TV programs, it seemed, agitated him into yapping shrilly and tirelessly, but he was, undeniably, a very loved dog. One that would be missed dearly.

Bogdan knew it had to be Lentil. Ever since the creature had made its latest demand. Poor Lentil. Bogdan could, with effort, wrap his mind around it, but not his heart.

He had always loved dogs. Growing up, there was an energetic fuzzball named Toto around his house, a loyal and devoted sidekick with a curiously human-like grin. When Toto died of old age, Bogdan distinctly remembered crying, mourning his faithful four-legged companion.

It was only the last couple of years in the old country that changed his mind. Since then, he could scarcely look at dogs. Despite Aimee's occasional prods, he couldn't even bring himself to entertain the idea of getting one as a pet.

Mrs. Woolworth seldom locked her door during the day as she went out on errands or grocery shopping. The opportunity was there, so was the motive. The means … All Bogdan had to do was steady his hands. Steady his heart.

The dog recognized him yet still unleashed a series of high-pitched barks. He didn't put up a fight, though. Not when Bogdan picked him up, not when Bogdan snapped his neck.

It was over so quickly. For something everyone clung to so dearly, life didn't take long to leave.

Bogdan didn't know he was crying, not until tears made their way down his cheeks and onto the terrible deadweight in his hands.

It was another one of those pivotal life moments, he knew. Nothing would ever be the same again after this.

He had done worse before, but out of desperation, out of a dire need to survive. For lack of options. This … this was different. Deliberate. As heavy as a sin.

Bogdan took the dead dog upstairs, back to his condo. Aimee was working late. All he had to do now was wait until dark.

He sat at the kitchen table, holding the still-warm lifeless body, and whispering apologies he didn't believe to matter, unsure whose forgiveness he was asking for.

9.

The night came quickly. But not before Mrs. Woolworth's plaintive cries for Lentil. Not before her coming up to talk to him, and his lying reassurances that he wore headphones while working and heard nothing. She went out searching, and he headed downstairs to the basement, feeling like a monster with each step.

The real monster was waiting for him below. Uncoiling from the trunk like a cobra from a snake charmer's basket and fixing its all-black liquid gaze upon him.

Bogdan took one last look at poor Lentil. Such a well-fed sausage of a dog. Nothing like the curs he remembered from before, roaming the streets, feral, with a starved glint in their eyes and viscous drool hanging from their mouths, ribs poking through the mangy fur. He remembered the time when dogs went from pets to food. In his darkest moments, he even remembered the taste.

He'd never forgive himself for this, he knew. He'd add it to his list of sins. No feather would ever balance out his soiled soul.

"Ah," the creature hissed. "Looks delicious."

Bogdan carefully laid out the dog's body before the trunk and backed away.

The creature reached for it, hungrily. "Want a taste?"

Bogdan looked up, hate simmering in his eyes.

"Oh, wait, I forgot. You don't do that anymore. You're all American now, Danny boy."

Aimee would sometimes call him that. He shuddered. The nickname was poisoned now.

The creature tore into the flesh, and Bogdan looked away. The sounds were enough. The sounds were everything.

"I've watched the home movies of your mind. I've sssseen all you've done. And yet this … this is what upsets you? Sssstrange. Sssssilly. You make no sssenssse."

The chewing accentuated the hissing. Or maybe vice versa.

The mastication sounded impossibly wet and gristly. Visceral.

"Why?"

"Why what, Danny boy?"

"Why are you here?"

"You mean, you haven't figured it out yet?" The creature sounded amused.

"Are you …" Bogdan found himself reverting to his mother's ways. Before her faith was put so savagely to the test. "Are you a punishment? A demon?"

"Interesting that you should think of me that way. Do you believe you deserve to be punished?"

How quiet this basement was, Bogdan thought. He'd never encountered any other neighbor. He knew they must have used it at some point. The other storage units held boxes, old bikes, things like that. But there was no one ever down here. What would they say? What would they see? Would they see the same thing as he was seeing? Or was this a private sort of nightmare? For his eyes only. Was this even real? Was any of it?

Lentil's dead body was real, he knew that. Mrs. Woolworth's sorrow would be, too.

And what of him? Was this still compartmentalizable or the proverbial last drop? Was his ability to separate and move on still intact, or did he finally overload it? What would it feel like, he wondered, if the floodgates were to finally open up?

"You have what you asked for," he said abruptly. "I'm leaving."

"Come back ssssoon," the creature taunted.

"And if I don't?" Bogdan chanced. "What then? More nightmares? *You* are the worst nightmare of them all."

The creature stopped chewing for a moment. "That is simply a failure of imagination speaking."

Bogdan met its gaze—dark, impossibly dark. The kind of blackness that denotes the complete absence of light. The kind of blackness that must have existed before any light.

The creature was already showing signs of a good meal ingested, becoming unsettlingly fleshier before his very eyes, turning disconcertingly more human in appearance.

"Say hello to Aimee for me." It grinned a terrible grin. "Or maybe *I* should one day." And with that, it went back to its gruesome meal.

Bogdan felt like gravity gave up on him. There seemed to be an unbearable lightness in his limbs, like he had suddenly become detached from reality and was drifting away.

A science-fiction movie image came to his mind, an astronaut unmoored, floating away into the stygian darkness of space.

On spongy legs, unfeeling and undone, he walked away from the monster.

10.

The nightmares accelerated slowly, but they were nothing compared to the worry Bogdan felt about Aimee. There were things he knew he could handle but Aimee couldn't. Shouldn't. Shouldn't *have* to.

She'd had such an easy, light, happy life. Cozy middle-class upbringing in a small, comfortable home in a large, safe country. Picket fences, trips to museums for culture, and the ocean for vacations. Small liberal college education, a useless but well-meaning degree in English. A procession of decent jobs leading to her present position as a high school teacher. No privation, no tragedies. First world pillow-soft cushion all the way.

The sheer thought of potentially marring that lovely existence haunted Bogdan, kept him awake more than the nightmares ever could. From the moment they met, all he ever wanted to do was to make her happy. She was so quick to laugh, so easily pleased, so easy to love.

He kept his darkness at bay, storing under lock and key to ensure it never touched her. And now it was here, in their basement, taunting him, threatening him. Threatening *them*.

Could he kill the creature? he wondered. Could the creature even be killed? It looked like a corpse once, but not anymore. Could they move? Should they move? Would it follow them? How could he possibly ever explain wanting to move away from this perfect place they had found for themselves?

Bogdan had always moved light. His possessions were few. On purpose. He came over to America with only an old beat-up backpack worth of necessities. Since then, he had never required so much as the smallest size U-Haul for any of the moves he'd been through. They rented one last time but only because of Aimee's things.

What Bogdan carried with him had no physical heft. Not in this world. His baggage weighed heavily on him, invisible to the eye. A human eye, at any rate.

His memories, his sins, his crimes, the terrible accumulation of it all would have been crippling if given material weight. Pound by pound, it would break him. He was no Atlas, merely a man. He could only shoulder so much.

Until recently, he had always thought he could manage, just buck up, take the enormous heaviness of it all, and persevere. Now, he was no longer sure. Now, the monster was in his head.

Bogdan stayed away as long as he could. Until the nightmares that paralyzed him after dark started featuring Aimee.

"Ah, I thought that might get your attention," the creature greeted him. It was almost completely out of the trunk and nearly fully human-like in appearance. Even its hair had turned lustrous and dark, a far cry from the white gossamer strands before.

It wore no clothes, betraying no sense of false modesty. Its skin still had the corpse-like mottled grey-green quality to it, but the build was solid now: muscles, fat.

The biggest transformation was in the face. Its features, no longer skeletal, now looked almost normal. A straight slightly too-long nose, large ears, a thin-lipped mouth, and a firm chin losing itself to the beginning of jowls. Bushy eyebrows and worry lines across the forehead above. If not for those black ink pools of eyes, it looked like a person.

Worst of all, that person seemed vaguely familiar. Definitely male.

Bogdan prided himself on his memory. It had always served him well in customer service—people liked to be remembered.

This man, he wasn't sure about. He thought he had seen the face or at least some variation of the face, maybe a brother or a son. It was one of those things liable to drive him nuts in different circumstances. *Currently,* he thought grimly, *it might be the least of my concerns.*

The creature stuck its tongue out —still a bifurcated hideous thing—as if to taste the air. Then retracted it with disconcerting speed.

"You want to kill me," it said. A statement, not a question.
Bogdan didn't reply.
"You can't."
"I want to know what you are."
"I am hope. The last thing left in Pandora's box."

"No," Bogdan shook his head.

"I am Rumpelstiltskin. You guessed my name, and I came."

"Tell me."

The creature tilted its head to one side with an eerie unoiled-hinges creak, regarding him carefully.

"I am what you made me," it said at last. "You dreamt me up, you built me up, in the darkest corners of your mind, in the deepest recesses of your heart. Where no light can reach, and no love can touch. I am your guilt, your shame, your sorrow. Look at me. Don't you recognize me?"

Bogdan looked and looked, refusing himself the permission to look away.

"This is what he would have looked like had he lived," whispered the creature. "Now watch."

The years fell away from its visage, like a CGI movie effect unfolding in real time before Bogdan's eyes. The man before him lost jowls and wrinkles, the flesh gained youthful tautness, the hair became longer and floppier and in a stilling horror of the night, Bogdan recognized, at last, the face he had so valiantly strived to forget all these years.

"You left him behind."

"I had to."

"You left him to die."

"It was me or him," Bogdan screamed. "Me or him. There was only one spot left on the train, only one chance. The Americans were pulling out. It was the only way. The only way."

"You lied."

"I had to."

"You cheated."

"I had to."

"You stole."

"I had to."

"He died."

"I know." Bogdan's voice broke down to a whisper. "I know."

They were never friends in school, Bogdan and Marko. They belonged to different social cliques. They knew of each other, attended some of the same parties, but didn't really become friends until the war.

With all social norms obliterated, for most people geography became their main connection. Marko and Bogdan lived in the same building. They hid in the same basement during the searches and through the endless artillery shelling. That sort of thing can bind people together more than any high school clique.

They whispered secrets to each other in the dark, shared their hopes and dreams and whatever food they could find. They became orphans together. Mourned their parents together. They waited together, praying, in the dark basement for someone to come and save them. They fantasized about it, told themselves they'd do whatever it takes to get out. They were equals in all things, partners in tragedy.

And then, when the time came, it seemed that Bogdan could go further than Marko after all. He found out there was nothing he wouldn't do to get out, to survive. Even lie to his best friend, steal his money to bribe a local official in charge. Even leave him behind to die.

Bogdan knew what he was doing at the time. Sure, he was scared, hungry, desperate, but—excuses aside—he *knew*. And he did it anyway. His greatest sin, the heaviest weight on his soul, the darkest stain on his conscience.

It would never let go of him, he knew that too; and so he learned to live with it over the years, putting it away, burying it deeper and deeper beneath the scabbed-over scars, distancing himself more and more, until it all seemed like some long-ago and far-away nightmare.

Now, decades later, in a very different basement in a very different place, it was as if the time fell away, as if the intervening years were nothing but a dream. Now, slapped in the face by reality, Bogdan finally woke up.

"You want to kill me *again*." The creature before him had completed its transformation into Marko. With its all-black eyes cast down, the similarity was uncanny. The voice was spot-on, too. "And bury me, this time. Bury me for good."

"What else can I do?" Bogdan asked quietly. "What would you have me do?"

"You can come with me. You can keep me company."

"Where?"

"In the dark place. It's lonely there. I could use a friend."

"I was a terrible friend to you."

"You were the best friend I ever had." The not-Marko shook his head, just the way the real one used to. "I would have probably forgiven you in time. If they hadn't found me so soon after you left."

"Can you … can you forgive me *now*?"

"I think we are beyond all that." Not-Marko extended his hand. His skin looked almost normal now. Almost real. "Come with me. I'm so tired of being alone. No more lying, no more trying. You've had your chances. Now come with me."

Everything came crashing down around Bogdan. All the walls, real and imaginary, everything he had built, all the life he had so meticulously created for himself, crafted from scratch and custom-made, fell away.

Until he was just a kid standing in the basement getting ready to make a terrible choice once again.

He reached out his hand, and a creature that looked just like his long-lost best friend took it and led him into the trunk. The space within it was infinite. It closed around them like a black glove. The lid slammed shut.

11.

Aimee hadn't thought to look in the basement. She'd never been down there, not once since they moved in. And Dan, as far as she knew, was no fan of basements. When their realtor asked him whether it was something they wanted in their future home, he was quick to dismiss it.

And so, when he wasn't there in the morning, she looked everywhere else. She checked around the condo, then outside. She phoned his work.

His car was parked outside. Did he go walking? She went searching for him in the park.

Later, panicking, she checked with ERs and police stations. Nothing.

It didn't make sense. Dan was steady, reliable, set in his routines. He wouldn't just disappear.

Mrs. Woolworth was no help, but then again, she hadn't been the same since Lentil went missing. With a vague, bitter, watery smile, she said something about how now both of their loved ones left them, and it made Aimee shiver.

Was it this place? Things had started to go strange between them since they moved here. It was meant to be the happiest time of their lives, and yet she felt the distance between them more than ever before. Not on her end, she stayed the same. It was Dan. Dan was pulling away. It wasn't in the things he said or the way he looked at her, and they still talked and made love. No, it was in his eyes, the distant, haunted, thousand-yard stare he sometimes got. Or maybe she was merely noticing it more lately.

She wasn't sure what was going on with him. He had never been particularly forthcoming. Honest, but reserved, not a man prone to discussing his emotions. He never talked much about his past either. She cobbled her own version of it from the bits and pieces he let drop over the years, piecing together some things here and there. She knew he was an orphan, knew where he was from, but there was still so much she didn't know. Dan never wanted to go into it, and she didn't like to press, but now she wondered if that had been a mistake.

She remembered an old story by Richard Matheson in which a character is asked, "Do you really think you knew your husband?"

Aimee thought she did. Well enough, anyway. Now she had no idea.

At the time it seemed right not to pry, to let each other have their secrets. Aimee had hers—one solitary indiscretion, one night of carelessness, the reckless drive back, drunk on Cosmos and remorse, the screeching of the brakes applied much too late ... She shook her head, clearing her mind like an Etch A Sketch. None of that mattered now. It was in the past. After all, everyone had their baggage. Their secrets.

She reported Dan's disappearance to the police. She couldn't think of anything else to do, though she was all too aware of how much her husband would have hated being looked for officially like that, how much he distrusted the powers that be. They agreed with her: the circumstances were suspicious, but at the end of the day, Dan was an adult, and these things happened. Their implications about his potential affairs upset her viscerally. She chewed her lip angrily while answering their questions, and upon leaving the station, could taste the bloody rawness of it, the ferrous aftertaste.

They'd be no help, she knew, the cops. They didn't care. Dan didn't have anyone to care about him but her. His business partner at the car dealership didn't count. They weren't friends, not really. It was just money and convenience.

The condo seemed empty now, suddenly much too large. Aimee felt like her very breath echoed, mockingly returning to her time and again. Alone, she was all alone, and she hated it. Nothing to be done but wait, she supposed. The sheeting rain outside seemed to agree.

She didn't go to the basement until next November. There was no reason to. Everything she wanted and needed was right there, inside the condo. She thought about selling but couldn't bring herself to do it. Couldn't even fathom the legal logistics of it. Technically, they co-owned the place as a married couple. Technically, Dan was still alive, just missing. To have him declared dead—to even contemplate doing so—seemed unbearable.

She trudged through her daily life with the sort of grim joyless determination Dan would have described as profoundly Eastern European. They would have laughed about it then. Nothing was funny now.

She went to work, she paid bills, she bought groceries. If she had stopped doing those things, the world would still turn. Dan's business partner at the dealership bought him out, providing her with a nice safety cushion. There was nothing for her to worry about now, but also nothing to look forward to. In her heart of hearts, she knew Dan was never coming back. In her darkest fantasies, she entertained various scenarios of what might have happened to him, but nothing ever made sense. She missed him like a limb.

Deciding to decorate for Christmas was spontaneous. The idea took her by surprise. Last Christmas, Aimee was so happy. She thought that maybe, subconsciously, she wanted to revisit some of that feeling. Either way, it was easy enough. She already had the tree.

She couldn't find the key to the storage unit, but in the end, it didn't matter—the door was unlocked. She found it with the hasp disengaged and the u-bar of the padlock swinging from its metal staple undone.

Creepy, Aimee thought. But it was only creepy in a typical basement fashion. Empty, poorly lit, cobwebby. All the other storage units had lots more things in them. Theirs only had their artificial Christmas Tree in a box. And wait, what was that? A trunk? There was an old-fashioned wooden trunk in the back, all the way against the wall. A solid-looking thing of dark wood and brass accents. A handsome piece, but not one either of them had ever owned. *The previous occupants of their condo must have left it behind*, she reasoned. Perhaps, it was too heavy to move.

She was almost going to leave it alone, but curiosity won over. She approached the trunk and studied it. It wasn't locked.

Aimee paused for a moment. She felt an undercurrent of unease, a sense of trepidation … but oh, what did it matter now? What could a simple trunk do to her after the year she'd had?

She lifted the lid resolutely. It was heavier than she thought it would be. There was a body inside. A strange, mummified body.

She felt a scream building in her insides, rising up, threatening to spill over and never stop, but then a voice, a sibilant whisper of a voice, spoke to her, paralyzing her into terrified silence. The body opened its eyes, and Aimee couldn't look away. Its gaze held her, paralyzed her.

The light flickered. The walls closed in. Suddenly, in the ascending darkness, there was nothing but the trunk.

REDDEST

I've never given any thought to graffiti until I moved here. Now I see it everywhere. In this strange city with its brutalist architecture, loud neon advertisements, anemic trees, and the dirty river that runs through it all, graffiti is what passes for art.

Some of it is art, I suppose. I'm no expert, but it's elaborate enough, interesting to look at. Some are just stylized names. Tags, I believe, is the proper word.

And some … some get under your skin worse than any tattoo ink, deeper than a stab wound, uglier than a scar.

I first saw the smile on my lunch break. I've taken to walking down to the river, because filthy or not, it was still nature. I'd go there, find a bench, and eat my apples and homemade sandwiches. It was never far enough from the hustle and bustle of the city, still within earshot of the street traffic rushing by, but it beat the windowless basement-level breakroom at work.

The river water was a different shade of brown each day depending on the ambient light. It carried along leaves and stray branches. Occasionally, a kayaker rowed through. Once I saw a dead rat floating by. A bona fide city river. Nothing like what I grew up with, nothing like what I left behind.

But then, I wanted this, didn't I? I chose this. A big city job felt like a step in the right direction. My ex used to accuse me of aimlessness, back when she still cared enough to cast accusations. Well, now here I was. Aimful. Pursuing proper goals. A mature adult through and through.

I tried reading, then listening to podcasts or audiobooks on my lunch. Nothing took. I settled for people-watching instead, chewing my food to the soundtrack of the city noise. But soon something began attracting my attention more than people ever could.

Graffiti, bright and wild, decorated the embankments of the river, shouting from the angles seemingly impossible to achieve. Numerous overpasses span the river at even, grid-like intervals. Graffiti climbed them like vines, twisting around the stones and beams in technicolor madness.

I found myself admiring the audacity of people who would do this, if not their artistry directly. It was daring, fearless. Tame and reserved by nature, I vicariously appreciated such thrill-seeking.

The art itself left me indifferent—there were no Banksys along the river—I simply enjoyed imagining the process.

Then I saw the smile.

From a purely technical perspective, it looked like any other graffiti. A closer look revealed madness beyond the swirls of color.

It was red. The reddest red I've ever seen. The red you see when you close your eyes after staring at the sun. Bright arterial red.

And then there was the design itself. A standard convex line of a smile rendered in blood. It looked like blood anyway. Like someone took a finger, dipped it into a wound, and drew. And just like any fresh blood, it ran in drips from the smile down in some horror show display of gravity.

Somehow the artist managed to give dimensionality to his design. You could see that the smile had lips and its blood had texture. It was distinctly the most unsettling image I had ever laid eyes on. And I had daylight on my side then.

From that day on, I began seeing the smile everywhere. It decorated the bricks of the buildings on my way to work or home. It appeared on the walls of the grocery store I frequented and the gym I didn't visit nearly enough. Once I saw it on the side panel of a passing bus.

From my limited understanding of these things, tags were meant to be representative of their artists. Presumably, the person behind the smile was just *that* popular.

But I couldn't shake the feeling that there was something more sinister behind the design.

Now I've come to expect finding the smile wherever I go. Anticipation does nothing to reduce the unpleasant jolt I feel every time I see it.

I don't know enough people in the city, not yet. My neighbors are ghosts; their presence heard and smelled, but seldom seen. My coworkers are nice enough but aloof and cliquey. I've not found my way into their confidences yet. My parents are kind, well-meaning people who do not understand my choices and seldom know what to say to me. Our conversations are usually weather and silences.

There's no one I can talk to about the smile. About its disturbing ubiquity. About the way it crawls into my nightmares. About how I can't unsee it now, how it has imprinted itself on the back of my eyelids, engraved itself into my psyche.

I tried the free therapist offered through work, but the person didn't seem to understand me at all. I could tell they were talking to me from their home. There were all sorts of domestic noises in the background which made me feel both unlistened to and isolated. She told me to get a hobby that involves other people. I thanked her and hung up. Then canceled the follow-up session.

Before all this, if you spoke to me of a disembodied smile, images of the Cheshire Cat would swim to the surface. Cute childish things.

But this bleeding smile is razorblading my mind. Each nightmare it visits is more intense than the previous one.

A few nights ago, I dreamt it opened its lips and licked them with a thin and much-too-long tongue, like it was getting ready to say something.

I do not want to hear what the smile has to say.

I've decided the only way out is to find the artist who draws them. So now I look.

I've taken some time off work for the first time, and I'm pounding the streets, ready to ask questions, even grease some palms if it gives me the answers I need.

Nighttime is when graffiti artists come out. I sleep during the day and look for them once the sun sets. They are the true urban legends, almost impossible to sight. The few I find know nothing of the smile, though they all admire it. Best red they've ever seen, they say.

Isn't it just? I can hardly look at the color red anymore. Certain shades of lipstick are triggering. Red lights bother me.

I've cut my hand recently on the edge of a soup can, and seeing the blood made me nauseous.

I'm running out of time off. Running out of ideas. I'm tired, caught in a perpetual hungover feeling of the day and night cycle turned on its head. When I finally spot the guy, I can hardly believe he's real.

But there he is, spraying a red nightmare onto a wall.

It's dark, and he's wearing all black, making himself seem like a shadow among shadows. He's tall and thin, but that's about all I can make out.

The wall he is working on is the side of yet another overpass, a hundred feet high, easily. Either he's wearing a suspension harness, or he is clinging to the wall like a bat. My exhaustion and his black clothing make the latter seem a distinct possibility.

There's a hill leading up to the overpass. I have no choice but to climb, grabbing at scraggly trees and rocks to aid my progress. My shoes are not meant for this. I am not built for this. I'm huffing and puffing like a marathoner by the time I get to the top.

I look, afraid I missed him. The smile is there, all finished. Its sinister grin drags across my mind like nails down a chalkboard. The man is gone.

I look around frantically and spot him across the road. He's leaning against the railing. I feel like he's staring right at me, but I can't see his eyes. Can't make out any facial features. It's like his face is wrapped in the same black fabric that cloaks his body.

Suddenly, I'm too afraid to speak. My thudding heart steals precedence from curiosity.

Before I can croak out a desperate "Why?", the man smiles at me. Which is to say a red, red smile appears and spreads across his face.

Then he opens his arms wide and topples backward, over the rail and out of sight.

I run across the street—at this time of night there is no traffic to dodge—and peer down. The river below is calm. No bodies. No harnesses hanging off the side of the rail. If this was a trick, I can't figure it out. And if he fell, if he died … *Could* he die? Was he even a man? Was he even real?

I make it home on autopilot and pass out on the couch.

The smile comes to me in my dream. Red, so red. Its lips part, and it whispers terrible truths into my ears. Things I can never unhear.

When I wake up, I go buy some Krylon cans. The reddest I can find. Once the night falls, I shall begin.

The End?

Notes on the stories

Smile So Red was the first thing I ever published and therefore is as special to me as only a firstborn can be. It is the anchor of this collection and the only universe I've come back to more than once now.

It was inspired by the real house, graffitied and inexplicable, that I came across on a hike in the real woods not too far away from where I live. The descriptions are from experience. Even the animal carcass was real. The rest … I may have taken some liberties with. When I came back to the woods to look for the house, it was gone.

Spindel was one of my first thrillers. I write across genres and always tell people I'm not only a horror author. I wanted Spindel to showcase that. As far as to what inspired it…

When we moved into our new place, one of the first things I noticed were the spiders. In the city, they were small innocuous things. Here, in the suburbs, they were huge and terrifying, like something out of a horror movie…or Australia. And yes, one day there was a crazy web hanging outside the window. And then a fly got caught in it, slowly wasting away. The spider never came for its victim. Eventually, the rain washed the entire set up away. Creepy, I thought, there's gotta be a story there somewhere…

Blues for the Soul was conceived to try doing something new with the "evil child" scenario. I play music, I love music, it's a huge part of my life. I find a lot of intersectionality between music and writing. And what better score for an unsettling tale than the blues? At the risk of being terribly corny, I hope it sings for you.

The Devil's Chord, since we're on the subject of music, was written for a specific anthology, but inspired, it seems, by a subconscious desire to revisit the *Smile So Red* universe. The devil's chord is a real thing. I learned about it during a music lesson, and it had stuck with me ever since. I knew it was going to make it into a story one day, and so it did.

Stump was inspired by seeing a particularly disturbing looking tree stump in the woods across from our house and wondering what secrets it may hold. The more I thought about the story, the more I wanted it to be a double-sided coin of the "quiet desperation" Thoreau wrote about. It was also informed by the news. I read them daily, and certainly things are impossible to ignore. Tobey and Finn are two very different individuals united in bleak circumstances and bound by a deadly weapon. The tree stump is merely the hiding place for the infamous Chekhovian gun.

Flamingos like a lot of my recent writing was inspired by a move to a small-town suburbia idyll after a lifetime of city living. The differences to this day are striking, wild, and yes, fiction-inspiring. The town the protagonist lives in is modeled on the one I live on the edge of. What crystalized *Flamingos* in my mind was learning the secret—swinger—meaning of those cute plastic birds in the yard. I don't know if it's real, but it proved to be just the right push for the story to materialize.

The Trunk just showed up. When my wife and I bought our place, we were told there it came with a basement storage unit. Neither of us went to check it out for months, but the seed of an idea was planted. This is the nightmare it spawned. When we finally ventured into the basement, the space was just as I had imagined it. Only there was no trunk … not in our storage unit, anyway …

Reddest was written specifically for the Crystal Lake Entertainment's monthly flash fiction competition. When I saw the theme, I knew it merited another visit to the *Smile So Red* universe. It worked, too. The story took second place. And yes, graffiti does fascinate me. The well-done, well-laced, artistic kind. I'm also a huge fan of Banksy, whoever he is.

That's it. I hope these notes have been of interest. I always read these things in books, so I figured I'd include them in mine. Cheers!

Acknowledgements

Without an audience, a writer is a mere scribbler. Therefore many, many thanks to everyone who reads, buys, reviews, recommends, and promotes my books. You are all magical!

Thank you to all the wonderful friends and BETAs who have helped me so much through this writing journey. You know who you are. And much gratitude to all the authors who provided the awesome blurbs.

Thank you to the wonderful Atticus Morton, a true fan and patron of the arts.

Thank you to Davida De La Harpe Golden for her eagle eye.

Thank you to Tony Anuci of Anuci Press for first bringing my book into the world. And to Brigids Gate Press for giving it a wonderful new home.

And the biggest, hugest, universe-sized thank you goes to my wife, Chelsea. My heart, my best friend, my first reader. For everything. Forever.

AUTHOR BIO

Mia Dalia is an internationally published, CWA-nominated author of all things fantastic, thrilling, scary, and strange.

Her short fiction has been published online by *Night Terror Novels*, *50-word stories*, *Flash Fiction Magazine*, *Pyre Magazine*, *Tales from the Moonlit Path*, *carte blanche magazine*, Jaded Ibis Press, Weird Wide Web; in print anthologies by Sunbury Press, HellBound Press, Black Ink Fiction, Dragon's Roost Press, Unsettling Reads, Phobica Books,

PsychoToxin Press, Wandering Wave Press, rebellionLIT Press, Bullet Points, Critical Blast, Off-Topic Publishing, Exploding Head Press, Sinister Smile Press, *Dracula Beyond Stoker Magazine*, *Mystery Magazine*, Headshot Press, Nightshade Press, WonderBird Press; Crystal Lake Publishing, Grendel Press, and more, and featured in narrative podcasts such as Zoetic Press' Alphanumeric, Sudden Fictions, and Tales to Terrify.

Mia's work has been selected as *Tales to Terrify's* top ten best stories of 2023, shortlisted for the Crime Writers Association's Daggers Award 2024, and praised by authors and editors such as Michael Marshall Smith - "One of the best novels I've read in years", Stephen Jones - "horror tour-de-force", Clay McLeod Chapman - "every flip of the page leads its readers deeper into uneasy dream", Neil Sharpson, M.R. Carey, A.C. Wise, Ian Rogers, Edward Ashton, and institutions such as Booklist's Starred Review: "Beautifully detailed characters and a subtle slide into dread…"

Her full-length works include the novels *Estate Sale* and *Have* (CamCat Books) and the novellas *Tell Me a Story* and *Discordant* (Anuci Press); *Arrokoth*, and *Do You Know The Muffin Man?* (Spaceboy Books)

Her upcoming work will be featured by PS Publishing, Crystal Lake Publishing, Dark Matter INK, Absinthe Press, Earthling Publications, Ellery Queen's *Mystery Magazine*, and more.

Find her at **https://daliaverse.wixsite.com/author**

https://linktr.ee/daliaverse

Twitter: @Dalia_Verse: FB: Read DaliaVerse

If you enjoyed this story, kindly take a moment to
leave a review on Goodreads, Amazon, etc.
Tell your friends.
Shout it from the rooftops.
Supporting indie authors is the surest way to
improve one's karma!

MORE FROM BRIGIDS GATE
PRESS

The Five Turns of the Wheel

Stephanie Ellis

Welcome to the Weald. The Five Turns of the Wheel has begun. With each Turn, blood will be spilled, and sacrifices will be made. Pacts will be made…and broken. Will you join the Dance?

In the Weald, the time has come for the Five Turns of the Wheel. Tommy, Betty and Fiddler, the sons of Hweol, Lord of Umbra, have arrived to oversee the sacred rituals… rituals brimming with sacrifice and dripping with blood.

Megan Wheelborn, daughter of Tommy, hatches a desperate plan to free the people of the Weald from the bloody and cruel grip of Umbra, and put an end to its murderous rituals. But success will require sacrifice and blood as well. Will Megan be able to pay the price?

COUNTRY ROADS

Colin Leonard

Something is outside; in the fields, by the ditches, on the roads. Something old and cruel and vicious.

When Luke Sheridan moves out of Dublin city to rural Kilcross with his wife and baby, he imagines the worst part will be his extended commute to work. They can look forward to enjoying the countryside and being part of a small community. After all, his old friend Declan Maguire lives in the house next door and is a Garda in the nearest town.

But Declan's devilish attitude towards drink, drugs and women means trouble is never far from his door. And worse, gruesome murders and the appearance of sinister figures at night mean the countryside is becoming a very dangerous place to live.

Country Roads—don't go outside alone.

THE PRISONERS OF STEWARTVILLE

Shannon Felton

Stewartville. A town living in the shadow of the prisons that drive its economy. Haunted by the ghosts of its past. Cursed by the dark secrets hidden beneath. A town so entwined with the prisons waiting outside the city limits that it's impossible to imagine one without the other, or to ever imagine escaping either.

When a teenage boy digs into the history of the town, he discovers a tunnel system beneath Stewartville, passageways filled with dark secrets. Secrets leading not to freedom, but to unrelenting terror.

Stewartville. Where the convicts aren't the only prisoners.

LOVE THE SINNER

Mo Moshaty

According to Dante, a sin is the misdirection of love - the human will, or essentially, the direction of our beings. *Love the Sinner* is an examination of just how those sins can kaleidoscope into horrific consequences creating a distorted and deadly landscape. These stories stand stark before you in full glaring misstep and macabre to show the human psyche in all its twisted reality.

From grief and its rage to medical meddling to ensure a new world order to bloody revenge within a quantum leap, these stories seek to solidify one absolute truth: man is the scariest monster.

Visit our website at: www.brigidsgatepress.com